SHADOWS

ALSO BY MEAGHAN MCISAAC

MOVERS

URGLE

SHADOWS

MEAGHAN MCISAAC

ANDERSEN PRESS • LONDON

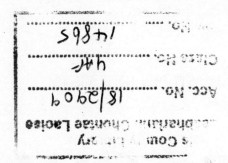
First published in 2018 by
Andersen Press Limited
20 Vauxhall Bridge Road
London SW1V 2SA
www.andersenpress.co.uk

2 4 6 8 10 9 7 5 3 1

British Library Cataloguing in Publication Data available.

ISBN 978 1 78344 621 6

Typeset in Minion Pro by Palimpsest Book Production Limited,
Falkirk, Stirlingshire

Printed and bound in Great Britain by
Clays Limited, Bungay, Suffolk, NR35 1ED

For Mae, my very own little shadow

PROLOGUE

Two black doors.

I stare at them, standing alone in a dimly lit hallway. It's cold. But still, I'm sweating.

Because I've stood here before.

I'm inside BMAC – the Bureau of Movement Activity Control.

But more than that, I'm inside the Movers' Prison.

I glance at the security scanner on the wall beside the frame. It blinks green, even though no one's placed their hand on it. The doors don't care if I have special clearance today. They want me to see what they're hiding.

The doors grin wide, an unfeeling sneer as they click open and beckon me inside.

My feet carry me forwards, as if I have no control, and I step over the threshold into the amphitheatre, cold blue lights lining the aisles of folded seats that encircle a glowing convex window. The last time I was here, the theatre was empty. Now, every seat is full. I recognise the faces – they're

1

from my school, my apartment building, the busy city streets I walk every day. They're all here to see something. Something I have a feeling I don't want to see.

Three figures stand in the front row with their backs to me. They stare down into the window. I know them.

Mom. My little sister Maggie.

And Special Agent Beadie Hartman.

'Mom!' I call out, but she doesn't turn around. 'Mags?' They're too focused on whatever's happening beyond the glass.

Agent Hartman turns and smiles at me – a smug, triumphant smile – and beckons me to join them.

Slowly I go to stand beside Hartman, staring down into the bright white glow of the operating room below us – dark monitors, sharp metallic instruments, and the cold steel bed where Movers are made to fall asleep. The restraints are unlatched, each furious little mouth hungry for the wrists and ankles of one of us. I watched what happened when they bit down on my friend – Rani – not long ago. When those jaws clamp closed, there's no escape.

A door opens. In walks a little man carrying a tray of syringes – three syringes. Those are the needles that send Movers to sleep. Icy dread prods my temples.

Someone is getting Shelved.

Right here. Right now.

I frown at Hartman. 'Who is it?'

She doesn't look at me, but her smile grins wider in the reflection in the glass.

There's a murmur from the onlookers as another door in the operating room opens and two BMAC agents enter the room. They're standing in front of the prisoner, so I can't quite see. But the people around me know who it is.

'Hurry along, let's get this done!' someone cries.

'Shut her down for good!' shouts someone else.

The jeers grow louder and my sister presses her palms to the glass as the prisoner is led to the bed.

The prisoner—

My heart stops beating.

The prisoner is Gabby.

BMAC has her.

The glass fogs up with my panicked breath, blurring out her face. I smear it away, and don't dare exhale again.

Gabby's arms are bound behind her so that the officers have to help her up onto the bed. She looks so small, so helpless – nothing like the way I saw her last, on the deck of the Avin Turbine with my little sister, the Movers' wind whipping through her hair and bowing to her command. She found her power then. Found her strength.

And now, BMAC is taking it from her.

She's only fourteen, like me. They can't Shelve her. The law says they can't. At least, it used to. When she lies back on the bed and the hungry restraints close around her limbs, there's a cheer from the crowd. I turn to look at them – faces twisted with a jubilant rage. Can Gabby hear them? I want to scream, to tell them all to shut up. They've done this to her for too long – hated her, chipped away at her, piece by piece, for her entire life. The unfairness of it makes my heart ache and all I want to do is make it stop. But there's no stopping this mob. They want to see this. Want to watch her sleep for ever.

Just like Hartman.

Without thinking, I hurl myself at the agent, arms throwing punch after punch for every nasty word, every unkind person, that ever hurt Gabriela Vargas. And then I'm punching for everything I've done – every time I was no better than the rest of them, every time I called her Gooba, or laughed at someone who made a joke at her expense. Because Gabby didn't deserve it, didn't deserve any of it. And someone has to pay. And that someone might as well be Hartman.

Blow after blow lands on nothing but air. Not a single strike finds its mark and all I'm managing to do is tire myself out with each missed fist. Agent Hartman doesn't even notice me. I'm no more bother to her than a fly. I'm useless. I'm nothingness. A ghost.

Hartman nods at the man with the syringes.

My eyes burn and I look to Mom – she can do something. Mom always knows what to do.

'Mom, please, make them stop this.'

But she can't hear me.

She hugs Maggie close and shields her eyes as the first needle meets Gabby's arm.

'Why are you doing this?' I scream at Hartman. But I already know the answer. I've known it since the day the lightning struck the school roof. BMAC thinks Gabby Moved her Shadow, the person in the future she shares a mental connection with.

And worse than that, they think Gabby is the reason I became a ghost.

The second syringe meets Gabby's other arm. Hot tears

spill down my face as the final syringe is picked up and held to her right temple.

This is the one that will close her eyes. The one that will set her sleeping for the rest of her life.

I press my hands to the glass and Gabby's eyes find mine. So dark they're almost black, flecks of gold glistening under the sterile lamplight.

'I'll fix this, Gabby,' I tell her, or maybe I'm telling myself because she can't hear me through the glass, can't hear over the angry voices, but I'm making the promise all the same. 'I won't let them do this to you. I'll fix it all.'

And she nods. Did she hear me?

The final needle empties, and her eyes close for what I know is for ever.

She's gone from me now.

She belongs to the Shelves.

PAT
2383

I wake with a gasp, eyes wet from the dream.

I lie there, listening to my accelerated breath and the *drip drip drip* of leaky pipes and drains. Night after night, it's the same dream. Gabby, strapped to the table in BMAC's operating room. The syringes. And my promise. *I'll fix it all.* It echoes through my mind, over and over and over again so that even if I wanted to get back to sleep, I couldn't.

It's been two weeks. Two weeks since we stood on the platform of the Avin Turbine, the tower that stands at the heart of the city. Since Gabby and my sister Maggie took control of their power. Since they destroyed Commander Roth, the scientist from the 2300s who had made himself a Shadow to both of them.

Two weeks since I found myself here, in the future, in 2383. Two weeks where anything could have happened to the people I love. It's the not-knowing that's driving me crazy. The only thing I *do* know is what I've managed to scavenge from articles and censuses. And what I've discovered haunts my dreams.

Gabby was Shelved. Three needles, and it's sweet dreams. I can still see them, the Shelves. Agent Hartman took me there not long ago, made me stand right in the middle of the giant silo, staring up at rows and rows of pale feet of convicted Movers.

I disappeared. And Gabby was made to sleep. And night after night, I promise her I'll fix it.

As for Mom, for my little sister, there's no record of them being convicted. Nothing written that says they were Shelved with Gabby. I hope that means they're safe. I can't be sure but at least I have hope. I'm so desperate to be back with them in our apartment, to be at home.

I stare up at the arched ceiling of the sewage pipe that serves as my room, rust and mould eating away at the metal. Underground. Hidden away. This is how Movers live in 2383.

There's a rumble outside, somewhere beyond the walls, a low humming I've become uncomfortably familiar with. I hear it most nights, after the winds of the Eventualies have calmed down. The Cure Bus.

People with Movement capabilities, a muffled voice blasts over a crackly speaker, *or those with communication to individuals of the past, the struggle of your condition need no longer persist.*

I hear this same speech every night, lying here on my soggy mattress. The Cure Bus rolls through the neighbour-hood around nine, after the roar of the Eventualies have dulled to a howl, promising to cure Movers and Shadows of their ailment.

The Cure for your condition is real, the voice continues. *You no longer need to hide outside the city limits if you register now with the Bureau of Movement Activity Control.*

BMAC.

This is how Avin is now, my home city, 300 years in the future, in 2383. After the war. The battle has been going on for centuries, my Shadow Bo says. Centuries of fighting between Movers and Nowbies. But eventually it ballooned into a formal armed conflict that raged for thirty years. Nowbie army versus Mover army. Six years ago, the Movers lost, and the Nowbies kicked them out to the fringes of the city, left them to the rubble and ruin like garbage. It's the same everywhere, all over the world. Movers and Shadows forced to live in hiding.

The Federal Information and Identification Licensing Electronic System, or FIILES, don't exist any more. Not for Movers, anyway. No birth certificate, or driving licence, or anything else to identify you as *you*. For Movers, there's only one thing BMAC needs to know. Are you a Mover, or aren't you? With so many Movers living in fear, and Shadows arriving and disappearing all the time, it's impossible to keep track of all of us. So that's what the Cure is for. Control. To take away the only advantage Movers and Shadows have left, and force them to live as Nowbies.

For most Movers and Shadows, the very idea is appalling. Living without a connection to your Shadow, or Mover – that would be like losing an arm, losing a leg. It's a part of you. Defines you. But BMAC promises a better life for Movers and Shadows in the city, if they sign up to live as Nowbies. And for some, that promise is enough to make them seek out the Cure. But Bo says it's all a lie. Even those who are cured are still only regarded as cured Movers. The ones that go into the city can only work for pennies, finding employment with whichever Nowbie is in the market for a servant. More often they end up homeless on the city streets or back here in the outskirts. But still, even knowing that, there are Movers and Shadows that come out, night after night, to be cured. For some of them, anything is better than being a Mover.

Register, and you will receive treatment. You will no longer be victims of a future you cannot see, or a past you do not want. Register, and you will belong to Now.

Bo grumbles angrily from his hole – that's what I call his room, because really that's what it is. A hole. A big sewer pipe that leaks something green. Across from Bo's hole, on the other side of the gaping, wet cavern that serves as the kitchen/living room is my hole, another giant pipe. This one gives a light but steady flow of rusty red water. I hope it's water. I listen to it trickle beneath my mattress every night. I've tried to stem the flow with gravel and dirt and stone, but nothing seems to stop it. Which is why I can't tell if the damp clinging to my body is from the mattress or my own sweat.

Several spider-looking robots shuffle across the floor, scrubbing as they go. Bo builds them, tiny little robots to help with household chores, and sells them, along with other gadgets and gizmos he's always tinkering with. As I watch the little insects work, I can't help but shake my head. This place is a den of rot. Their artificial brains must be so over-whelmed, I'm surprised they haven't short-circuited.

Bo's lying with his back to me, and I notice him glance

over his shoulder. His wrinkled old face is wearing a stern frown. He grumbles something, a guttural command in a language he knows I don't speak, but I understand its meaning anyway. His mind is connected to mine, and so the foreign words travel on his thoughts and into my head. *Do you ever stop thinking? I'm trying to sleep.*

Bo's my Shadow. I'm his Mover. It's been hard for us, keeping our thoughts to ourselves now that we're both in the same time. When I was home, in 2083, my brain was connected to my Shadow here in 2383. That's a lot of years that separated us. Lots of distance for thoughts to travel. Now that we're together, in one time, our thoughts are easier to hear than either of us would like.

I'm sorry, I tell him.

Another nightmare?

I don't say anything. I don't have to. It's in my thoughts and he's seen it.

He harrumphs, and turns over, too tired to deal with me. But I can still hear his thoughts, however much he tries to keep them to himself. He's mad because it's been two weeks of the same thing – my nightmares and thoughts waking him up. Two weeks he hasn't got the rest he needs. Two weeks of regret. Sometimes, I catch him wishing he never Moved me. Wishing he could just send me back.

I wish he could too. More than anything.

But that's not how Movement works. We're both in the same time now so neither of us can Move the other.

Movement has rules. A Mover can Move their Shadow back in time. Never forwards. But Bo and I broke those rules. My Shadow Moved me forwards.

We're connected to each other by particles called pungits. Roth's device, the Punch, can strengthen, steal and reverse pungits. The Punch reversed my pungits, when Roth was trying to steal them, and Bo saved my life by Moving me forwards to his time. And I'm grateful, of course I am. But I have to return to my own time now, I must save Gabby, I want to be back home with my mom and sister.

I need the Punch; it's my only hope to get back home. I need it if I'm going to break the rules again. Back before Roth came. Before he changed everything. I have to fix it *all*.

Another harrumph from Bo. *There is no going home.*

But he's wrong. He has to be. I've seen what a Punch can do. I've felt it. Felt the burn of it reversing my connection so that I could travel here. And I need a Punch to do it again so that I can travel back.

Patrick, Bo says sternly, *even if you could reverse your pungits, the Move between you and me has been spent. Which means you will have to steal someone else's pungits, and who's going to let you do that?*

I can't think about that now. I just have to find the Punch first. But I have no idea how.

I close my eyes, inhaling the mouldy funk of Bo's lair. I need Gabby. She's so much smarter than I am. She'd know how to find it.

I wish Gabby was here.

GABBY
2083

Stomp them out.

Scratch them from existence.

He's inside my head. My Shadow.

Stupid, ignorant, useless Nowbies.

Angry again.

Always angry.

Wasting precious time.

They will fall. All of them. Fall at our feet and grovel for . . .

I close my eyes. Force myself to sing something. Anything to focus my mind and drown him out. *A b c d e f g* . . .

And just like that, he's gone from me. For now. But he'll be back. He always comes back.

My eyes open. I've been too quiet for too long. There's a burning under my skin. I'm blushing. I have to be.

I glance up from my notes.

You're stupid, pathetic, a glob.

But no one in Mrs Dibbs' class has noticed I haven't been talking. No one's paying attention to me at all. Leelee

Esposito whispers something to Val Ogden. Janna Martins and Sophie Lu giggle over their droidlets. Matt Doig is counting the speckles in the tile at his feet. Even Mrs Dibbs is scrolling through her droidlet. Ollie Larkin plays games on his. And behind him there's Pat Mermick, staring out the window, imagining being anywhere but here.

None of them ever pay attention to me.

Because you're disgusting. You're useless. A goob.

I want to be anywhere but here.

Suddenly, his eyes are on me. Pat Mermick. No one else is looking. But he is.

I clear my throat. 'So, like I was saying. The rays I'm working with, they're just light rays. Like the light we see every day. They're just on a different wavelength.' I fumble with my pungit ray. The cathode connections look loose. 'The rays pass through the glass tube. And out through this end here.' Pat Mermick's eyes drift to his droidlet. I'm on my own again. 'Um, and when they are aimed at a Mover, hopefully they pick up the pungits.'

A new pair of eyes is on me. Ollie Larkin. Finished with his game, I guess. He's grinning. I hate it when he grins. It usually means something bad is—

'Goooooooooooooba.' He grins wider. Staring. Waiting for me to react. The class starts to laugh. I drop my eyes to my notes.

You will scratch them out.

Starting with him.

I close my eyes again.

And then I see it. I'm grabbing Ollie Larkin by the hair. Shaggy blond locks held tight in my fist. I bash my forehead into his nose. And the blood – so much blood—

14

A b c d e f g, h i j k . . .

And the image disappears from my mind. The image I didn't think up on my own. My Shadow put it there.

When I open my eyes, there's Ollie. That grin.

'Goooooooooooooooooooba.'

More laughing.

And then Kevin Prenders joins in. 'Goooooba.'

I hate that word. That ugly, made-up word. The word that means nothing. Just a sound. An ugly, fat, sluggy sound. The word they made for me.

Because you're disgusting.

Everyone's laughing. I can't move. Can't speak. Afraid to breathe. No matter what I do, they'll only laugh more. Is he laughing too?

I glance up. He's smiling. Pat Mermick. He thinks it's funny.

Thinks you're funny. A joke. Just like the rest of them. What else could *he think?*

I turn back to my project. What was I saying? I reach out and touch the cool glass tube that encases all the wires and oil and the motor and all the months of research and work that went into it. This is mine. I made it. And it will free me. I hope.

'The idea is kind of like an X-ray,' I say. 'Only X-rays don't really pick them up. Neither do normal light rays. So by finding the right frequency, hopefully I can expose the pungits so they can be measured and better understood.'

Mrs Dibbs stands. 'The what?' She sighs.

'P-pungits,' I say. 'The particles that I believe are connected to Movers, the particles that make a Mover Move.

I have a theory that the Mover manipulates these particles, which is why they have the ability to pull their Shadow from the future here to the present. If I can figure out how to see these particles, or even measure them, then we would be better able to understand Movement phases. For example, a Mover who is Phase 1 would have a low pungit count, while a Mover who is Phase 3 would have a high—'

Mrs Dibbs cuts me off with a sharp clap of her hands. 'All right, Miss Vargas. Thank you for that.'

'I, uh, wasn't finished.'

'That's all the time we have, Gabby. Please take your seat.'

She never wants to hear me. None of them do. And I can't understand why. They all think Movers are such a problem. I'm trying to fix the problem. If she'd just listen, she'd know that.

I want to scream. Make her hear me. Make her see.

I'm angry.

And my Shadow can feel it. He's creeping back into my head.

Useless Nowbies.

He wants me to say it. Wants me to yell at Mrs Dibbs.

I grab my pungit ray and head back to my seat. I can't yell at Mrs Dibbs. It will make her hate me even more.

Let her hate you.

I sing inside my head. I want to push my Shadow out. Push his anger back. Or does it belong to me?

'And, Miss Vargas?'

What now?

'Tomorrow is the first of the month,' says Mrs Dibbs.

'I trust you have your Phase Licence Renewal Forms ready for Officer Dan?'

You do not answer to her. You answer to no one.

I nod and take my seat. Back of the class, beside Pat Mermick. He's watching me.

My Shadow seethes behind my thoughts.

And a part of me wishes my Shadow were right. Wishes I didn't have to answer to Mrs Dibbs. To anyone. Does that make me like him?

Yes, you are like me.

No. I'm not.

We're a pair, you and I. Linked through time and space.

Get out of my head.

We need each other.

I close my eyes and sing the alphabet. Mouth the words. Focus. Focus.

'Mr Mermick?' snaps Mrs Dibbs.

I glance over at Pat.

'I hope I'm not expected to place *another* phone call to your mother about your phase forms after last month's fiasco.'

Pat hunches low in his seat. 'No, ma'am, she knows.'

The class is giggling. Is it bad, that I'm glad it's not at me, for once?

'Good,' says Mrs Dibbs. 'Because her slippery memory when it comes to your phase status, I don't need to remind you, Patrick, could land us all in jail.'

His cheeks are turning red. Teeth grinding. He grinds his teeth when he's angry. You can see it in the way his jaw goes tight.

'Remind her when you get home, please.'

'Yup,' he says, turning to watch the storm clouds outside the window.

'I beg your pardon?'

And then he shouts, 'Yeah, I'll remind her!'

I hold my breath. Mrs Dibbs' face goes blank with fury.

'I. Beg. Your. Pardon?'

She waits. I do too, watching Pat Mermick's tightening jaw. Mrs Dibbs wants an apology. I don't want him to give it to her. Finally, Pat rolls his eyes. Slumps further in his seat. 'Yes, Mrs Dibbs.'

There's laughter from the class. But I don't laugh.

I wish I had the nerve to yell at Mrs Dibbs.

I wish I had the nerve to be more like Pat Mermick.

PAT
2383

I want to go with you.

Out of the question, Bo snaps, loading gadgets and wires and other parts into his sack. It's the third Monday I've been here, in 2383. And the third time Bo has decided to leave the lair. The first time, I was too weak from the Move to get out of bed. The second, he told me no. I listened then. But this time, if I'm going to find what I'm looking for, I have to leave the lair.

Maybe I can help you. I can carry your stuff . . .

He laughs. *It's just SpiderBorgs and AvinGates. They aren't exactly heavy.*

No. The spidery robot things are no bigger than a fist – not heavy at all. And the AvinGates are like air – thin, junky-looking tablets no heavier than a couple pieces of paper stuck together. Bo makes them. And there're plenty of customers at the pawn shops in the Movers' sector looking to buy. Information in 2383 isn't a right, it's a privilege. In 2383, Movers don't have any privileges. That means no internet. Or,

I should say no CyberAvin. That's what they call the internet now. It's heavily guarded and monitored by the government. Movers are not allowed access. That doesn't stop Bo though. The AvinGates allow anyone onto CyberAvin undetected by the authorities somehow. I don't know the technical details, but it's worked all right to help me find what little I've found on Gabby and my family. Which is very little. The only historical information available on CyberAvin is what BMAC chooses to make public through their online library. And they've chosen not to mention the Punch. Not anywhere that I can find. So an AvinGate isn't enough any more.

You'll only get yourself into trouble, he tells me. *And me, while you're at it.*

I'm ready to pull my hair out. We've been talking in circles for an hour. *I have to get out of here! I have to find SOMETHING that can help me. I have to go home!*

AGAIN with the going home. You can't go home! I've Moved you, you're here. I can't put you back.

Exactly! I have to find someone who can.

No one can!

Not yet. That's why I need the Punch. And where Bo's going, with all those AvinGates, maybe someone familiar with the tech of 2383 will know how to help me.

Bo sees my thoughts and scoffs. *What you're looking for won't be at the pawn shop, Patrick. I can guarantee you that.*

I want to see for myself.

Bo doesn't say anything, just slings his sack over his shoulder and heads for the door.

'You can't keep me here!' I shout at him. 'I'm not your prisoner!'

Prisoner?! Bo whirls on me, eyes wide with anger. He's shouting in his language too, spit flying from his mouth. *Do you know what BMAC will do to you if they find you? Do you know what they'd do to a Mover who was Moved by his Shadow?*

I don't answer. Because I honestly have no idea. It's never happened before, as far as either Bo or I know. But Bo has a guess. I can see it crawling up through his mind like smoke – memories from the war. Memories of his life as a younger man. It's only a glimpse – lots of shouting, and running. Bright lights and towering buildings. Lots of wind. And BMAC uniforms. I've seen these images from him before – when they startle him awake in the middle of the night, when we've been quiet for too long and his mind wanders to whatever happened all those years ago. He doesn't talk about it. Doesn't want me to ask. Even now, I don't. He pushes the memories back, trapping them deep down inside himself where I can't find them.

Trust me, Patrick. In here, inside my home, this is the only place you can be free.

I'm not afraid of BMAC. But I am. I'm very afraid. And Bo knows it. He can see it inside my head. But fear can't matter. Not if I'm going to get home. *Either take me with you or I'm leaving.*

Bah! You wouldn't last five minutes outside these walls.

I'll take my chances. I shoulder past him, heading for the exit hatch.

All right wait. I turn back, and he's frowning at me, fists twisting the strap of his sack. He's inside my mind. I can feel him there, searching and prodding for any sign of a

21

bluff. But he won't find one. Because I'm not bluffing. If Bo won't help me, I'll do this on my own.

I'll take you, he says, finally. *And you'll see that I'm right. And then you can stop with this ridiculous 'going home' nonsense once and for all.*

I nod, but Bo's angry frown stays fixed to his face. Because we both know that I won't. No matter what happens, I can't stop until I figure out how to get back home. Get back to my little sister, my mom. Back to Gabby. And fix it.

Bo and I move from alley to alley, along rain-drenched, muddy pathways lined with makeshift homes. Most don't have windows – too much work to brace them against the strength of the Eventualies. The lights of tiny hearth fires flame and flicker through cracks in the recycled walls.

It's unsettling being outside. The streets – if you can even call them streets – are nothing like the time I left. The skyscrapers that used to climb into the clouds have mostly crumbled, except for the cluster of a dozen or so I see glowing on the horizon towards the heart of Avin. They are monstrously tall, shiny and new. Not broken and scarred like everything here in the outskirts. Nowbie territory. For the Nowbies, the power still flows like it did in my time, its electric light illuminating the underside of a stormy night sky. Standing in the centre of the cluster of giant buildings is one I'd recognise anywhere – all 553 metres of it – the Avin Turbine. Its blades are gone, replaced by a shiny ring flickering on top that Bo says does the same things the blades used to – power the city

22

– just more efficiently. But even with this small change, it's still the Avin Turbine. The same one I've been looking at since I was just a little kid. In 2383, it makes me feel just a little less alone.

That, and the cool Eventualies winds, driving the evening's drizzle into my face. *The Movers' wind*, it reminds me, rushing into my ear. It blows for me.

There's a grunt from Bo as he shuffles along ahead of me. *Blows for you, does it? Stand in the street at high noon and see if you still feel so romantic about it.*

I try not to blush. I always forget how powerful the Eventualies are here because it's not the way it is in my time. In my time, there are fewer Movers and Shadows, so the winds are weaker. Here, the Eventualies can get dangerous. During the day I can hear them howling over Bo's lair, hear the rattle and ping of debris they've torn loose from homes. They're so strong that you can't stand outside without protection. This is why everyone only leaves their shelters at night, when the Eventualies have eased off for the day. *A hundred and sixty miles an hour on an average day*, Bo never tires of telling me. *Do you know how much power a hundred and sixty miles an hour generates through the Turbine, Patrick?* I don't, but Bo does, he won't tell me how he knows this. He has a special metre he keeps outside the lair for measuring each day's top wind speed. And every evening he shares his findings with me, despite my complete lack of interest. *You'd be smart to listen to me, Patrick. The world always needs more educated people. You'll find these teachings useful to you when you grow up.* And it's that kind of talk that makes me ignore his attempts to teach me. Because he doesn't just mean when I 'grow up'. He means, when I 'grow up *here*'. And I have no intention of staying *here*.

Bo stops, and winces, rubbing at his left leg, the one that makes him walk with a limp. I don't know how he got it – another thing he doesn't have any interest in telling me. But I can see from the strain on his face that it's hurting him.

'You OK?'

He waves me off and grumbles something that's supposed to mean *It's fine*, even though I can feel his mind telling him it's not. I slow down, walking in step beside him as he struggles along. It's frustrating, forcing myself to keep pace with him, but I don't know where I'm going, so all I can do is let Bo lead the way.

We make our way through the busy bit – Dune's Thoroughfare. I guess it could pass for 'downtown' in this Movers' sector. Shops are opening up now that the winds have slowed and people have emerged to purchase and trade whatever they need as quickly as they can before the Cure Bus rolls through. It smells of life here, enough to make you believe this broken place could actually function as a town if it tried hard enough – smoky fires and savoury foods, spices and even coffee. It reminds me of Hexall Hall, the Movers' refuge back home in my time. Crows perch on shutters and rooftops and flap around on the street amongst people's feet. Where there are Movers, there are crows. One lets out an ear-piercing *caw* and swoops low by my face so that I have to duck out of the way. I watch it soar upwards, getting lost in the black of the sky, and think of my sister. She loves crows. One in particular.

Bo's stopped walking and excitement flutters through my chest. 'Are we here?' He moves towards a shack on our left, people queueing out the door.

'Bo?'

He ignores me, pushing his way to the front of the line. People are already crowding around him, shouting over each other while he tries to get through. I look up at the sheet metal awning, a handwritten sign dangles from it in a language I've never seen before. Words followed by prices. A goods list.

I guess we're here.

I follow after Bo as best I can, elbowed and shoved by everyone else who's clamouring for what he has in his bag.

Inside the shop, it's cramped, with rows and rows of shelves packed with what looks like nothing better than junk. Rusty pieces and cords, circuit boards and grubby-looking plastic. But everyone's sifting through it carefully like it's treasure. Maybe it is. If Bo can make robots and AvinGates out of this stuff, it's definitely worth something. To me, it all just looks like garbage.

Bo's at the back counter, negotiating with someone who I assume is the owner – a frail old lady who's carefully inspecting each piece she pulls from Bo's bag. I head towards them, keeping my eyes on the shelves in case I find the one piece of garbage I'm here for.

Two guys in black hoods, a few years older than me, watch as I pass and I keep my head down. I don't like being noticed. Not here, in 2383. What are they looking at, anyway? That's when I notice what I'm wearing – my filthy red sweatshirt and jeans. The same ones I was wearing when I left home. Everyone else is wearing dark coloured fabrics that look home-made, patched together from materials I don't recognise – leathery plastics and scaly metals. I stick out.

Bo glances back for me, a buzz of alarm in his mind as he looks me up and down. *We'll find you something else to wear,* he promises, while his background thoughts are about how stupid he is for overlooking my outfit.

Keeping my gaze on my feet, I nudge my way in next to Bo, annoying the people around him who are trying to trade for some little black cube, the same kind Bo places by the exit hatch every day before bed. Security, he'd told me. Keeps the borgs away. I'd figured they don't work very well since his SpiderBorgs crawl all over them, but from the way the old woman is staring at this one, I guess they really do.

'*Ah blicto stun,*' she says, firmly. There are a lot of different languages in 2383. English is just one of many. Between the Movers migrating from city to city looking for a better life (and never finding it), and all the Movers and Shadows arriving from times where language has changed and evolved, almost everyone in 2383 has to speak three languages or more. Bo himself speaks seven, his least favourite of which is English, which he stubbornly refuses to speak with me. Unfortunately for me, English is the only one I've got. And it's frustrating.

Bo shakes his head and laughs, speaking in her language. *Keep that sum for the next person offering you a Pulse Block. I'm sure you can find plenty of other people who can build them for you.*

She folds her arms across her chest and sighs. She spits out another price I don't understand.

Bo's still not satisfied. This could take a while.

'Do you have any Punches?' I ask her.

She frowns, no idea what I've said.

Don't be ridiculous, Bo seethes at me.

Would you just ask her?

I told you, you won't find such a thing here. If I've never heard of anything like it, it's a certainty she hasn't.

Why does he have to make it so difficult?

Then what's it matter if you just ask her?

The woman leans over the counter on her elbows, eyes darting between me and Bo. I wonder if she knows we're communicating silently.

With a frustrated sigh, Bo asks the question in her language. And her brow furrows. Before she shakes her head, I already know she has no idea what I'm talking about. If there's a Punch here, she doesn't know about it.

There, thinks Bo. *Are you happy?*

He knows I'm not.

'Does she know where I could find one?' I say out loud.

Bo almost laughs, which only makes me more annoyed, but he asks the question anyway. The woman shrugs and says something, casting me an apologetic look.

She's never heard of it, says Bo, a little too pleased with himself.

Maybe she knows someone who might have, I counter desperately.

Bo's grin goes away and he just blinks at me.

'Ask her, Bo!'

He clears his throat and turns back to her, asking the question. She thinks for a minute, and then she holds up a finger, eyes brightening as she answers him. Bo nods, and then starts talking to her about the Pulse Blocks again.

'Wait a minute,' I interrupt. 'What did she say? Does she know someone?'

No, nothing.

She said something, Bo.

Bo elbows me back. *Nothing useful, just CyberAvin searches. No help. Go wait for me by the door. I'll just be a minute.*

I step back, but I don't understand. She looked like she had an idea. Was it just to check CyberAvin? I've done enough of that, Bo knows it's no use to me. And I hate that I can't know for sure what she said. All I have to go on is what Bo told me. A weight settles onto my shoulders as I head back the way I came. I don't know where to go from here. Not that I held a lot of hope that I'd walk out of the shop with a Punch in my hands. But I thought at least maybe she'd have heard of one. Roth was a maniac, but I have to admire his work as a scientist. The Punch was an amazing invention, I can't believe BMAC would let it just disappear. Someone must know about it. I run my hands over the objects on the shelves. Nothing looks anything like a Punch.

'*Fiano act set sowa?*' The boys from earlier are standing in front of me, a shelf separating us.

I shrug, not understanding.

The smaller of the two, the one who spoke, tries another language. Like I said, there are a lot of languages in 2383.

The big one just scowls at me. I shake my head and move further down the aisle.

The small one tries again, 'Those are some raw threads you're rocking.'

My clothes. It's more noticeable than I thought. I smile awkwardly.

'You looking for something?' he asks.

'Just, uh, browsing.'

The tall one begins to laugh, eyes shifting side to side. He was scowling just a moment before – what's he laughing at?

'It's not here, is it?' the small one says. 'What you're looking for.'

I guess I look surprised, because he smiles.

'It's all over your face,' he says. 'I know cos that's how my face used to look. Before.'

'Before what?'

He rests his elbows on the shelf, eyes shifting from left to right to see if anyone's watching us. I glance over my shoulder. Bo is.

'Before the Unit found me.'

The Unit – Shade Unit, the last bastion of resistance for Movers and Shadows against the Nowbies. 'Are you guys Shade Unit?'

He snorts and shakes his head. 'Something like that. You might think of us as the new generation – tired of waiting for the decision-makers in Shade Unit to get off their asses and actually stand up to BMAC.'

That's how broken Avin is now. Even Shade Unit can't stay together.

The tall one isn't paying attention. He's back to scowling as he watches the door. His friend hits him. 'Show the kid,' he says.

The tall one obeys, flashing me his wrist without taking his eyes off the entrance. There on his wrist is a black hand tattoo, a crow's wings sprouting out the sides.

The short one grins at me, rolling up his own sleeve to reveal a matching tattoo. 'We're the Dark Unit. And we can help you find what you're looking for.''

'How do you know what I'm looking for?' I ask, defensively.

'Cos we're all looking for it,' he says. 'An end. To all this.'

That's not what I'm looking for. Not exactly.

'Rads!' A girl appears in the doorway wearing the same black jacket and hood. Her hair cascading down over her shoulder is unlike any I've ever seen – blue, like midnight. 'Gamma, it's time!'

The tall one, Rads, nods and pats the one who's been talking to me, Gamma. 'Time to go.'

Gamma ignores him. 'You a digithead?'

'A what?'

'The Unit is always looking for new digitheads. Wouldn't have to sift through this crap, either. You'd have all kinds of Norm tech and hardware at your fingertips in the Unit.'

Nowbie hardware. Like a Punch?

'What kind of tech?'

'Gamma,' says Rads, nodding at the door.

'You want in?' Gamma asks. 'Then follow us.'

Do I? Was this what the old lady was saying? That this Dark Unit of theirs might have a Punch? I take a step to follow and a hand clamps down on my shoulder.

Bo.

You boys want to play at your foolishness,' he growls at them in one of the many languages that he knows and I don't. While I don't speak it, I understand his words anyway because my mind is connected to his. *'You go ahead. But you do it alone.'*

Gamma says something back in a tone that doesn't sound very friendly.

I know better than you what kind of work Shade Unit does. Bo's skin has gone red, his eyes almost bulging. *I've been seeing it since before you were born!*

I've never seen Bo so angry. And I see the memories bubbling up again – the screaming, the running, the wind.

Gamma says something else, two short words that I'm pretty sure don't mean 'fair enough', and Rads bursts into laughter, a strange manic laugh as his eyes flick from Bo to Gamma.

'Rads!' The girl in the doorway. 'Knock it off. We have to go.'

And as quick as his laughter started, it disappears, replaced by an unnerving seriousness, turning away and heading for the door.

Gamma shakes his head and leans into me. 'You ever want to join up, kid,' he says. 'Our gang is always around here.'

And then he leaves with Rads and the blue-haired girl, out into the street.

This is what I meant, Bo says when they've gone, jabbing a finger into my chest. *You'd only get yourself into trouble.*

People in the shop are looking up from their items, watching Bo poke me and my frustration with him switches to anger.

I smack his hand away. *What'd you have to chase them off for? They said they could help me—*

Oh, I'm sure they did. You're lucky I interrupted you when I did.

'Lucky?!' I almost shout. 'Like I'm lucky you didn't tell me what the old woman said?'

What?

She told you something that could help me, Bo. Told you the name of someone who could help me. I know she did. Was it the Dark Unit? Is that what it was?

He throws up his arms, lets out an angry 'Bah' as he steps around me.

'What do you care if the Dark Unit helps me? You certainly don't want to!'

Dark Unit, Shade Unit. It's all the same fools! He grabs me by the collar and drags me to the door. *You want to see how they'll help you? You want to see what help from Shade Unit will cost you?*

Before I can answer, he's dragged me into the street.

And I can hear the roar of the Cure Bus descending from the sky.

PAT
2383

Even with his limp, Bo's too strong for me to get away from, and he pulls me to a mound of trash, piled up against the wall of the pawn shop. With a firm shove, he throws me into it. *Keep your head down*, he warns.

People with Movement capabilities, the familiar voice blasts over a crackly speaker somewhere above the clouds, *or those with communication to individuals of the past, the struggle of your condition need no longer persist.*

The people out on the streets run in all directions, seeking shelter. Doors lock, windows are shuttered. But still a few are left idling in the street. *Fools*, Bo thinks – it's on loop in his mind as he takes in all the people with their eyes turned skywards, waiting.

'Who are they?' I ask him.

But he shoots me an angry glare. I shouldn't be talking. *Volunteers*, he says into my mind.

They've come for the Cure. I search each face. For what, I don't know. Doubt maybe? Fear? I can't bring myself to believe they actually plan to deliver themselves to BMAC. But there they are, standing out in the open. Waiting for the bus.

I don't see Gamma or Rads, or the girl they left with.

The Cure for your condition is real, the voice continues. *You no longer need to hide outside the city limits if you register now with the Bureau of Movement Activity Control.*

Bo grumbles angrily under his breath as an older couple splashes by us, heads hung low and clutching each other's hands tightly. The woman glances nervously in our direction, her eyes meeting mine, and I can see she's scanning for judgement.

She's right to. I *am* judging. Just like Bo. I can't understand what she and her friend are thinking, running towards BMAC.

If there's one thing I know, it's that Movers should *always* run away from BMAC.

The humming and the voice on the speaker grow louder, and the wind picks up. Not the Eventualies. It's coming from above us.

Like a shark breaking the surf, the Cure Bus explodes from the clouds, bright white searchlights blinding me. Bo grabs my shoulder and pushes me down further beside the trash.

I've never seen the Cure Bus before, and only now do I realise it isn't a bus at all. It's some other vehicle altogether. No wheels, it floats above the ground in the middle of the street. A hovercraft, sort of. Armoured, like a tank. Black. With the BMAC symbol glowing on its side.

Three BMAC officers, just as armoured as their bus, stand on top. There's an officer in the middle using the loudspeaker, his voice echoing over the wind and rain. More officers file out of it, guiding the volunteers up a ramp that leads them into the bus.

There's shouting, I can hear it faintly over the echo of the speaker. Someone's yelling. Multiple someones. *What is that?* I ask Bo. *Do you hear it?*

Bo just frowns, his mouth pulled into a grim line.

Beyond the cluster of people who are getting on the bus is another group, their faces covered, hurling things at BMAC.

This is how Shade Unit helps, Bo says.

And then I realise it's them – black jackets and wiry frames. Dark Unit. The one at the front, leading the charge, I recognise – it's Gamma. There's no sign of Rads or the girl with strange blue hair, but Gamma is there with others dressed just like him. Dark Unit is attacking the bus.

And I feel a rush of excitement, an urge to join them. I rise up a bit, trying to get a better look. They sprint towards the officers, screaming battle cries and showing no fear. I want to rush the bus too. To fight BMAC. To do something.

Bo grabs me by my hood and pulls me down just as a blast of blinding white light explodes from somewhere on top of the bus. I've seen that kind of blast before.

Light engulfs a few Dark Unit members. Gamma takes the brunt of the blast.

The stricken Dark Unit soldiers freeze, bodies shaking, before they drop to the ground.

Commander Roth. He could shoot light just like that. I can see him in my mind, lightning exploding from his palm – exploding from the Punch.

Bo looks away, disgusted, and I can hear his thoughts. *And that's it for them.*

'Are they,' I barely whisper, 'are they dead?'

Bo shakes his head. *Frozen. It's the light that does it. Paralyses the pungits and the person for a time.*

Paralyses the pungits. Roth told me that same thing not long ago.

One blast from a shock cannon that powerful, Bo says, *and the victim won't move for hours. Long enough for BMAC to arrest them without a fight.*

The BMAC officers continue shooting, more Dark Unit members dropping, others fleeing, until there's no one left but the frightened volunteers, huddling around the boarding ramp. Bo and I watch the officers drag the fallen Unit members onto the bus. Arrested.

'Does that mean they'll be . . .'

Shelved. Bo looks at me. *That's what Shade Unit gets you.*

If Bo hadn't stopped me, would I have gone with Gamma?

Do you want to end up like them? he asks.

No. He knows I don't. I can't let BMAC Shelve me or cure me.

I need to focus on getting home; I can't be side-tracked by the fight in this time.

There's a surge of anger in his mind. *If you don't want to end up like those morons, then it's time you stopped with this going home nonsense.*

I can't.

They're gone, his mind rages at me. *All of them. Everyone you've ever known is long dead and buried. You have a new life here. It's time you accept it.*

I look away, watching the officers carry the last of the fallen Dark Unit on board. I can see the Avin Turbine blinking in the distance – a beacon in this time, and in mine. Somewhere, back in history, it glows for Gabby too, for Maggie and Mom. *I can't accept it*, I tell him. *I have to go back. I have to find a Punch.*

You won't find a Punch, he growls in his language.

'How do you know?'

Because I've never heard of such a thing.

'You have! You were in my head the whole time when Roth—'

Here, Patrick. I've never heard of a Punch here, in this time.

'And you know everything, do you?'

There's another surge of anger and I think he's going to shout at me, but he doesn't. Something shifts inside his mind – there's a sadness there. And it's all for me – for my search and the heartache he's sure it will end in. *No I don't*, he admits. *But I know someone who does. Or close to it anyway.*

I frown, waiting for him to say more, but his mind is fighting with itself as the last of the volunteers are loaded onto the bus and the engines start up again. The street is empty now. The bus lifts up into the clouds, and it's just me and Bo and the crows.

Fine, Bo says at last. *You want to find this Punch of yours, I know someone who can help. I can't keep fighting you about this and I can't keep you out of trouble for ever. You need to learn some sense. And if the Archivist can finally talk it into you, then it's worth the trip.*

The Archivist?

Bo winces, forcing himself up from behind the garbage. *The guardian of history, you might call him.* He rubs at his leg and sighs.

And you think this guy will know where to find a Punch?

I think if he doesn't, then no one does. And if that's the case, there's nothing left but to drop it. All right?

I agree, but he knows I'm lying.

GABBY
2083

The bell rings. Everyone runs for the door. Everyone but me. I'm always the last one to leave. I guess I'm the only one in no rush to get home.

I disassemble the pungit ray, wrapping the fragile bits in pieces of clothing I brought from home.

'Miss Vargas?' Mrs Dibbs doesn't look up from her desk. She's scribbling on a piece of paper. Real paper. Real pen. Must be important to use real paper. 'I do hope you've made a reminder to yourself about tomorrow.'

I don't need to remind myself. The whole city of Avin is one big reminder. Commercials, billboards, posters. Each one demanding Movers remember their phase forms. 'Yes, ma'am,' I say anyway.

She nods and folds up the note, placing it inside and sealing an envelope. She gets up from her desk. Walks over to me. 'As Phase 2, I know you know how important it is that you submit on time.' She hands me the envelope. I hesitate. 'Give this to your parents when you get home, please.'

A handwritten letter. For my parents. My fingers itch at the thought.

'What's it for?' I ask.

'It's for them,' she says, sternly.

My hand trembles and I take the envelope. It's dry and crisp. It smells like sawdust. I stare at the pure white. Whatever's inside, I know my parents won't be happy.

Mrs Dibbs scoffs. 'Let's go now, Miss Vargas. I'd like to get home myself, you know. The more you dawdle, the longer I'm stuck here.'

I tuck the note into my pocket. Hurry to pack away the rest of the pungit ray. Mrs Dibbs watches me. Arms folded, tapping her foot impatiently.

Why did she give me a letter? She didn't give the other Movers in our class a letter. Matt Doig. Pat Mermick. She just let them leave. Why am I the only one?

Because you're Phase 2.

My Shadow seeps in, reading my thoughts. *You're more powerful than the others.*

Your power frightens her.

What power? Phase 2 may be stronger than 1, but that doesn't mean much. All it means is that I hear my Shadow. Inside my head, all the time. Filling my head with his anger.

Which he thinks makes me better. Makes me stronger. But I'm not. I'm being worn down. Every angry, hate-filled thought from him eats away at me. Makes me weaker.

Phase 2 doesn't feel powerful. It's crippling.

You cripple yourself.

'No, you do!'

40

Mrs Dibbs clears her throat. My face feels hot. Did I speak out loud? She watches me with a raised eyebrow.

I did.

Humiliated, I scramble to grab the last of the pungit ray parts. I don't bother to wrap them. *Just get out of here.* I toss them in my duffle bag. Head for the door.

Outside the classroom, the halls are packed. I feel hot. I can't breathe. How could I have done that? How could I let him get to me like that? Engaging your Shadow makes you a stronger Mover. Everyone knows that. How could I let myself respond to him?

Because I'm right.

abcdefg...

I press my back against the lockers. Breathe deep. Focus on the letters. Push him back. Push him out.

You're fighting yourself, he tells me. *I'm part of you.*

I don't want him to be. I don't want this part. I didn't ask for it. I have to get rid of him.

You might as well fight your own eyes. Your liver. Your heart.

No. A boil. A cyst. A tumour. You can remove a tumour.

You can't remove your heart.

'Go away!' I whisper. Hit my head against the locker – once, twice, three times. Jog him loose from my mind. But I can feel him in there. Coiling in tighter, like the roots of a tree, twisting and tightening around my brain.

And then a scream cuts through the chaos in my head.

'VAAAAAAAATOR BOMB!!!!'

I open my eyes. Pat Mermick is launched into the air, Ollie Larkin and a red-headed boy I don't know propelling him upwards. He soars over the heads of the other students. The doors to the elevator open with a ding, and he falls inside, landing on top of the other passengers. Some kids are laughing. Others cheering. Others are angry.

The doors close. And he's gone.

Vator bombs are against the rules. But Pat Mermick doesn't care.

I wish I didn't care like Pat Mermick.

My Shadow's grip tightens. I wince, his hold is so strong. *He makes fun of you too,* he reminds me. *He laughed like the rest of them.*

I remember Pat's face. The way he laughed when Ollie called me Gooba.

He's no different from the others.

He is though. That's something I've always known. Since that day in third grade, Pat Mermick was different. The class was sitting in a circle on the carpet, I was sitting there too. Listening to my Shadow whisper to me. I wanted him to leave me alone. So I sang my abc song. Out loud. And everyone in the class started laughing.

A little girl – Evie Mills – called me Shelf-Meat.

Everyone laughed more.

Except Pat Mermick.

'What did you just say?' He stood up from his seat on the carpet. 'Do you know how many Movers get Shelved every year?' he shouted. Our teacher told him to sit. He didn't. 'Do you know what BMAC does to Shelve a person? Do you?!'

No. None of us did. We were all too little. No one wants to tell little kids how Shelving works. But Pat Mermick knew. His dad was Shelved just four months earlier.

'They stick a needle in your head!' he yelled.

That made Evie start crying.

'Say you're sorry,' he told her. 'Say you're sorry!'

That made Evie cry more.

And our teacher had to have a meeting with Pat's mother.

All because he stood up for me.

He didn't stand up for you today, my Shadow reminds me.

No. I guess he didn't.

'Gabby?' Leelee Esposito is walking over to me. She's smiling. She's very pretty when she smiles. I'd like to look like Leelee. But there's something wrong about the way she's smiling. Nicely. Too nicely. She wants something. 'Have you done the math homework for tonight?' she asks.

I shake my head.

'I've got judo, and I just know I'm not going to get it done,' she tells me. Like we talk all the time. Leelee Esposito never talks to me. She tilts her head, blinking big lashes.

Here it comes.

'Could you message me the answers later?'

I look down at my feet. This is the third time in two weeks.

Tell her to blow off.

Leelee's smile fades. 'Look, I'm really in a bad spot, Gabby. And you know you'll have it done in, like, five minutes, so what's the big deal?'

My Shadow burns. He doesn't like the way Leelee is talking to me.

Neither do I.

'It's not like you've never done it before.' she says, impatiently.

And then I see it. What my Shadow wants me to do. I'm grabbing Leelee by her curly blonde locks. Pulling her head down as my other elbow comes up. Her nose crunches. And when she staggers back from me, blood pours down her face.

I grin. I don't mean to. But I do. I'd never do something like that. I couldn't. But the thought of it – I feel a little stronger.

It would serve her right.

'So we good?' she says, misreading my smile.

I nod.

'Great,' she says, too-nice smile returning. 'Thanks.' And she bounces off down the hall.

I won't do her homework, I promise myself. I can stand up for myself that much, at least.

It isn't enough, my Shadow insists, coiling tighter. *They'll keep using you, keep laughing at you. Keep hating you.*

Maybe. But at least I won't have to do Leelee's homework if I don't want to. She'll hate me for it, but who cares if she does? Pat Mermick wouldn't care. I don't have to care either.

My Shadow's grip. It's so tight. I've never felt it this strongly before. I groan.

Alone, you are powerless.

You're hurting me.

You're hurting yourself. Hurting us. By keeping us apart.

The pain is so bad. I lean against the locker to keep from falling. There's a tightening in my stomach. Way down deep. A nagging urge.

Move me.

And that's what it is – the nagging in my gut. It's a muscle. The muscle that wants me to Move. It's flexing. Why?

I'm Phase 2, I remind him and myself. ***I'm too weak. I can't Move.***

My stomach twitches.

I think you can.

I breathe through the pain. Fast, panicked spurts. Sing sing sing.

'A b c d . . .'

The squeeze on my brain leaps to a crushing pressure. I cry out. Sing faster.

'. . . e f g, h i j k . . .'

Push him back. Push him out.

His grip begins to loosen

And then he's gone. Because I forced him out? No. I think he let me go on purpose. I've never felt him that strongly before. Never been so . . . hurt. I've acknowledged him too much today. Let him too far in. I can't let him bait me. I have to ignore him.

If I don't, I'll only make him stronger.

I rub at my head. There's a dull ache where he released me.

I can't let him get stronger.

PAT
2383

The streets are deserted. Eerily still, save for the rush of the Eventualies. Like the Cure Bus stole the very breath from Dune's Thoroughfare. Bo and I walk in silence, each of us trying to quiet our thoughts from the other. I can still hear his though. However much he tries, he can't silence his uncertainty. He's not sure he should bring me to the Archivist. Not sure he should risk exposing me. Not sure he wants to open himself up to the old man's questions. What questions, I don't know. Questions about me, maybe. Who I am. Where I come from. I'm not really sure how to answer those either.

Though from the shape of Bo's thoughts, it seems like these are questions that have nothing to do with me. And everything to do with Bo.

So this guy, I say, tired of trying to ignore Bo's thoughts. *This Archivist. How do you know him?*

An old friend. The memories are bubbling up again – the wind, the Avin Turbine, the screaming – and he pushes them down.

And what makes you think he'll know anything?

Bo sighs through his nostrils. *Before the war, as tensions were building and BMAC's power became more and more corrupt, a number of individuals had the foresight to preserve as much historical information as they could.*

We turn down another street. This one is dark. None of the dwellings that line it have any lights on. The crumbled remnants of old office towers and singed apartment buildings paint a picture of the fighting.

He who holds the power controls the information, says Bo. *So before BMAC could seize complete control over the city and CyberAvin, men and women calling themselves Archivists preserved what they could. Through the war, they kept strict records and documented history. And still do today. If a Mover wants information, an Archivist is their best hope.*

Bo stops, rubbing at his leg and I realise there's nothing around us, not even any crows. We're standing in front of a collapsed building. Beams, cinder and rubble piled up in a mess.

What is this? Are we here?

Bo shuffles up to a slab of concrete lying askew next to the pile.

Bo? There's nothing here.

He waves me closer and when I'm beside him he points to a scratch in the concrete. A circle. And there's a faded black handprint in the middle. Just like the one I'd seen on Gamma's wrist, without the crow's wings.

Shade Unit.

'What?!'

He puts a finger to his lips and sets to work clearing away some rubble at the side of the slab.

Bo, what are we doing here? I thought you said we were going to the Archivist?

This is *the Archivist.*

On the side of the concrete slab is a piece of gnarled metal: the splintered bone of a chewed-up old building. But when Bo grabs hold of it, I see that it is really a door handle. He pulls it open and reveals a warmly lit staircase that goes down into the earth.

I don't understand. *This* is the Archivist? Marked with the symbol of Shade Unit? Does the Archivist work for those guys? I look nervously at Bo. Why would Bo take us to anyone associated with Shade Unit?

You're looking for answers, Patrick. Well then, Bo nods to the stairs, *go get them.*

I glance back the way we came, afraid someone might be watching. This feels dangerous.

It is dangerous, Bo says, reading my thoughts. *But you wanted this.*

Yes. I do want this. I want the answers. I want to find the Punch.

I step down into the stairwell, and Bo follows, closing the heavy door behind us.

It's quiet inside, and warm. The air is still and dense with heat. The walls down here must be really thick. There's a rustling somewhere below us and a voice – high-pitched and nasal – calls out.

'Houjun?'

I look back at Bo who nods for me to keep going.

'Hello?' the voice tries again – there are many languages worth trying in 2383. 'Olakon?'

'Carlin!' Bo answers.

'Bo?' The owner of the voice, Carlin, peeks his head into the stairwell – an elderly man, maybe even older than Bo, with glasses that make his eyes bulge bigger than an owl's and a balding head with tufts of hair sticking out wildly behind his ears. His mouth spreads into a gap-toothed smile and he throws open his arms, speaking to Bo in words I don't understand. The man pulls me forwards, through a doorway and into a cramped room before he steps around me to greet Bo properly. The old men shake hands and laugh as if I'm not there at all.

The room is a mess of clutter – notebooks, binders, file folders and boxes stacked in towers from floor to ceiling along the walls, in the corners, and in random piles all over the floor. Papers stick out everywhere, scattered here and there in absolute chaos. Candles placed precariously on many of the stacks light up the room. I'm overwhelmed. Paper – real paper – isn't something I see a lot of back in 2083. I would guess it's even scarcer now. Too rare and expensive for anyone to bother with. Everything is digital. But even still, there must be millions of pages here, compiled and clipped and stapled and folded with what looks like no rhyme or reason to their organisation.

A desk sits against the far stacks, several binders lying open beside the candles clustered there. The Archivist's desk.

I step closer and glance down at one of the open pages – a BMAC seal is stamped on the top left corner. The year 2383 printed below. It's current, whatever it is. There are three columns, each one a list of names and a year printed beside it. Bentley Schiff, 2347. Boris Wilte, 2376. There must be a hundred names per column, and in the bottom right is written 'page 3 of 52'. There are a lot more names where these came from.

The binder that's lying open next to the lists shows an article, the title printed in big bold font – *Finally! Blue Ashlinn apprehended by BMAC, Avin rests easy*. I glance back at the list of names. 'Blue Ashlinn, 2339' has been circled in black ink. *Apprehended by BMAC*, my mind repeats as I glance back at the stamped symbol. Below the year, I notice something I hadn't before – *Silo 3*. My lips feel dry just thinking about it – the cold, dry air, the clank of the metal grates as I walked, the marbled frozen feet, one on top of the other, climbing up and up and up through the round tower. The Shelves. This list is a current account of the Movers and Shadows sleeping on BMAC's Shelves.

The binder slams shut, pinching my fingers, and I leap back from the table. The Archivist leans over the desk, staring at me over the rim of his glasses. 'Another Blue Ashlinn fan, I take it?'

'What?' My hand clasps my stinging finger, my heart thudding from the surprise. 'I don't know who that is.'

The Archivist raises an eyebrow and looks at Bo. He asks him something in Bo's language – I guess even the Archivist knows about Bo's distaste for English. I can feel Bo's answer inside my head when he speaks. *The boy isn't well-read on current affairs.*

'Not well-read?' chuckles the Archivist. 'Strange sort of establishment to come to then, for the not-well-read. But I wouldn't have thought one need be well-read to have heard of the infamous Blue Ashlinn.'

I glance at Bo, not sure what to say. He answers for me. *Still on the hunt for Blue Ashlinn, are you, Carlin?*

'It would go faster if you agreed to help me.'

The warmth that was in Bo's head, the comfort and familiarity he felt being down here, instantly freezes over. *I don't know anything about Blue Ashlinn.*

'You know her daughter.'

An image flashes across Bo's mind: a woman with long blue hair. Bo pulls it back as quickly as he can, but I've seen it. And I'm wondering who she is. How Bo knows her. How this Carlin man knows him.

And Bo can feel my questions.

Careful, Carlin, he warns.

'All right, all right, I won't get into it.' The Archivist turns back to me. 'Still, though. Strange you haven't heard of her. Didn't you want to be Blue when you played "BMAC and Outlaws" on the street as a child?'

Patrick isn't exactly from around these parts.

My mouth drops. Why would Bo tell him that? Why would Bo even hint that I'm a Moved person? We don't even know this man!

This man is my friend, Patrick, says Bo inside my head. *Trust me.*

The Archivist purses his lips and lowers his glasses to the tip of his nose, his eyes squinting as he appraises me more closely. 'That so? A Shadow, are we?'

Not exactly.

That's right, Bo lies for me in his own language. *Patrick here is a recently Moved Shadow.*

But I'm not a Shadow, I think to Bo.

He doesn't need to know everything, Patrick.

I frown. *I thought you said he was your friend? To trust him?*

I told you to trust me. *I don't need to tell my friends every detail about my life.*

The Archivist glances from me to Bo, frowning. I quickly look away, afraid the Archivist will be able to tell we're communicating silently right in front of him.

'I'm a recently Moved Shadow,' I say.

'Where's your Mover, then?'

That's a good question – another one I have no answer to.

Picked up by BMAC, Bo says quickly. *Would've caught the boy here, too, if he weren't such a fast runner.*

The Archivist harrumphs and turns back to Bo, saying something in Bo's language.

I am telling you the truth, Bo tells him.

The Archivist points an accusing finger at Bo, speaking faster, stern.

What do you want me to say, Carlin? Bo says calmly. *The boy turned up at my door, scared out of his wits and desperate to get back to the future he came from. I wouldn't lie to you.*

The Archivist grumbles something in a dubious tone. I don't blame him. Taking in a random frightened kid doesn't exactly sound like Bo's style.

I can be charitable when I want to be, Bo tells him.

The Archivist doesn't look convinced when he turns back to me. 'Tell me then, Shadow Patrick. What is it you've come to me for?'

'A Punch.'

'A Punch?' He taps his chin, scanning the shelves over his head. 'Punch, punch, punch. Where have I heard that word before?'

'It's some old tech my uh . . . Mover told me about,' I say, careful to be as vague as I can. 'Something to do with pungits.'

The Archivist motions at me to follow him, into the stacks. 'Well, if it's pungits you want, I've got plenty on them. The last six rows here.' My heart sinks. There are six rows of floor-to-ceiling shelves packed tightly with papers and binders, still more piled in stacks cluttering up the aisles. 'These three front rows here are mostly pungit theory and history. And the back shelf is focused on current pungit applications. If it's anywhere, it's in here.'

With a phlegmy cough, The Archivist shuffles by me, heading back to Bo and his desk, offering him something to drink.

In here. Somewhere. Hidden inside these thousands and thousands of pages. It could take me years to find even a mention of a Punch in all of this.

Bo's inside my head, reading my thoughts. *Then best not to waste too much time gawking.*

With a sigh, I set to work, scanning the titles on the spines of the first shelf's binders. Bo's right. For a Mover, there's no sense wasting any time.

PAT
2383

A kick to my foot jolts me awake.

I'm sitting on the floor of the Archivist's library, my back against the pungit history shelves and a binder lying open in my lap. Bo stands over me, scowling, a cup of something hot and spicy-smelling in his hand. The Archivist is huddled over his desk, jabbering on about whatever it is he's reading. I assume he's talking to Bo but it doesn't seem like Bo's listening.

'What time is it?' I ask, wiping the drool from my chin.

Late, he tells me silently. *The sun is down.*

I look at the books piled beside me. We've been here nearly an entire day. I spent all last night and this morning trying to get through as much reading as I could. By noon my head had been bobbing into my chest while I tried to fight sleep. I must have lost the battle and dozed off.

The Cure Bus will be out soon. At least Bo won't be in a rush to go anywhere.

Bo hands me the cup.

'What is it?' I ask.

He shrugs. *Archivist cooking*. And then he leaves me to lean against the old man's desk, pretending to listen to whatever the Archivist is gesticulating wildly about.

I look into the mug, pleasantly hot against the skin of my palms. It looks like coffee but it smells like some kind of spicy soup. I swirl it, expecting to see chunks of beans or noodles but there's nothing. Only liquid. I can't tell if it's a drink or a soup, but it doesn't really matter. The scent makes my stomach growl and I take a sip.

It sets me coughing immediately. Flecks of spice cling to the back of my throat and singe like hot coals.

The Archivist pauses his rant to turn and look at me. 'My thirty-two-spice mull,' he says. 'It's good for you. Cough through the pain, Shadow Patrick, it's good.'

Thirty-two spice is right. I can taste the granules of each and every one but I can't identify any of them. My throat and chest are hot, the fire of the soup spreading down through my body and burning in the pit of my stomach.

Slowly, I get to my feet, breathing through the heat, and walk over to the desk where Bo and the Archivist are sitting.

'I'm saying she expected to get caught.' The Archivist says, reclining in his chair and placing his feet on the desk. 'Blue Ashlinn would still be at large if she hadn't insisted on targeting First Avin bank.'

Bo shakes his head. *If it wasn't First Avin, it would've been the next bank after that*.

'No, Bo! It wouldn't! She'd managed hundreds of robberies before this one. What went so wrong this specific time?'

BMAC got wise to her plans.

'Of all people, you can't really believe that.'

I glance at the papers strewn beneath the Archivist's holey socks. More articles on Blue Ashlinn. *Outlaw Blue Ashlinn Strikes Again, East-Fourth Branch of Secure FIILES Bank Hacked!* A FIILES Bank isn't like a money bank they'd have in the old days. A FIILES Bank isn't really a bank at all. It's a data centre. Every person in Avin has their own FIILES – birth certificate, driver's licence, financial records. Even my school grades used to be stored in my FIILES. FIILES are an Avin citizen's entire life.

'Blue Ashlinn was a FIILES thief?' I ask.

Bo nods.

'She was more than that!' The Archivist pumps a fist into the air. 'She was the greatest fighter Shade Unit's ever had! She didn't care about being caught by BMAC because being caught doesn't matter to someone with her level of Movement ability!'

I've had just about all I can take of your crackpot extra-Movement ability ideas, Carlin.

'What do you mean?' I ask.

They both ignore me, Carlin leaping up from his chair and rifling through the papers on his desk in a frenzy. 'Crackpot theories, are they?' He pulls up a paper like he's won some kind of victory and pushes it into Bo's face. 'Whose face is that then, huh? Date marked fourth of January 2018.'

Bo squints at the image, and his frown morphs into surprise.

'Ah ha!' shouts Carlin. 'There, you see?' He shows the

image to me, as if I can help support his argument. It's an old photograph, really old. A president stands on a podium at a rally, crowds of people cheer behind him. Carlin's finger points to one face that's frowning – a girl with hair the same colour as the girl from the pawn shop: midnight blue.

An ancestor, suggests Bo. *A relative*.

'A relative!' balks Carlin. 'Blue Ashlinn's identical twin, maybe!'

'But how is that possible?' I ask.

It isn't, says Bo.

'Breezes, Bo! Speak English for the boy's sake, you stubborn old fart!'

Bo doesn't, knowing full well I can understand him fine, and carries on in his language of choice. *Carlin, you're a conspiracy theorist, your anomaly Movers don't exist.*

'I'm a historian, Bo. And a damn good one. And I'm telling you, this is proof that there are Movers out there with talents that surpass Phase 3 movement capabilities.'

Another phase. Stronger than Phase 3. BMAC thought Gabby was a new phase. I remember sitting with her in my apartment, as the news broadcaster warned all of Avin to watch out for her. My chest aches.

'And if I could just find Blue's daughter Constance, I know I could prove it.'

Well, you won't find Connie, says Bo. *She finds you.*

'She'd find you, Bo,' says the Archivist. 'If you would just send word that you're looking for her.'

Don't make me say it again, Carlin.

'But why not? You used to worship her! You were one of her best—'

There's a flash of anger across Bo's mind. *I said be careful, Carlin.*

But I'm not listening any more. A year on one of the binders at the bottom of the stack turns my blood to ice.

Silo 2 – 2083.

The year I left. My time.

I run to the stack and tug the binder from the bottom, nearly toppling all the ones above.

'Steady now!' the Archivist cries, leaping up from his desk. 'Hey, I have those organised, you know.'

Dropping onto the floor, I flip open the binder, pages and pages and pages of names flipping by in a blur of black and white until I come to the Ms: *Mermick*. My name. It's there. Just the one name. *Michael Mermick*. My father. No Maggie. No Mom. They aren't here. BMAC didn't Shelve them.

Frantically, my fingers pull through the pages, to the back of the binder. To the Vs.

Gabriela Vargas – 2083.

I press my palm to her name. *Gabby*. It's true. The proof is right here. It's not that I thought the things I've read were lies, I just . . . I just hoped they were wrong somehow. Hoped she was still where I left her, on the observation deck of the Avin Turbine, confident in her power as a Mover, taking back her life. But this binder makes that image disappear. And all I can see are her feet, pale and marbled next to thousands of others. She's on the Shelves because of me. Because I'm here.

The Archivist's shadow falls over Gabby's name as he stands over me. '2083? That year's a doozy,' he says.

I look up through watery eyes, surprised. 'You know it?'

'Of course I know it. It's the year Beadie Hartman discovered pungits.'

I trace the G with my finger. Beadie Hartman did not discover pungits.

'Lots of interesting, though primitive, pungit research and tech came out of 2083, from Beadie Hartman and her BMAC lab. Fascinating stuff, the dawn of pungit under-standing . . . Now, let me see . . .'

He disappears behind some shelves, muttering to himself before finally crying out, 'Ah ha! Here we are.' He comes back with a thick binder and opens it to the first page. 'BMAC Technologies Inventory. I've had some late nights with that one, I must admit.'

I take the new binder from the Archivist. A technologies inventory from 2083. It's organised much like the Shelving list, columns and columns of listed items, with brief descrip-tions and suggested further reading beside each entry.

And there it is. A few page flips in. The Punch. The notes beneath it are brief. *Evidence leftover from the Vargas case. Future tech brought in by renegade Shadow. Weapon – fatal to those with no Movement capabilities. Effect on Movers/ Shadows unclear.*

They don't know what it does. At least not in 2083. Could they have figured it out later?

Kept for further investigation. Warehouse 4.

'They kept it,' I whisper. 'Would BMAC still have this stuff? From 2083?'

The Archivist shrugs and pushes his glasses further up his nose. 'Depends on what it is. I suppose they might still have some of them, though I think it's policy to destroy anything that's been idle for ten years.'

'Where is this?' I ask him, holding up the binder and pointing to the page. 'Warehouse 4? Do you know where it is?'

The Archivist chuckles. 'Oh they haven't used warehouses in more than a hundred years, boy. If BMAC has hung onto anything you find in there, they've probably got it tucked away nicely in the Time Cache.'

'Time Cache?'

'It's a vault, son. BMAC keeps its greatest treasures in there. Everything they've stolen from the rest of us. Regular pirates, they are.'

'Where can I find it?'

The Archivist looks at me like I've sprouted a second head before glancing at Bo. Bo shakes his head. *There is no finding it, Patrick. The Time Cache is inside BMAC Headquarters, in the heart of Avin.*

'I need to go there,' I tell him.

You can't, says Bo, and I can feel his patience wearing thin.

'You can't, young man,' the Archivist says, not realising Bo has told me this in his mind. 'You don't think BMAC just lets Movers and Shadows waltz into their greatest treasure trove, do you?'

No, of course not. I'll have to break in somehow.

There's a pulse of frustration from Bo as he catches my thoughts.

The Archivist is rifling through a stack of papers by the front door, and pulls out several pages for me. 'Here, son,' he says, dropping the papers onto my binder. 'Perhaps you need a bit of a history lesson on Nowbie/Mover relations.' The pages look like copies from a textbook, summarising the war between the Nowbies and Shade Unit. 'When the Nowbies won the war, BMAC confiscated everything the Shade Unit had: weapons, documents, research, everything in our arsenal. They threw it in the Time Cache, to be studied and dissected to help the Nowbie cause. To be used *against* us. They don't want Movers and Shadows in there, unless it's our skeletons. Getting close to the Time Cache is a massively dangerous endeavour, my boy. Not even Blue Ashlinn would try something so bold.'

'I don't care if it's dangerous,' I snap. 'It's what I need, so will you please just help me?'

The room is silent except for the howl of the Eventualies. Bo and the Archivist just stare at me, surprised by my outburst. I'm a little surprised too. I know they're just trying to tell me the truth. But the reality is, it can't matter how dangerous it is to get the Punch, can't matter how difficult, or impossible. All that matters is the Punch and getting my hands on it. I know where it is now and Bo didn't think we'd even find that out.

A rumble calls their eyes to the ceiling. I listen. It's the same sound I hear every night – the Cure Buses are on the move.

'What's so important about this Punch gadget to you, anyway?' asks the Archivist, still looking up towards the sounds of BMAC. 'Why do you think it's worth risking your life over?'

I stare down at the papers in my lap. 'It's my only hope of getting home.'

'Getting home?' says the Archivist, throwing up his arms. 'Well, let the breeze take him. Bo, this boy is out of his mind.'

Bo watches me, brow furrowed. He knows I'm not. Because he felt what the Punch did to me – what it did to us. He felt the pungits reverse.

'I can do it,' I tell the Archivist, annoyed by his tone. 'As long as I have the Punch, I've seen it. I know how it works.'

Bo cuts me a warning glare. It's comments like that one that give away what time I'm from.

But the Archivist never looks away from the ceiling. It's like he hasn't heard me at all. He spins on his heel, forgetting Bo and I entirely, and disappears into the stacks.

Bo lets out a frustrated growl, rubbing his hands over his face. He speaks in his own language, too frustrated to keep it inside his head. I hear the meaning of his words: *Why can't you just accept that this is your life now? In this time? I said I would help you, and I have. But what you're asking for is too much, Patrick. I can't support this! You don't understand what you're up against. I do.*

'I need to fix it, Bo!' I say. 'Gabby is on the Shelves because of me. I need to go back and make it right. What else am I supposed to do? Just leave her there? Just forget about my family?'

Yes! He shouts in his mind. *What you're talking about, storming BMAC's Time Cache, is suicide. Honestly, Patrick. You're talking just like those fools in the Shade Unit who are stupid enough to think they can take out armoured BMAC vehicles all on their own. I thought you were smarter than that, Patrick. You have to be smarter than that!*

Bo turns away from me and I feel hopeless. I hate that he compared me to the young people in masks that storm the Cure Buses. I've felt how Bo thinks of them. To have him lump me in with them stings.

Patrick, says Bo, *you don't even know for sure that the Punch is in the Time Cache. It could have been destroyed decades ago.*

'If-if I may.' The Archivist emerges sheepishly from his stack of shelves holding an armful of binders, one balanced open beneath his nose. 'It would seem that this Punch device of young Patrick's is indeed still alive and well.'

What are you saying, Carlin?

'Well, I had known that I'd seen that word before – Punch. But then I heard it outside. The Cure Bus. Listen.'

The voice on the speakers is faint, barely loud enough to make out the words. But we all know them by heart anyway.

'And I remembered where I'd seen it mentioned before. It had something to do with the mechanism that equips the Cure Buses to freeze pungits. So I went into the archives to see what I had on the evolution and structure of the Cure Bus and . . . well, look.' He places the binder down on the desk and motions us over. There's a diagram of the Cure Bus, with notes and lines breaking down its make-up. 'See here?' The Archivist points to the paragraphs next to the drawing of the cannon that sits on top of the bus. 'It says the technology comes from a much earlier, more primitive device that was part of the early era of pungit experimentation. A device that has been preserved by BMAC's antiques collection, known as a Punch. Look, see here? The year of publication for this text is 2378. Only six years ago. Where else could BMAC have recovered such a device if not from the Time Cache?'

My cheeks spread into a grin and the Archivist nods at me. 'I think you may be in luck, young Patrick.'

But Bo isn't smiling. *Luck? What luck, Carlin? The Punch is still locked away in the Time Cache. Do you know what kind of tech they've got guarding that thing? What kind of AI?*

The Archivist raises an eyebrow. 'Well now, doesn't that sound like exactly the sort of challenge that would excite the greatest digithead Shade Unit has ever had?'

GABBY
2083

I step into the elevator. My brain still aches where my Shadow squeezed. Move me, he'd said. Demanded it. And I felt my muscles flex. Felt them ready to do it. I hug myself as more students file into the lift. But I wouldn't have done it, would I? I couldn't. I'm only Phase 2.

The monitor above the door plays through BMAC's Movers Threat public service announcement. 'The Bureau of Movement Activity Control – Patrolling your Present. Protecting your Future. The Mover threat is a very real and ever-present danger. It is carefully monitored and treated according to an individual's Movement capabilities, or phase status.'

Two, I tell myself. I'm Phase 2. I'm too weak to Move my Shadow. Too weak, too weak, too weak.

You're stronger than you know.

My hand flies to my head, like I can physically jog him loose. Someone snickers.

I look up. Ollie Larkin is standing by the buttons. Grinning.

'Goooooooooobaaaaa . . .'

Everyone turns and looks at me. My cheeks feel hot.

I don't like them looking at me. Don't like them noticing. Don't like having to stare back at them. I fish into my pocket and pull out the letter from Mrs Dibbs. I open it, busying myself with reading.

Mr & Mrs Vargas,

I am writing to inform you that I will be recommending Gabriela for phase re-evaluation to her BMAC Officer.

My breath stops. My heart pounds. Re-evaluation?

'Goooooooooooooooba . . .'

While she currently holds a Phase 2 status under the BMAC Phase System, it is my personal view, after months of observing Gabriela's behaviour, that she would be more appropriately classified as Phase 3. Her BMAC officer will contact you with further details on Gabriela's re-evaluation and any changes to her status upon final review of my report.

Jean Dibbs

The room starts to spin. My parents – they'll be mad. More than mad. Mother will cry, asking God what sin she committed to deserve a child like me. Father will go silent. Terrifyingly silent. The storm that only I seem to churn up in him will cloud over his face.

If my status changes, they'll hate me.

They are insignificant.

They're my parents.

They are your burden. Let me free you of them.

'Phase 3,' the video warns. 'Highest threat level to state and environment. The Phase 3 Mover poses the risk of Movement activity, allowing a traveller from the future to infiltrate the present.'

If I get an upgrade, my parents will think of me as a criminal. They'll think I did it on purpose. Somehow, this will all be my fault.

With me by your side, you have no need to fear them.

My stomach. Deep down in my gut. The muscles twitch.

Reach out for me. Pull me close.

The twitch grows into a spasm. I gasp.

Ollie Larkin sees me. 'Steady there, Goobs.'

I'm not steady. Nothing's steady. It's like the ground is falling away. I grab my stomach. I close my eyes. And start to sing.

I can hear Ollie laugh.

My Shadow pushes back against my mind. *Stop singing that!*

But I don't. It's the only thing that works. Since I was a little girl and he first seeped into my mind. Focus on something else. Anything but him. Focus on the song. The song will push him back.

But he's not falling back. He's coiling tighter.

You're not a little girl any more. You can't just sing me away.

But I try. As hard as I can, I try.

Everyone watches me.

'Goooooooooba,' moos Ollie. 'What are you doing, you freak?'

There's a *ding* as the elevator doors open. I push my way through. Just keep singing.

My elbow knocks Ollie's and he shouts after me, 'Are you talking to yourself?'

I run across the front foyer. Shoulder my way through the revolving doors. The Eventualies rush my ears, cooling my face. I just have to get home. Home to my room.

You feel the pull. I can feel you fighting it.

'A b c d e f—'

STOP SINGING!

'Goobs!'

I glance back – Ollie Larkin is behind me. Ollie and Matt Doig and Sean K.

'Who are you talking to?'

I quicken my pace. Just have to get home.

'Who are you talking to, Gabby?'

My Shadow squeezes down on my brain. The pain. It shoots through my skull like a hot needle. I cry out.

'Who are you talking to?'

'I'm not talking to you!'

'I never said you were talking to me!' Ollie Larkin laughs.

My Shadow's grip tightens – how is he doing this? How is he hurting me?

Phase 3.

The muscles in my stomach tense. Brace themselves. And I want to release them. Want to let them lash out. The pain will stop if I do. I know it. On instinct. I know he'll stop if I just let go.

You can't escape what you are. What you were meant to do. Built to do.

I close my eyes tight. Hold my breath. And bend in half, trying to stop the contracting muscle. 'I won't do it! I won't!'

'Won't do what, Goobs?' Ollie calls.

You will, my Shadow assures me. *One way or another. You will.*

And he releases me. The throb in my brain is gone. And the muscles in my gut relax. He's falling away from me. But for how long?

I break into a run. I have to get home. Home to my room. Home to my experiments.

I'm in such a hurry, I don't even see them. And I knock them both off the sidewalk.

'Watch it!' Pat Mermick. Standing beside his little sister. I nearly pushed them over. Humiliation floods over me. I just want to be home.

'Goooooooooooobaaa!' The hideous nickname echoes after me.

'Shut the hell up, Ollie!' screams Pat.

I glance back, surprised. That boy who stood up for me in third grade. He's still in there somewhere.

Ollie holds up his arms. 'What gives, Mermick?'

She's watching me. Pat's little sister. Carefully. Head tilted to the side as she reaches for her brother's hand.

I turn away before Pat notices me looking, and race home as fast as I can.

My Shadow is gone from me now. But he'll be back. Back with the same strength he had today.

I can't let him hurt me like that again.

Won't let him.

I have to find the pungits. Now more than ever. I have to find them. And make my Shadow go away for good.

PAT
2383

Bo stands there, glaring at the Archivist, fists clenched at his sides. Shade Unit, the Archivist said. *Bo?*

'You're one of them?' I ask.

No.

The Archivist puffs air through his bottom a lip, a *pffffft* sound, and I feel a push of rage radiate from Bo. His memories are bubbling up again too, the ones he doesn't like me seeing. Running. Mud. Screaming. And wind.

'But you used to be?' I press him.

'I really don't understand why he insists on ignoring the past,' says the Archivist. 'He's a Shadow, for the love of crow. The past is a pretty big part of your life, don't you think? Bo?'

Don't push me, Carlin.

I've never seen Bo so furious, but I have to agree with the Archivist. What is he so angry about? Why is he keeping secrets if he can help me get home?

'Bo,' I interrupt, 'if you can help me—'

I can't.

'You can!' I shout, because it's all over his face. Whatever it is in his past that's making him so angry, whatever he did for the Shade Unit, the Archivist thinks it can help me. And so does Bo. 'You wouldn't be trying so hard to keep your past a secret if you couldn't.'

Patrick, I'm doing more to help you than sending you into BMAC could possibly do.

'How?'

By keeping you safe!

'I don't want your protection, Bo! You're not my father!'

Bo's anger disappears, and he looks at me, surprised. I've surprised myself. And I can see a colour bubble up from Bo's mind, a calm turquoise, it's warm and welcoming like tropical water – it's Bo's memory of him, my dad. The way he saw and knew my father, through my mind, before BMAC took him from us.

I want to reach for it, to hold it to me, but Bo pulls the colour back down into himself, hiding it away.

I know I'm not, Patrick, he tells me inside my head. *Better than anyone, I know that.*

A lump swells in my throat, my own memories of my dad bubbling up inside me. I don't know why I said what I said. Bo does know my father. He knows because he experienced every memory with Dad that I did, through me. If anyone knows how much I miss Dad, it's Bo. I know Bo's just trying to take care of me, even if he's a grump about it. But if he can feel how much I miss Dad, then he can feel how much I miss Mom and Maggie and Gabby. He knows, better than anyone, why I need to go home. No matter how dangerous it might be to try.

'Please, Bo,' I say quietly.

Bo just frowns, eyes on the floor, unshaven jaw clenched.

The Archivist speaks in Bo's language, just a few words. But it's enough to make Bo run for the door, shove it open with a bang and leave me and the Archivist alone in his library.

'Where are you going?' I call after him, but he doesn't answer. I look over at the Archivist. 'What did you tell him?'

The Archivist shrugs. 'I just said he can't keep running from his past . . . Apparently, he means to show me that he can.'

I jump to my feet and run after Bo. The Archivist calls out, 'Now wait just a minute there, Shadow Patrick. You heard them out there! The Cure Buses are about! Wait!'

But I don't wait. I'm already up the stairwell. With his limp, there's no way Bo could get up here very quickly. I throw open the door to the street, expecting to see him right in front of me. But he isn't there. It's dark, no moon or streetlights to help me see, but my eyes adjust and I scan for him. To my left, there's just quiet, tightly packed shacks and rubble. To my right, the Dune's Thoroughfare is quiet, the shops and cafes shuttered. Business must be over for the night. I don't see Bo anywhere. I have to get back home before the day-time Eventualies.

'Bo!'

There's nothing but the howl of the wind.

I set off at a jog towards the Thoroughfare. If he's heading home, then this is the way he'd go.

A dark figure shuffles across my path just up ahead, between the boarded-up street stalls. 'Bo?'

No. The figure, hunched and quick, is too small and fast to be Bo. The face, I notice, is masked.

Dark Unit.

There's a light clatter to my right – empty cans and garbage kicked underfoot. Two more masked figures hurry along in the shadows.

My pulse races. They're setting up for something. The Cure Bus – I'd forgotten. I listen, and I can hear it now, hear the faint mumbling of the loudspeaker. I have to get off the streets. But what about Bo? My mind reaches for him and there's a flash across my mind – a mental shove. He doesn't want me in his head. But without that, there's no way I can find him.

The voice gets louder, shuttered doors begin to crack open. People poke their heads out – they want to volunteer. I've got to hide, with or without Bo.

I head for the nearest awning, bumping into people who are moving towards the sound of the approaching bus. In the shadows of the awnings, I see masked heads. Dark Unit. They're waiting for the bus. This is about to get bad.

I turn and head for the other side of the street – a set of steel barrels overflowing with garbage look like a good place to duck and hide.

Something slams into my stomach, and I stop. A little girl looks up at me, rubbing her forehead. Her hair is curly brown, knotted and tangled in all directions. She wears a purple T-shirt.

My little sister, Maggie, is in my head, and loneliness opens up inside me.

'Asha!' A woman stands not far ahead, a baby in her

arms. She waves an impatient hand at the girl, telling her to hurry up in a language I don't know. The girl runs after her mother and I watch them go. I want to yell out, *Stop! Turn around!* But I know there's no point. Their mother wants the Cure. She's made up her mind for Asha and her brother. After living here for two weeks, I can't say that I blame her.

White light blazes into the Thoroughfare, silhouetting the volunteers moving towards it like moths to a flame. I wince at the brightness.

People with Movement capabilities, the speaker voice begins.

The black armoured tank hovers just feet above the street, its hulking mass gliding slowly along as easily as a fish through water. The size of it sets me shaking. I've seen it before, but not this close. All I can do is stare.

And then Bo's in my head – *Where are you?* He's urgent, worried. My sudden panic must have scared him.

I can't think properly, can't form a response, I'm so intimidated by the vehicle gliding towards me. But Bo sees it, through me. *Don't move!* he tells me.

I'm frozen, my breath coming in panicky spurts. *Don't run, don't run, don't run*, Bo repeats again and again. My legs are buzzing with the urge. *If you run*, he warns me, *you'll look like Shade Unit. If you run, BMAC will fire on you.*

The voice of the officer on the loudspeaker continues, calmly and coolly. *The Cure for your condition is real. You no longer need to hide outside the city limits if you register now with the Bureau of Movement Activity Control.* The front opens up like a giant yawning mouth, a grated black ramp lowering to the ground. A dozen soldiers spill out, two posted at the opening, the others moving into the crowd of volunteers and directing them all onto the bus.

Where are you?! my head screams for Bo. *Where do I go?*

Before he can answer, there's a nudge at my back.

'Keep moving, boy.' A BMAC soldier stands behind me, holding his shock cannon, a handheld version of what's on top of the bus, across his chest. I nearly leap out of my skin at the sight of him – his body armour is plated like the bus across his shoulders, chest and joints. His helmet is black and covers his face so that he barely looks human. 'Don't hold up the line.'

Don't get on that bus, Patrick, says Bo. *Whatever happens, do not get on that bus.*

But I'm not in any position to argue with the soldier. He nudges me forwards and I do as he says, falling in step with the other volunteers, the space around me closing up as the crowd shuffles together. The faces of the people around me are a mix of nerves and excitement. A boy on my right looks me up and down. His left eye is a startling shade of red. He looks smug, confident, like he can't wait for the change the Cure will bring to his life. I guess no one told him things aren't going to get any better for him. The hard metal grate of the ramp clanks beneath my feet as the shadow of the bus falls over me. I'm staring into its throat.

Patrick, says Bo. *Where are you? What are you doing?*

I can't get away, I tell him, staring up at the dark hole that's going to swallow me up. In front of me, a head turns in my direction – the little girl from before, Asha, holding her mother's hand as they enter the Cure Bus. Her eyes are wet and wide as she looks up at me. She's frightened.

She should be.

I'm frightened too.

Movers should *always* run from BMAC.

And here I am, walking right into their hands.

PAT
2383

The soldiers posted at the door tell me to go right, following behind Asha and her mother, to a series of benches. It's dark, save for the glow of floor lights marking the aisles, and intricate panels of buttons and switches glowing on the walls between big long mirrors. I can see every angle of the room, every person reflected in the dark glass. There's a side room in which several soldiers are fussing with bags and tubes of a fluorescent blue substance. The Cure, I guess.

I can't breathe. I shouldn't be here. I *can't* be here. Shaking, I take a seat on the bench beside Asha. I glance back at the entrance, at all the volunteers filing inside, the soldiers posted at the doors, still more at the end of each row.

Bo's with me. I can feel him darting around my head, scooping up all the information my brain is registering about my surroundings. I close my eyes and hope the Archivist is right about Bo's past.

Can you get me out of this? I ask him.

There's nothing from his end for a moment. Then finally, *I don't know.*

Across from me, more volunteers take their seats on the opposite bench, rolling up their sleeves and placing their arms on the metal rests. I glance over Asha's head, at the rows farther back – a BMAC agent and an armoured soldier make their way down the line. The agent holds a small tube, almost like a pen. He clicks a button and aims it into one of the volunteer's faces. It doesn't take me long to figure out what the pen is. Immediately, I glance at the mirror behind the volunteer's head. The agent is looking too. Because there they are – tiny black flecks fanning out from the man's head – pungits. The man clicks the little tube off – a pungit ray, Leonard built one back in my time – and the black flecks disappear from the reflection.

My breath catches in my throat and instinctively, my hand flies to my head. Pungits. They are going to look at my pungits. What are they going to see? After what Roth did to me, did to Bo, the flow of them won't look right. Pungits move out in organised lines from the head, in a tight connection through space-time to your Shadow or Mover. Or, if you've been Moved, or Moved someone, your pungits aren't tight any more. The lines are wobbly, floppy. That's for normal Movers and Shadows. What about me? My pungits have been tampered with, sabotaged. I'm a Mover who was Moved by my Shadow. There's no way my pungits won't look suspicious. BMAC will know there's something wrong with me.

The agent pulls out a small black disc, a white light glowing in its centre. He holds it up to the inside elbow of the volunteer's arm. There's a click, and a ring of light spreads out from where it presses into the flesh. An injection.

In 2097 Gabriela Vargas discovers the Cure for Movement. And here, in 2383, BMAC is in control of it. *Oh Gabby*. What would she say if she saw what they were doing with her life's work?

The volunteer jerks, a tremor moving through their body. The cords in his neck look ready to snap as his eyes roll back and the light fills the whites. He jerks, the soldier bracing him against the seat with his arm as more light haloes his head. Finally, the light fades, and his body relaxes, the soldier releases him. I stare. The man groans in his seat, barely able to move.

I grab my arm, clutching the spot where the Cure is going to enter. How do I stop this?

There's a mechanical grinding noise, and the light in the bus is dimming. I look back to the door – the last of the volunteers are shuffling inside, and a soldier has his hand on a hefty lever as the ramp pulls up inside the bus. The door closes with a clank.

Bo's pulled back from me, but I can feel his concern, it's radiating out of him. I can feel him trying to keep his hopeless thoughts to himself, but we're too close to each other now. I can read his thoughts on this whether he wants me to or not. He can't help me.

I'm on my own.

Sitting across from me is the boy with the red eye. He stares, his head resting against the back of the bench. He rolls up his sleeve – one less step for the BMAC agents – calm and confident. He's so much more together than I am, and he can tell. It's then that I realise how much I'm shifting. I sit back, trying to get a hold on my panic.

An agent and soldier start making their way down our row and my eyes flick around the bus, desperate for something that can help me, something that can help Bo, give him an idea. My eyes fall on the lever for the door. That's the only way out. And there's a soldier posted right beside it. I don't have a prayer of getting over there and pulling it. BMAC would be on me in a second.

Asha whimpers quietly beside me, biting on her nails. Her mother shushes her and the agent and soldier make their way through the row. Finally, they come to Asha's mother who holds up the baby for the pungit ray. The little black flecks reflect in the mirror and the agent nods. Asha's mother holds out the arm of her baby. The agent presses the disc to the little fleshy arm and I drop my gaze to my lap. I don't want to see it. The baby screeches before its cries are strangled by whatever the Cure is doing to his little body. Asha's whimpers turn into a sob. When I glance up, the baby is sleeping and the mother hands him off to Asha, before she looks into the pungit ray. More flecks in the mirror, and the agent nods. Asha's mother rolls up her sleeve.

'Mama . . .' Asha sniffles. But her mother ignores her, watching as the disc is pressed to her arm. Immediately, Asha's mother locks up, her eyes rolling. Asha looks up at me, tears streaming down her face. She reminds me so much of my sister, I want to hug her, tell her it's going to be OK. But it isn't. Not unless I can come up with a way to get us out of here.

My eyes flick back to the lever. It's the only chance I have.

Don't be stupid, Bo warns.

Asha's mother groans, swaying in her seat as she comes to. She rubs her face and blinks at the room as if seeing it for the first time.

'The baby, ma'am,' says the soldier, motioning at the infant in Asha's arms. Her mother reaches over and takes the baby, and the agent aims the ray at Asha. When I glance at the mirror, I see the flecks. Hordes of them, stretching out across time. Phase 3. The strongest kind of Mover. No, not a Mover. The flecks are flowing into her head. Not out. She's a Shadow. The agent reaches for Asha's arm. She cries out and pulls it back from him. The agent and soldier stand over her, frowning.

'Asha,' snaps her mother, saying something in a different language, but I can tell it has something to do with rolling up Asha's sleeve.

'No, Mama,' Asha whimpers.

Her mother grabs Asha's arm and holds it out for the agent. The little girl screams and pulls but the agent has a firm grip on her. Still she squirms and I'm terrified for her. The soldier bends down, pressing his forearm across her small chest to keep her from moving and the sight of his armour plating against her purple T-shirt sends the fear blasting out of my bones, replaced with nothing but anger.

Before I even know what I'm doing, I'm on my feet, pushing the soldier back. He's just as surprised, because he can't regain his footing and he goes sprawling backwards.

A hush falls over the bus and every eye turns on me. Bo's just as shocked – there's anger at his end, he can't believe I've done something so rash, but it's mixed with something else. Is he impressed? The boy with the red eye watches me with half a smirk.

'I-I'm sorry,' I stammer. 'I just . . . She doesn't want to do this. I didn't—' Two soldiers grab me, and drag me roughly over to the wall.

'What are you doing?'

They don't answer. They press me up against the cold metal, pulling down heavy bars that lock around my shoulders and chest. They leave me there, a prisoner. If they prick me with the Cure now, there's nothing I can do.

Keep quiet, Bo instructs me. *They'll deal with you when they've finished with the volunteers. Don't give them a reason to do it sooner.*

What are they going to do to me?

Bo doesn't answer me. He's not sure.

The boy with the red eye is staring. I guess I've given him quite the show. He cocks his head to the side, like he's trying to figure me out. I frown at him and he smirks again, leaning back lazily against his seat.

The soldiers gather around Asha – she's thrashing now, her mother shouting at her to stop it.

Fight them, Asha. Fight them.

It will be easier for her if she doesn't, Bo tells me.

She doesn't want this.

It doesn't matter what she wants.

While she fights, the boy with the red eye leans forwards, stretching, like he couldn't be less bothered by what's happening. He drops something at his feet – small metallic spheres, about the size of golf balls.

He leans back in his seat with a yawn, as if he doesn't notice.

No one notices. They're all too distracted by Asha.

The spheres – six of them – begin to roll. They spread out along the aisle, moving out to every corner of the bus.

The boy lifts a scarf from his neck, wrapping it around his nose and mouth. He catches me watching – and winks. I jump. His red eye – it's glowing.

And then there's shouting. Smoke rises up from different corners of the bus, one plume not far from me. One of the spheres sits on the floor beneath the gas, a red light the same colour as the boy's blinking eye at its centre – the spheres are releasing something into the bus. People are coughing.

Cover your mouth! says Bo. *Don't breathe it in!*

Quickly, I tuck my neck into my chest, pulling my shirt up over my nose. The smoke stings my eyes and there's a smell – sweetly chemical.

What is it? I ask Bo.

Shade Unit.

The soldiers start to drop. One after another they hit the ground with a thump, and the volunteers slump in their seats. The men gathered around Asha fall to the floor, her mother already collapsed on the bench. Asha is still squirming but she's slowing down, until finally she curls up, falling asleep despite herself.

The boy with the red eye lifts himself off the bench and saunters over to the door.

I can feel the smoke tickling the back of my throat. It's getting through my shirt. I cough.

Hang on, Patrick, says Bo.

The boy pulls the lever and the door opens, men in masks running onboard.

The first up the ramp, a big man with tubes sprouting out the back of his cowl slaps the red-eyed boy on the back. 'Well done, Pilot.' He shouts orders to the other masked men running onto the bus. 'The bus is ours, Unit! Volunteers are a priority. Drag 'em out. Keep families together. BMAC, disarm and restrain.'

The men are quick to obey, taking BMAC shock cannons and guns, binding their hands behind their backs. Others drag the sleeping volunteers down the ramp and off the bus.

My eyes feel heavy, I can barely hold myself up.

I'm coming for you, Bo tells me.

The boy whistles, and I blink back sleep at the sight of his red eye glowing. The silver balls roll towards him, gathering in a line at his feet, a red light glowing out from the centre of each. He isn't paying much attention to them. His red eye is on me. He steps over the balls and walks over, and they follow in a silver line. He grins, watching me fight sleep. 'Well,' he says, 'how'd a guy like you end up on a Cure Bus?'

But I can't answer him. My tongue is fat and lazy in my mouth and my lids are too heavy to hold up any more. There's no fighting it – my head drops and sleep carries me away.

GABBY
2083

Home.

The relief I feel walking down our floor's hallway is short-lived. I put my key in the door. It's unlocked. Mother and Father are home. Fear wraps itself around my shoulders. I thought they would be at their meeting by now. I check my droidlet. 4:20. I'm early. I don't get home until half past most days.

I close the door quietly behind me. I smell takeaway pizza – onion and salt and sweaty cheese. I peek into the kitchen. The new pizza boxes are open, stacked on top of the old ones. Empty, save for a couple of chewed crusts. They've eaten it all. I'm on my own for dinner again tonight.

The TV blares. I watch my parents through the hatch to the living room. It's dark, untidy, every knick-knack out of place. Pictures line the walls, all of them framed posters or pamphlets from twenty or thirty years ago to now. The familiar anti-Movers slogan *We Are Now* written in big letters on every single one. Mother reclines on the couch, a plate of pizza on her lap. Father stands, arms folded across his chest, transfixed by whatever he's watching.

I hug my bag. I just want to work on the pungit ray. Just close the door to my room and bury myself in my experiment. I don't want to be yelled at. Not after everything that's happened today. But my father's blocking the hallway to my room. I can't sneak by without him noticing.

Father kicks the coffee table. I jump. 'Out of control!' he growls. He points at the TV, turning back to Mother. I hide behind a cupboard. 'Did I tell you, or did I tell you? The Movers problem is spiralling out of BMAC's control!'

Mother nods, taking another bite of pizza.

I glance at the TV. The latest headline on *Avin News* scrolls along the bottom of the screen. *Movers Update – Phase Upgrades at All-time High.*

The note from Mrs Dibbs feels heavy in my pocket.

'I said this would happen!' Father rages. 'All these Movers having children, then *they* have children. On and on it goes. They'll overtake us at this rate!'

Mother nods again.

'It's ridiculous to assume that the rise in phase upgrades is the result of a rise in the instance of people developing higher Movement abilities.' A BMAC representative in a well-tailored suit and crisp haircut is being interviewed. *'I think, Brenda,'* he tells the anchor, *'that we can attribute this rise to greater vigilance within the community. And I for one am encouraged by that.'*

'Greater vigilance,' Father huffs. 'This man's a quack. Write down his name. Miller. I want to bring him to the attention of the group tonight.'

My eyes roam over the We Are Now posters wallpapering the room. I can't help but feel sorry for Agent Miller. Once you have the attention of Mother and Father's WAN chapter, you never shake them.

'I'm sorry, Agent Miller,' says Brenda, *'did you just say you were encouraged by the growing population of high-phase Movers?'*

'Yes, I did. The cooperation between BMAC and school boards across the nation, and our relationship with large corporations like AvinGrocers and Acron, is a new social phenomenon. Before that, say ten, fifteen years ago, phase status was left to be reported by a Mover's parents, or in some cases the Mover themselves. Often times, not at all. In today's community, it's much harder for an individual with Movement abilities to hide from the Bureau and the control mechanisms we've been able to put in place.'

I'll say.

'Typical BMAC moron,' Father huffs. 'So smug and confident. What controls have they put in place? There're more Movers than ever! The system is broken. If it were working, we'd be seeing a decline in upgrades, not an increase.'

'He has to say this kind of garbage, Arthur,' says Mother, cheeks stuffed with food. 'BMAC doesn't want the city in a panic.'

'Avin *should* be in a panic. It's time we all took our heads out of the sand and started acknowledging that the Movers threat is growing. It's banging on our doors. Living inside our walls for God's sake.'

I shrink back. He means me. I'm the threat inside the walls. Mother slouches and puts down her pizza. Just mentioning me has darkened her mood.

'Protect the present. That's BMAC's mandate,' growls Father. 'If they won't do their job, then it's up to us.'

'What are you thinking?'

'That we need to get people's attention. We need to show them how dangerous Movers really are.'

'We can protest again. Picket out front of the BMAC building—'

'No protests. Nobody listens to protests. We need to strike. With force.'

'Is that wise? That Mermick woman has lodged enough formal complaints against us as it is.'

She's talking about Pat Mermick's mother. Mother and Father despise Mrs Mermick.

'If she catches even a whisper of us planning something—'

'She's a Mover sympathiser, Mary,' roars Father. 'A traitor to the Now. You really think people are going to side with her over us?'

Mother shakes her head. Because no. People wouldn't side with Mrs Mermick.

'Her husband is a convicted Mover,' Father reminds her. 'She's guilty by association.'

And I have to wonder if Father would feel the same way about Pat Mermick. Probably. As far as my parents are concerned, the apple doesn't fall far from the tree.

Except for me. To my parents, this apple is a different fruit entirely.

'What are you doing?'

Father stands in the breakfast window. He's scowling. He always scowls at me.

'N-nothing,' I stammer.

This scowl is different. Darker. Angrier. I feel the letter, practically burning in my pocket. Does he know?

'You're eavesdropping.'

'No, sir.'

'Then what are you doing, standing silent in the kitchen all by yourself?'

'I was—' What am I doing? Answer him. Quick. Or he'll get angrier. 'I was looking for something to eat.'

'We're going out,' he grumbles. 'You'll have to fix something for yourself.'

I nod. I always do.

'I want your Phase Forms ready to sign when I get home.'

I swallow.

He watches me, eyes hard, mouth tight. 'You're not going to cause me any more grief, are you?'

'No, sir.'

With one last squint, he turns away from me. 'Let's get going, Mary.'

When the door closes behind them, I allow myself to breathe again. I close my eyes, and let the air fill my lungs. Alone at last. But they'll be back. I pull the letter from my pocket and read it again. I can't show them this. Can't even imagine what they'd do. But one line scares me more than all the others.

Her BMAC officer will contact you with further details on Gabriela's re-evaluation and any changes to her status upon final review of my report.

How long will I be able to hide this from them?

You don't need to hide from them. My Shadow's grip takes hold, making my brain throb. *Not with me beside you.*

He squeezes harder.

Just MOVE me.

Now the squeezing is more like a stabbing. Slicing through my mind. White. Hot. Searing. I fall to my knees. Grab hold of my head.

I see them there. My parents. Inside my thoughts. They're screaming. Eyes wide with fear. Fear of me. Because I'm stronger than them. Better than them—

I scramble up from the floor and double over into the sink. I throw up.

'Stop it,' I groan, wiping my mouth. 'Stop putting thoughts in my head!'

The pain relents. But I still feel him there. Circling my brain like a shark. *I'm trying to show you what you can be. If you let me help you.*

'I don't want your help!' I shout, grabbing my bag and running for my room. I slam the door and pull out the pungit ray. I have to make it work. Have to find my pungits. Find them and destroy them. Before my Shadow hurts me even more.

PAT
2383

I wake up on my back, my eyes blinking up at a ceiling so high I must be inside some kind of hollowed-out tower block. The walls are scorched and cracking, weedy plants and vines climbing their way skyward. Bo's in my head, ping-ponging around my skull in a fit. *Where are you? Why didn't you get off along with the others?*

The others? I don't know what he's talking about, my mind is a fog.

The other volunteers, he says impatiently. *I looked for you among the sleeping bodies. You weren't there. Where* are *you?*

Where am I? I have no idea. I'm lying on something soft – a cot. There are grinding noises and slamming, men shouting at each other. It sounds like a construction site. I move to sit up and a wave of nausea forces me to think better of it.

'Hey, you're awake! Cap, he's awake!' Someone shoves a metal bottle in my hand. 'Here, it's water. You must be thirsty.'

I shake my head against the spinning and look up to see the boy with the red eye standing over me.

'Chloroform packs a nasty punch, eh?'

'The gas?' I say, trying to remember the last thing that happened. 'The gas came from those spheres . . .'

'Yeah,' says the boy, 'Tungsten.' He takes a seat beside me on the bed and motions at the creature sitting at his feet. I blink. It's the silver spheres, but they've joined together, as if by magnets, into one train. No, not a train. It rears up, like a cobra, the first ball glowing with two beady red eyes.

'Not a bad little borg, is he?' says the boy. 'Bit of a defiant streak, but I try not to hold that against him. Especially since he comes in so handy against BMAC. Ain't that right, Tungst?'

The robot snake's eyes blink and it tilts its head as if considering what's just been said. And then, to my surprise, it nods.

'Its eyes . . .' I say. 'They're like the one you have.'

He taps the skin beside his eye. 'How else would I give him his marching orders?'

'You control him? With your eye?'

'Well,' laughs the boy, 'communicate with him, anyway. More my mind than my eye. But they had to hook him up to me somehow, didn't they? In through the eye and up into the brain.'

I try my best not to think of what kind of surgery could accomplish that.

'Pilot!' a voice shouts and the boy jumps to his feet. The Cure Bus is parked in the centre of the massive room, they're gutting the whole thing. The man with tubes coming out of his cowl – I saw him on the bus when Shade Unit came in – stands at the ramp of the Cure Bus, arms full of some important-looking parts. 'Did you get him some water?'

'Sure did, Cap!'

I glance at the bottle in my hand. It's cold, and I realise how parched my throat is. I take a sip and as soon as I do, I can't stop, chugging as quickly as I can.

'Good,' the man nods. 'Be right there.'

I can feel Bo with me, absorbing the information, but it's not enough. He doesn't recognise the place and I'm no help since I've been asleep. They could have taken me anywhere.

I gasp for air, the water bottle nearly empty, and the boy slaps his hand on my back. 'Easy there, buddy. No one's gonna take it away from you, if that's what you're worried about.'

'Where am I?'

'Unit outpost.' He nods towards the ceiling. 'Call this the Block. Neat, huh?'

Shade Unit. I'm with Shade Unit.

The Block, I tell Bo. *Do you know it?*

No.

I grab my throbbing head. *But you're one of them, how do you not know it?*

I am not one of them. He's just as frustrated, and my tone isn't helping. *Shade Unit has hundreds of outposts, Patrick. Few of them I've seen personally.*

My gaze climbs the decaying walls – hundreds of feet of crumbling concrete and scars from battles long since passed. That's it then. Getting out of here is up to me.

Just stay calm, says Bo. *Learn what you can and we'll figure it out.*

I breathe deep, trying to settle down, but I can feel his concern and it isn't helping.

'You OK?' The boy sits beside me again, watching me with a frown. The red eye is dull, the light inside not glowing like it did on the bus. His other eye is brown.

'But where *are* we?' I ask him. 'What am I doing here?'

'Uh . . .' He looks around, like he's not sure what he should say, and it's then that the man with the tubes comes strolling up to us. His mask is gone, his face dirty with grease. His hair hasn't been cut in a while, hanging in black strands over his eyes.

'So, how's he doing?'

'Bit of a headache, but no permanent damage,' the boy reports.

The man nods. 'Good. That's good.' He kneels down on one knee so that his face is level with mine. He's a young man, too young to be in charge of an entire bastion of Shade Unit, but from the way he gives orders and the other Shade Unit people watch him, it's clear that he is. 'What's your name, kid?'

'Pat.'

He nods and extends his hand. 'I'm Captain Bash. Pilot told me what you did on the Cure Bus for that little girl.'

'Asha,' I say, remembering her frightened face. 'Is she OK?'

The red-eyed boy – Pilot – grins. 'Oh yeah. BMAC was out before they got the chance to stick her with the Cure.'

I feel a swell of relief, even if it's just a little. I can't tell

94

where I am, but I do know that Asha is OK. That's a small victory, at least.

'But there will be a new bus,' says Captain Bash. 'And a new opportunity for her family to take her Movement away. Once a person decides they don't want to be one of us any more, it's hard to stop them.'

He says it with a heavy dose of resentment. I don't know why. It's hard to blame anyone for not wanting to be a Mover any more, especially here.

'Which brings me to the strange case of you, Pat.'

'Me?'

Pilot nods. 'Never met a volunteer who didn't think the whole world should sign up for BMAC's Cure. Except you.'

I can see their point: how strange I must seem to them. If I believed enough in the Cure to step onto the Cure Bus, why would I try to stop Asha's mom from doing what I should have thought was best for her kids?

'So how 'bout it, Pat?' says Captain Bash. 'Wanna tell me what you were doing there?'

Careful, Patrick, Bo warns me. *Keep your situation to yourself.*

Yeah, you're an expert at that, aren't you? As soon as I've thought this, I immediately regret it. He wants to help me. But keeping secrets from me isn't helping anything.

Pilot coughs and I realise I haven't said anything for a weird amount of time. Captain Bash smiles. 'You part of the rogue attacks on Dune's Thoroughfare? Part of Dark Unit?' he asks. 'I admire your determination but you're wasting your efforts. More likely to get cured or worse, the way those kids carry on.'

No, Bo snaps. *Tell him that's not what you were doing there.*

'You want to make a difference in the fight against BMAC,' he continues, 'you'd be much better served joining the real Shade Unit, don't you think?'

Bo's screaming at me to deny it, but I don't open my mouth. Both Pilot and this Captain Bash are being so nice – I'm afraid to sacrifice that, especially when maybe they can get me back to Bo.

'It's a good time for it,' says Pilot, rolling up his sleeve to show his Shade Unit tattoo, the same one Gamma had shown me, a black hand, but without the wings. 'You caught wind that we're ramping up, didn't you?'

'Ramping up?' I ask.

'To take on BMAC! Shade Unit's been so fractured, so disorganised and scattered since the last conflict. Captain Bash here is working to unite everybody again. Get the Unit in real working order.'

I remember Gamma, and what he said about finding answers. Is Bash the man with the answers he was talking about?

'Gamma,' I say, 'is he OK?'

'Who's Gamma?' asks Pilot.

'I watched him. Watched him try to take on a Cure Bus. BMAC started firing . . .'

Bash nods, soberly. 'Ah, a Dark Unit friend of yours?'

I nod.

Bash shakes his head. 'These rogue protest gangs, their hearts are in the right place, but they're too disorganised, too many hotheads. Every assault they launch only seems to vindicate BMAC's perception of Movers. And it tarnishes Shade Unit's name,' says Bash. 'Hurt themselves just as much as they hurt our cause.'

'Why aren't they here?' I ask. 'They are Shade Unit, aren't they?'

'No,' says Pilot, 'they started out that way. But they don't stand for Shade Unit. Not any more.'

Bash sighs, a frown on his face. 'The kids in the Dark Unit gangs are too impatient for what Shade Unit is trying to do. They want to fight and they want to do it now. I can't say that I blame them. But I don't know how many of their friends they need to lose to BMAC before they figure out their way isn't working.'

'And your way is?' I ask.

For a second I'm worried I might have offended him but Bash only grins.

'Our way's the only way,' says Pilot. 'We're going after BMAC's Cure facility.'

'What's that?'

'It's where they manufacture the Cure,' explains Captain Bash.

I sit up a little straighter, my mind instantly on the Time Cache. 'Where is it?'

'We don't know,' he tells me. He pivots on his knee and waves a hand at the gutted BMAC vehicle. 'That's why we hit one of the Cure Buses. Gives us access to the onboard computer, and the Cure equipment. Maybe something here can tell us where they're cooking up this junk.'

The way he says it, *junk*, leaves no question about how he feels about the Cure. The same way Bo feels – like it's a punishment. But I can't help but think of Gabby. Would they hate the Cure so much if they had a Shadow like hers?

'Cap!' One of the men is running down the boarding ramp of the Cure Bus. 'You're gonna want to see this.'

'Be right there,' says Captain Bash, getting to his feet. 'Pilot, take this.'

He hands over a folded, paper-thin sheet of plastic. 'I need you to get it to the Turbine by tomorrow.' Pilot nods and folds it away in his breast pocket. The Turbine – I wonder if Bash means the Avin Turbine. 'In the meantime, why don't you show Pat around? Get him something to eat. And uh,' he looks me up and down, and I'm aware of my sweatshirt. My very 2083 sweatshirt. 'Some clean clothes too – I can still smell the chloroform on him.'

Bo's already saying no, over and over, as if he can convince me it's my own brain coming up with the answer. But watching Captain Bash jog back to the bus, the men and women gathering around him with questions and reports, I get why they all admire him. He's trying something. Trying to resist BMAC.

And doesn't care who he hurts while he does it, snaps Bo.

He saved me from the bus, didn't he? I shoot back.

Pilot stands up, his metal snake coiling around his ankle. They both look at me expectantly. 'You coming?'

PAT
2383

Pilot and his little silver snake lead me away from the Cure Bus, deeper into the Block. The damage of war has nearly gutted the whole tower so that I can see up through the floors – there must be thirty – to the very top. Shade Unit has set up mostly on the ground floor, though I can see figures moving on the edges of the crater-sized hole in the middle of the first. As Pilot walks, I can see that the Block is like its own contained city, with makeshift tents and piles of supplies, all lined up so as to make laneways weaving through the place. Shade Unit members mill about, men and women, young and old, all of them with purpose.

'Those are some pretty raw threads,' Pilot says. Those were the same words Gamma used. 'Where does an outfit like that come from, anyway?'

Does he know I've been Moved? 'I dunno. What do you care?'

Pilot laughs at me as he marches down another row of tents. 'I don't. Relax, Pat. You're one of us now.'

I don't know how to tell Pilot I'm not here for this, not one of them, without sounding ungrateful. 'Uh, I don't – I mean – I'm not sure I'm ready for this.'

'Ah, don't worry,' says Pilot. 'You don't think Bash would just throw you into the thick of things without proper training, do you?' I follow him and Tungsten as they weave through little hearths and campsites, ducking out of people's way as they hurry by carrying intricate machine parts and glowing AvinGates. He finally stops at a wall of green canvas. 'Bash expects everyone in his Unit to know exactly what they're doing before they head out for their first real mission. He'll make sure you're ready.'

He pulls back the canvas to reveal rows and rows of tables, the smell of cooking, and Shade Unit members laughing and eating together. Pilot grabs two trays and slams them on a counter. They're slopped with what I guess is creamed corn and a grey-looking meat. He hands me one of the trays and hunkers down at the end of one of the long tables, shovelling a fork into the yellow-white sludge. Tungsten sits coiled on the table beside the tray, watching the fork move from plate to mouth, plate to mouth.

'Go on,' says Pilot. 'You must be hungry.'

I'm not. My stomach is tied in knots.

'You all right?' Pilot asks through stuffed cheeks, looking at my untouched food.

'I can't stay here. He's gonna be so worried about me.'

'You got someone waiting at home for you?'

'My . . . uncle,' I lie. 'I didn't tell him where I went. He's going to lose it when I don't come home.'

'That's no good.' Pilot's chews thoughtfully. 'Where is he? Near where the bus picked you up?'

I nod.

Pilot picks at his food, thinking. 'I could run him a message next time I'm out that way.'

'A message?'

'Yeah, that's my job. I'm a runner.'

I wait, not understanding.

He leans back in his chair, staring at me curiously. 'Never heard of a runner?'

I shake my head.

Tungsten's glowing red eyes blink at me, and he tilts his head. Did I say something wrong?

Pilot folds his arms. 'You talk kinda funny too.'

'I do?'

'Yeah. You called Tungst "spheres". Never heard anyone call him that before, like he was just a bunch of pieces. Like you've never seen a borg before.'

Heat rushes to my cheeks.

'And your clothes . . .' he says.

I fold my arms over my chest, as if that will somehow conceal what I'm wearing.

'You a Shadow? A Moved one, I mean?'

That's the same conclusion the Archivist came to. It's wrong, but it's the best explanation I can give for how out of place I am here. So I nod.

Pilot leans across the table. 'Hey. It's all right. Tonnes of people here come from some other time, you know. You're still one of us.'

I'm a little taken aback by his kindness. Where I come

from, if someone told you they were a Moved Shadow . . . you'd be terrified. Moved Shadows mean BMAC. Moved Shadows mean trouble.

But here, with Shade Unit, Moved Shadows are friends. It makes me like Pilot more.

'What about you?' I ask. 'What, uh, I mean, are you a Shadow or . . . ?'

'What do you think I am?'

I shrug.

He grins. 'Come on, if you had to guess.'

I honestly have no idea. But this seems to be a game he really enjoys, so I take a shot. 'Shadow?'

His grin spreads into a smile and he shakes his head. 'I'm a Mover. People always guess Shadow.'

His smile fades a little and he takes another spoonful. 'My connection is only phase 1, though.' He says it like he thinks this news would disappoint me. I have no idea why. Where I come from, if you have to be a Mover, you want to be a weak one. 'Me and my Shadow, we're working on it though. We'll get stronger. And then I'll Move her here.'

I blink at him, surprised that he's just admitted this to me.

'And when she gets here,' he goes on, 'we're going to run for Shade Unit. Both of us. Work our way up. Maybe be captains one day.'

'How do you know she wants to do that?' Phase 1s can't talk to their Shadows. I know. I used to be Phase 1. They only have an impression of them. Like a blurry reflection in water.

'I know,' he says confidently. 'I can feel how she feels.'

I don't doubt that. I remember how it was for me and

Bo. I didn't know what he was thinking, but I always knew how he felt.

'Look,' Pilot says, 'you better learn what a runner is, because I'll bet my rations that's where Bash is gonna start you.'

You have to tell them, says Bo. I shove him back from my mind, annoyed. Doesn't he think I know that?

'Basically,' Pilot goes on, pulling the plastic I'd seen Captain Bash hand him earlier from his breast pocket. 'I'm a mailman. Digital communication is way too risky these days, especially for us. It's just too easy for BMAC to track, and the information we're passing around is too sensitive.' He taps the plastic. 'So Shade Unit uses guys like me to send messages to each other.'

I push at the corn on my plate, thinking. 'Bash mentioned the Turbine . . . Did he mean the Avin Turbine?'

Pilot nods. 'BMAC Headquarters. Bash sends me all the time.'

I lean forwards, interested. 'BMAC Headquarters. You've actually been inside?'

'Mm-hmm.'

'Have you been to the Time Cache?'

'What, like *inside* it?' he laughs and places the note back into his pocket. 'Nah, that thing's under GuardBorg protection. I don't go near that.'

I sit back, disappointed.

'Nah,' Pilot goes on. 'I just get in, get out. Don't want to spend more time than necessary in the hornet's nest, you know what I mean?'

'What are you getting in for?' I ask him.

He glances at me, chewing his food carefully. 'I'm not supposed to say.'

I nod. 'It sounds dangerous.'

He shrugs. 'I'm good at it. Plus, I get to meet new people all the time – important people. I met Constance Ashlinn once.'

The name strikes me as familiar. 'Who's Constance Ashlinn?'

'Who's Constance Ashlinn!' His eyebrows raise, like I've just asked who's BMAC. Then he shakes his head. 'What year *are* you from, anyway?'

2683. I jump at Bo's voice suddenly back inside my head, and my hand knocks my fork onto the floor, sending Tungsten coiling in fear around Pilot's arm.

'Jumpy, aren't you?' says Pilot, pulling the little robot off him. 'Gonna have to get a handle on that. Can't have a jumpy runner. That's how mistakes get made.'

Of course it is. I pick up the fork, embarrassed. What am I even worried about? Like Shade Unit would want to take on someone like me.

'Constance Ashlinn,' Pilot goes on, 'is Blue Ashlinn's daughter.' He waits, and I realise I know that name. The Archivist was obsessed with the Blue Ashlinn person.

'That's that FIILES thief woman?'

Pilot grins. 'Exactly! See? You're picking up on the times. You'll fit right in. Most Shadows who get here from the future have never heard of Blue Ashlinn. Well done.'

I can't help but feel a little proud of myself. It's nice to not be completely clueless for once. 'So, what's Constance Ashlinn's story?'

'She's taken up her mother's place in Shade Unit. If you thought Bash taking the Cure Bus was aggressive, you should hear about some of the stuff her Unit used to pull off.'

'Used to?'

He nods, shovelling more food into his mouth. 'Her and Shade Unit, they tried to pick up where Blue left off. Tried to succeed where her mother Blue failed, and rob First Avin Bank. Almost pulled it off, too.'

'What happened?'

'Some of her men got caught.'

There's a chill of resentment from Bo. *The runner got himself caught. That's how BMAC found the others.*

How do you know? I ask.

There's silence on his end, and I'm frustrated with him, exhausted from having to ask questions he'll never answer. Before I shut him out of my head, a faint whisper of his memories wafts across my mind. Running. Towers. Screaming. Winds. And then I see it for the first time – or maybe it was always there and I just didn't notice before now – writing chiselled neatly into a stone and marble wall, *First Avin Bank*.

'She managed to escape capture, though,' says Pilot, 'so she did better than her mother I guess. But she had to go into hiding after that.'

Coward that she is, huffs Bo.

This is it, isn't it? I press him. *This is what you don't like remembering. This Constance woman. You were a part of what he's talking about, weren't you?*

Bo doesn't answer me, but he doesn't need to. His

feelings have betrayed as much and he's mad at himself for it. He falls back from me, not wanting me to find out more, but there's so much more I want to know. *What exactly happened to you, Bo?*

Pilot waves a hand in front of my face. 'You've got a drifting kinda mind, don't you?'

It must seem that way. I have to get better at focusing on what's happening in front of me when Bo is inside my head. 'So,' I say awkwardly, trying to show Pilot I've been listening, 'you met her, then, Constance Ashlinn. She's still around?'

'Sure,' says Pilot. 'If you know who to ask. She's still got her own Unit, west of Avin. I would've joined up with her if I could.'

'Why didn't you?'

'She never seems to be recruiting. Her Unit hasn't been active for a long time. But Bash, and what he's doing here, seems to have caught her interest. She's one of the first Unit leaders that Bash has managed to bring on board.'

'Pilot!' A woman stands at the far end of the table, a no-nonsense expression on her face. 'This the new recruit?'

'Pat, meet Opal Spitz, my favourite enrollment officer,' says Pilot. 'Opal, Pat.'

'I'll treasure this moment,' she says impatiently. 'Bash wants him processed, ASAP. You couldn't wait to stuff your face?'

'Uh, I've had kind of a big day, in case you didn't hear. I took the Cure Bus.'

'All by your lonesome, was it?'

'Well,' says Pilot, 'Pat helped, actually.'

Before I can deny it, Opal is already grabbing me by the arm and hauling me to my feet. 'Great, spectacular, what a hero. Let's get this over with, I've got a lot of work today.'

She takes off at a determined pace, expecting me to follow. Pilot and Tungsten are beside me, and the three of us hurry after Opal together.

'Processing what?' I ask him.

'You,' he says. 'For Shade Unit.'

'What? I told you—'

'It's no big deal. Standard procedure,' he says. 'Health assessment, aptitude test and phase review.'

'Phase review?'

'You know, where they examine your pungits and get a record of your phase and class.'

'What? What for?'

'Safety,' he shrugs. 'Gotta make sure you are who you say you are. Make sure you're not a BMAC spy.' He winks.

My armpits flash hot. They'll see what I didn't want BMAC to see. They'll see I'm not a Shadow at all. I'm something else entirely.

PAT
2383

Opal leads us through a line of people – men, women, boys and girls – Shade Unit soldiers waving them forwards one at a time and showing them behind white curtains. It looks uncomfortably like the line of waiting volunteers in front of the Cure Bus.

'Are they all trying to join Shade Unit?' I whisper to Pilot.

'Sure,' he says. 'I told you we were ramping up efforts. We can use as much help as we can get.'

There must be thirty or so people waiting. Maybe it won't be so bad for me to just say I don't want to join. It looks like they've got plenty of people who want to be a part of this. What's it matter if I'm here? *All the help they can get*, Pilot said.

As Opal leads us to the front of the line, there are groans and eye rolls from the people waiting.

'Opes!' shouts one of the Shade Unit guys standing by one of the monitors. 'What the hell?'

She shrugs. 'Bash said.'

'I can get in line,' I say.

Opal ignores me and leads us along the line. A woman emerges from behind one of the curtains. 'Opal, I've been looking for you. Can you come look at this, please? I can't get a read on this guy's pungits.'

Opal rolls her eyes. 'Can you give me a sec, Polly?'

'Well, he's been waiting . . .'

'Try replacing the bulb in the ray. I'll check on you in a minute.' She grabs me by the arm and pulls me along.

'Really,' I say, 'I can wait if you want to help her.'

Opal pulls back a curtain and there's a chair sitting against a wall, a mirror behind it, an AvinGate sitting on a little desk, and beside that, a tiny tube – the pungit ray.

'Take a seat,' says Opal.

I look nervously at Pilot who smiles encouragingly. Bo's squirming through my head, I can feel him trying to come up with a way out. This could be really bad for us.

'Are you sure?' I say. 'I mean, should I be jumping the queue like this?'

'Not in my opinion,' says Opal, scrolling through the AvinGate. 'But, orders are orders.'

'Special treatment,' winks Pilot. 'For your Cure Bus heroics.'

'You really don't have to do this. I don't mind waiting.'

'Don't worry about it,' says Opal. 'Processing you or the next guy, it's all the same to me. As long as I get through all of these people today, the order doesn't matter much.'

Great.

'Mover or Shadow?' she asks me.

'Uh, Shadow.' I guess.

Opal's eyes are focused on her AvinGate as she types something in – a file on me, I suppose. I try to focus on staying still, to keep from squirming, but everything about this reminds me of BMAC, of phase testing, of being in trouble for being what I am. How long before she points the ray at me? And what's going to happen when she does? She'll call Captain Bash first, that's most likely. But then what will he do? The stories Leonard told me about his days in Shade Unit suddenly flood back to my memory – their experiments with pungits. Commander Roth was Shade Unit. Commander Roth's experiments with pungits were what started all my troubles. How many more Commander Roths are waiting for me in Shade Unit's laboratories?

'Don't be nervous,' says Pilot, eyes on my shaking knees.

'I'm not,' I lie.

'All right,' says Opal. 'You taking any medications I need to know about? Any conditions that could prohibit you from doing some of the work Shade Unit could call on you to do?'

Conditions. Conditions. I don't have any that I know of, but that's hardly the point, is it? I just have to lie. I just have to pick the right condition.

'Asthma,' I say quickly.

Opal nods and makes a note silently. She purses her lips as she does, and I think maybe I've pulled it off.

Pilot nudges my knee. 'Don't worry about it. Tonnes of runners have that one.'

That's not quite the relief Pilot thinks it is. I try to think up something else, but my mind's a blank.

Tell her you get nosebleeds, says Bo. *And migraines. Tell her your Mover can get aggressive at times, to a point where his intrusion makes you lose motor function for a minute or two.*

What? Can that happen?

I've seen it. It's indicative of a volatile Phase 3 connection.

I've seen it too – in Gabby. The way she'd grab her head, the way she'd talk to herself. She told me about the ugly thoughts Commander Roth would put inside her head. What would she think of me pretending to have the kinds of problems she had to deal with all her life?

It's problematic in the field, says Bo. *Causes a lot of trouble. This woman won't like hearing that.*

How many Movers and Shadows like Gabby are out there?

'Also,' I say. 'I, um, get nosebleeds sometimes. And bad headaches.'

She glances up at me for the first time since we sat down. 'And your Mover? What's your relationship with them like?'

'Not . . . great.'

Pilot looks at me with a cocked eyebrow, but Opal has more questions. 'Define "not great". Are they hostile towards you?'

'Sometimes.'

Opal makes another note, her lips still pursed and I'm a little worried about going down this road. I'm just inviting more questions, more lies I'll have to tell and keep up with. I'm not a great liar, it won't be hard for her to see through me.

It's the only lie you can tell, Patrick, says Bo. *Better this and have them turn you away than getting enrolled and having them learn what you really are.*

What I really am. A Mover who was Moved by his Shadow. A freak of nature.

'Opal.' The woman from earlier, Polly, pokes her head in. Opal scowls at her. 'I'm sorry, I know. It's just I replaced the bulb and I'm still not getting anything. I think . . .' She glances at me and Pilot.

'Go on,' says Opal, impatiently.

'I think this guy might be a Nowbie . . . might be . . .' She puts a hand beside her mouth and whispers, 'Might be BMAC.'

'Polly, you said that about three recruits last week. And they were all just Phase 1s, remember?'

'I know, and I did everything like you showed me. I'm really being careful. But I'm telling you, there're no pungits on this guy.'

Opal's out of her chair, shoving the AvinGate at Pilot. 'Here, take over for me. I'll be right back.'

The two women disappear behind the curtain and it's just me and Pilot left alone. BMAC is here? I look to Pilot, who takes Opal's seat across from me, Tungsten weaving between his legs. His face is grave.

'You think it's like a spy, or something?' I ask him. 'What will that mean, if BMAC's found out where you guys are?'

'It's not BMAC,' says Pilot. 'Polly's a new recruit herself. She has a hard time seeing the sparse pungits of Phase 1s. Opal will clear it all up.'

He seems so sure, I want to believe him. But his grim expression is making me nervous.

'What is it?' I ask.

'You talked about your Mover to Opal,' he says. 'You

made it sound like your Mover was giving you the headaches, on purpose. That your Mover was hostile.'

'So?'

'You told me you're a Moved Shadow. So your Mover must be here somewhere.'

'He is.' At least that's not totally untrue.

'You said you want to go back to your uncle,' he says. 'That's your Mover, isn't it?'

I hold my breath. I've been caught in a lie. How many more will Pilot sniff out?

'Pat,' says Pilot, 'if your Mover is so hostile to you, why do you want to go back to him?'

I look at my fingers. I have no idea how to answer that. I've weaved a web here. No matter how I answer that question, the whole thing is going to unravel.

'He's not so bad,' I try.

Pilot sighs and makes a note on the AvinGate. 'Bad enough for you to run from him in the first place.'

'I wasn't—'

Before I can say anything else, he holds up the pungit ray – I didn't even see him grab it – and points it in my face.

On instinct, I leap out of my chair and duck out of the way. But it's too late. Pilot's jaw hangs open, his eyes wide. He's seen them.

'I can explain,' I blurt out.

'Your . . . your pungits,' he says, his voice strangled. 'What? What happened to your pungits?'

A cold chill runs up my spine. I haven't seen them yet. I don't know what they look like. Quickly, I grab the ray from

Pilot and point it into my face. When I turn to face the mirror, I'm not prepared for what's reflected back at me.

The lines of little black circles, they aren't straight like they were the last time I saw them. The last time I saw them was before Bo Moved me. The pungits on a Moved person are supposed to be more chaotic, the strings that connect them to their Shadow or Mover are too close together so everything gets floppy and weird. Since Bo Moved me, it would make sense for my pungits to look like the pungits of a Moved person. But they look different than that. They're not just arranged in a floppy messy way – they look tangled. Like a frayed ball of fishing line threaded with black pepper. And they're frozen. My breath comes in fast as I stare at the little flecks. Pungits are supposed to be in motion – fast or slow doesn't matter, but they should be moving. My nose practically touches the glass of the mirror as I stare at the flecks above my head. They look like they're vibrating. Like they want to move but something is holding them in place.

I need Gabby here. She understands pungits better than I do. What did Roth *do* to them?

Bo circles my mind. He's scared too, but then I can feel him lean into it. *Curious*, he muses, the way he does when he tinkers with his SpiderBorgs or his Eventualies readings. *It's as though you've been hit by the Cure Bus's cannons . . . I always wondered what the pungits looked like after. But this is . . . very curious.*

This is not one of your experiments, Bo! I blast him. *What does this mean?*

Just stay calm, Patrick.

Stay calm. Yes. I have to stay calm.

114

The curtain pulls back and Opal walks in. I click off the ray and sit back down, knees back to jiggling.

'I just can't figure it out,' she's muttering. 'What is SO hard about increasing the wattage on a pungit ray? I've shown her how to do it *three* times and she still can't ID a Phase 1 Mover.' She sighs, a hand on her hip as she looks between the two of us. Pilot is staring at me, his eyes practically bulging out of his head.

'How's it going in here?' she asks.

I bite my lip and keep my eye on Pilot. He hasn't looked away from me.

'Pilot?' says Opal.

'Huh? What?'

'I asked how it's going. How far along are you?'

He glances down at the AvinGate and starts typing. 'Good, yeah. Real good. No major health concerns, normal Phase 3 Moved Shadow. Not much left to do but the aptitude test.'

Why is he lying for me?

'What about the Mover relationship?' asks Opal. 'The headaches?'

Pilot stands up, handing her the AvinGate. 'It's nothing. We talked about it. I've agreed to keep my eye on him, but I don't think it's going to be a problem.'

Opal watches me, lips pursed, and I press my hands between my knees.

'Anyway,' says Pilot, 'I've marked up his chart, you can read it. I can deal with the aptitude test. Everything else checks out, so we should get out of your hair.'

'You're sure?'

'Yep, real sure. Let's go, Pat.' He can't get out of here fast enough. He doesn't even look at Opal as he ducks out through the curtain.

I stand awkwardly, ready to follow him. But Opal holds up her hand to stop me. 'Your headaches get any worse, I want you to come see me, you understand?'

I nod and she lets me pass. I couldn't be happier to be out from behind that curtain, away from the pungit ray.

But still, Pilot saw.

I scan the crowded queue area for him, and he's heading back the way we came in, Tungsten trailing behind. I hurry after them, not sure why he lied for me. But glad that he did.

'Pilot, wait!'

He glances over his shoulder and he's still got that wide-eyed look. He waves me along, telling me to catch up. We round the corner and he ducks in between two tents, stepping over lines and pegs and when we emerge, we're on our own in a tight corridor against the wall of the Block, the backs of the tents running the length of it.

He paces on the spot, back and forth, running his hand along the grey brick.

'Pilot,' I say, 'thank you. Thanks for not telling.'

'What was that?' he says. 'Your pungits. I-I've never seen pungits like that. I mean . . . Pat . . . what *are* you?'

I don't know how to answer him. Bo's already nagging at my brain, ordering me not to tell him the truth. But the lies aren't doing me much good either.

'I had an accident,' I tell him. It's not exactly a lie, but it's not the whole truth either. 'A bad one. And it messed up my pungits.'

'An accident? What kind of accident?'

'It doesn't matter. The point is, I have to get back to my Shadow, I mean, my Mover. I have to get back to Bo because he knows how to help me.'

'He can fix your pungits, you mean?'

I nod. Because even though that's not really true, it's the easiest answer I can give him, and hopefully it's enough to make him understand why I can't stay.

'He's a doctor, then?' Pilot says. 'This . . . Bo?'

There's a surge from Bo: *Why did you give him my name?*

I hadn't really thought about it, and I'm mad at myself for not being more careful.

You shouldn't be giving people my name, Bo warns me.

But Pilot doesn't seem bothered, he just stares at me, waiting for an answer. So I nod. Because it doesn't matter what Pilot thinks Bo is. All that matters is getting back to him. 'I can't be Shade Unit, Pilot. I've got too many problems right now to be any help to you guys.'

Pilot leans back against the brick. 'So all that stuff you told Opal, about the migraines, the nosebleeds. That wasn't true, was it?'

'No.'

He thinks about that for a second, and then, despite himself, he laughs. 'Man, you're a bad liar.'

I smile too, relieved to see his grin back.

'You *really* don't want to be part of this, do you?'

'It's not that I don't,' I tell him, which is probably the truest thing I've told him yet. 'It's just . . .' It's Bo. It's the Time Cache. It's my family. And it's Gabby. It's so much, and I don't know how I'm going to fix everything but I know I have to try, and I can't do that if I'm running around for Shade Unit.

When I don't say anything more, Pilot nods. 'I get it.'

He doesn't. How could he? I haven't explained anything. But I appreciate that he doesn't seem interested in pushing me.

He rubs a hand over his hair, and lets out a long breath while he thinks. 'Look,' he says, 'I've got a run I'm supposed to do tomorrow. I was gonna hitch a ride with the supply caravan part of the way when they head back to town to stock up on food and fuel and things. I can probably sneak you out then, get you back to Dune's Thoroughfare, and you can get back home from there.'

'What do we tell Bash?'

Pilot taps his head against the wall a couple times. 'We don't.'

'What?'

'Telling Bash will just mean you having to answer a lot more questions,' he says. 'It's easier for everyone if you just go. I'll tell Bash you ran away after you're gone.'

'*Ran away.*' I don't like the sound of it. It's cowardly. I don't want Bash to remember me as a coward.

'It wouldn't be the first time,' says Pilot. 'Plenty of people join up only to realise they can't handle it. You'd just be another one.'

I try not to think of the disappointment on the captain's face after he personally welcomed me to Shade Unit.

'Don't worry,' says Pilot, smirking. 'I'm a better liar than you, I promise.' He's being so nice to me, even after I lied to him. And I don't understand it. Who am I to him?

'Why are you helping me?'

He lets his head rest against the wall and he stares up towards the ceiling, hundreds of feet above us. 'You need it,' he says simply. 'I know what it's like to be alone, be scared. Know what it's like to wish someone would help. But no one was really in a position to help me. Now I find myself in a position to help others. So I have to, don't you think?'

'You don't *have* to,' I tell him.

'Yes, I do.' He pushes off the wall and leads me further down the line of tents. 'It's my own rule. Why else would I be here?'

I follow him, wondering what happened to make him dedicate his life to helping people. I don't think I've ever heard a person say anything so selfless. It's a bit intimidating, and makes me feel even more ashamed about abandoning him and Shade Unit. Is it selfish of me to want to go home?

No, I tell myself. Because I'm not just going home for me. I'm going home for my family, for Gabby. I'm going home to save them.

GABBY
2083

I've been adjusting the exposure for hours. I still haven't managed to see my pungits.

And you won't.

My Shadow lurks on the edges of my mind. Watching. Waiting. Assuring me I'll fail.

I can't fail.

I glance at my droidlet. It's nearly midnight. Mother and Father's WAN meeting has run longer than usual. They should have been home ages ago. They could walk in any minute. And if they find me still awake, I'll be in trouble.

It is foolish for you to fear them. It's you they should fear.

They don't fear me. They hate me. And they hate me even more when I don't follow the rules. I should have been asleep ages ago.

I need to hurry up.

I flick on the ray for the thousandth time. There's a buzzing, the whole thing rattling from the power.

I stand in front of the ray, watching myself in my bedroom mirror.

Please please please please.

You are wasting your efforts.

I stare at the space above my head. There's nothing. Just like always. No pungits. Nothing but the empty air around me.

All this precious time, squandered on something that can't be changed. We're connected, Gabby. The way nature intended. You are mine and I am yours. You can't stop what nature wanted. I won't let you go.

And then I see it. A distortion in the mirror just above my head – like a ripple of heat rising from the road on a hot summer's day. It's faint. Barely visible. But still, it's there.

I'm getting closer.

Pain – searing and hot – shoots through my mind. I'm on the floor. Grabbing at my head.

My Shadow. He's taken hold. Squeezing. Punishing.

'Stop it!' I scream.

But he doesn't. He just squeezes harder. And a thought radiates out from him. Over and over and over and over. Furious and loud, so there's no room for anything else.

Mine.

Mine.

MINE.

And the muscles in my stomach constrict. They want to flex. To end the pain. To Move.

MINE.

MINE.

My Shadow releases me suddenly. Voices have invaded the silence of the apartment.

Father and Mother. They are laughing.

I rub my head, the pain fading.

I can hear them in the kitchen. They are loud. Excited. Must have been a good meeting.

My other hand finds my stomach. The twitching muscles are quiet now. But still, I'd felt them flex. I hug myself, on the floor of my room, letting my head fall back against my desk.

What if Mrs Dibbs is right? What if I do need an upgrade?

I can't be Phase 3. Oh please, oh please, don't let me be Phase 3.

The voices in the kitchen go silent.

My heart stops.

The note from Mrs Dibbs. What did I do with it?

I was in the kitchen—

The door to my room bursts open. Father. His face is twisted. And I see what hit him – he's got it clenched in his right hand. The letter from Mrs Dibbs.

'What is this?' His voice is dark and quiet, like black smoke rising from his throat.

I don't have an answer. He's read it. He knows about the upgrade. I'm a worse daughter because of it. A greater burden. A bigger disappointment. My mouth hangs open. No answer comes. There's nothing I can say that won't make it worse.

'Well?!'

I glance helplessly at Mother, standing in the hall behind him. Her eyes are cold, narrowed. They wait for me to speak, their silence a black hole hungry to swallow me up and be rid of me for ever.

'I—'

You what? What is there to say to Neanderthals like these?

My gut tightens.

They are 'Now'? They are relics. Dust. Isolated to one time and space, lacking any reach throughout the ages. They are a blink in time. But you, you are timeless.

'Answer me!' Father shouts.

'I—' I can't think. My Shadow is in my mind, showing me my parents, their headstones, the names etched into the stone, fading from the elements over accelerated time, the stone itself crumbling to dust until there's nothing left. I close my eyes, trying to focus on pushing the image away. 'I'm sorry,' is all I manage to squeak.

'I'm *sorry*?' Father rages. 'I don't want to hear that you're *sorry*. I want to hear how you let this happen! How could you dare to let yourself become like those – those—'

'Criminals!' supplies Mother.

My stomach clenches, my Shadow seething at the word.

'Exactly,' agrees Father, his nostrils flaring as he stares down at me. 'Thieves of the present, stealing our time, our resources, our *world* for those vagrants from the future.'

My Shadow bristles.

'Bad enough that my own daughter is a Mover. But now,' he throws the note at me, 'I learn you've let yourself become strong enough to be Phase 3? The worst, most dangerous kind of Mover there is?!'

Mother hugs her middle, as if shielding herself from me, like my condition is contagious. 'How did you let yourself become worse?'

How? As though I tried to do it?

You did. You reach for me, you listen for me. You're stronger because you want to be.

I glance at the pungit ray. Father doesn't miss it. In two strides he's across the room, standing over my device. 'What is this? Some kind of Mover mischief? Something else to embarrass us?' He grabs the ray in his trembling fists.

'No!' Without thinking, I reach for it.

He pulls away from me. 'Don't you tell me no!' he bellows. 'This is my home! And I will not have Mover mischief in my house!' Father is wild, eyes animalistic with fury. 'You thought you could get away with this?'

Move me.

'Away with what?' I beg. 'Father, please.'

'You thought you could hide your disgusting condition from me? Under my own roof?'

Move me.

'You'd better think long and hard about what you are doing here, Gabriela.'

'I haven't done anything!'

But Father doesn't want to hear me. He's lost in his own paranoia. Years of We Are Now brainwashing pouring out of him in a furious torrent.

'Lines will be drawn, my girl,' he says. 'After tonight, all your fellow Movers will learn that we won't just stand by and let you steal the Now. Not without a fight.'

I don't understand. But my body quakes at the look in his eyes.

If it's a fight he wants, a fight he'll get. Move me!

'After tonight,' Father goes on, my pungit ray clutched tightly in his hands, 'there will be nowhere for Movers to hide. And it's time you stopped hiding too.'

'I'm not hiding anything!' I beg him.

'Then what do you call this?' His forearms flex as he grips the ray tighter, and I'm afraid it's going to snap. On instinct, I reach for it again and Father pushes me back, hard.

My Shadow swells inside my brain, grabbing tight. *Move me!*

'You think I don't know what you're up to?' he yells. 'You think I don't know you're just like the rest of them?'

My stomach clenches. *Do it, now.*

A part of me wants to. Staring helplessly at my life's work in my father's grip, I want to Move. I want someone to help me. To make my father give it back.

'I blame myself,' says Father, his voice quiet. 'I've looked the other way for too long, and this is what I get for it.' He looks disgustedly at the pungit ray, nostrils flaring. 'Well, no more. No Mover is going to make a fool out of me, least of all my own daughter!'

His hands come up over his head and I scream. But there's no stopping it. He slams the ray into the floor, pieces shattering across the room, my hope for a cure breaking with it.

And my heart opens up – an endless swollen hopelessness. That ray was my chance. My freedom. And it's gone now. All of the time, all of the spare change and scavenging for pieces and parts. All that work. Gone.

Because he took it from you.

Yes. I paw at the carpet, staring at the broken bits of the ray. Father took it from me.

He shouldn't get away with it.

I feel the pull in my gut. Feel my muscles flex.

A breeze tickles my hair.

Father feels it too. 'What are you doing?'

What *am* I doing? The wind picks up, but there are no windows in my room. This breeze isn't from outside. It's from me. And it grows as the pull in my gut gets stronger.

'Gabriela!' Mother stands beside Father. 'You stop this, right now.'

But I can't stop it. It's falling out of my control. My body is taking over.

And my Shadow is gleeful. His triumph is amplifying in my mind as though he were laughing right beside me.

I close my eyes. I can't do this. Can't let him have this.

The air whips around the room. I've stirred up the Eventualies, sending the contents of my room flying.

My father's hand clamps down on my arm. Fingers bruising my skin. He hauls me to my feet. 'We said stop this!' he screams, shaking me.

Stop. Yes. I have to stop.

There is no stopping it!

But this Move belongs to me. I have to take control. With all of my strength I focus on the clench in my stomach. Grit my teeth against it. My body wants to keep going. It needs to keep going. Like a yawn, or a sneeze, but ever so much bigger. As I resist, a pain radiates out from my stomach and I cry out but I have to hold strong.

Don't do this, Gabby.

My Shadow's shrinking back. Moving away from me.

You're giving the Nowbies what they want.

The winds are dying down.

At last, the muscles in my stomach relax, and I gasp for air, exhausted.

The room is silent. My father still grips my arm. When I look into his face, rage and horror glisten in his wide eyes.

Mother wrings her hands. 'A Move. You tried to Move.'

I'm just as frightened as she is. That was close. Too close. I've never done anything that close to Moving before. And the strength of it. The pull to my Shadow – it terrified me.

Father releases me suddenly, pushing me back from him. He looks at me like he's never seen me before. Like I'm some kind of animal. A diseased one. Ready to bite him.

I shudder, bracing myself for whatever comes next.

'Get out of my house.' His voice is breathless, so quiet I almost don't understand him. 'Get out!' he screams, kicking what's left of my pungit ray and sending pieces flying in my face. 'Get out before I call BMAC!'

I don't wait for him to say it again. I scurry by him, shielding myself from the contents of my room he's throwing around in a rage. I race for the front door, and nearly trip over several boxes blocking the hall. I pull at the door handle but one of the boxes at my feet stops it opening – the box is full of jars, white stickers on the lids all saying the same thing: *Nitromerc*.

I kick the box aside and slam the apartment door shut behind me, swallowed by the silence of the hallway. I'm alone. I can't hear my father rage. My Shadow has fallen back. And all that's left to take their place are two questions – where do I go? What do I do?

I wait for the answers to come to me. But all I'm left with is the stillness of the hallway.

The quiet is deafening.

PAT
2383

Pilot and I are back in the open space where I first woke up in the Block. The Cure Bus is down to nothing but its frame. Every inch of it has been torn apart and I have to wonder if Captain Bash and his men have found what they were looking for. I hope so.

Pilot strides across the floor like he owns the place, Tungsten leading the way. I try to look as confident as he does but I'm too nervous to pull it off. I watch the people coming and going, sorting through the piles of ruined bus. I don't see Captain Bash among them. That's a small relief. I'm afraid of running into him. Afraid of having to lie again, right to his face.

'Where are we going?' I ask Pilot.

'The hangar bay,' he says. 'It's where all Shade Unit's vehicles are. Just through here.'

The hangar bay is just a big empty space beyond the Cure Bus. No tents here, just rows of junky looking cars and other kinds of vehicles I can't identify. Some have BMAC crests on their sides, the Shade Unit mark painted over the top. All of them look like nothing I've ever seen in my time, but still, I can tell they are old and outdated. Their shells are eaten by rust, lights and windows missing. Compared to the Cure Bus, these vehicles look ancient. They must all be salvaged. Most look pieced together from the random parts of many different vehicles.

'This way.' Pilot leads us across the hangar, passing rows and rows of Shade Unit zombie vehicles until we come to the far wall and what looks like some kind of makeshift air traffic control. There's a line of large monitors here, and panels and panels of buttons that remind me of the cockpit of a spaceship.

'What is this?'

'You said your Mover is a doctor.' He takes a seat and pulls himself close to the panel, typing away at the buttons. Tungsten slithers up beside him, watching Pilot's fingers. 'Bash keeps a log of doctors in all quadrants of the city in case there's any kind of emergency. We might have his address listed. Bo, right? Bo what?'

He doesn't need my name, says Bo.

You won't be listed anyway, I remind him. *You're not really a doctor.*

Don't give him my name.

I couldn't if I wanted to. I don't know Bo's last name.

'Pat?' Pilot watches me, expectantly.

'I don't know his last name,' I say, glad to not be making something up for once. 'Look, I've got a friend nearby I can stay with until Bo picks me up. He's an Archivist.'

There's a grumble from Bo – he's in no mood to see

129

Carlin tomorrow – but it's the only place I can think of, so he doesn't have a choice.

'At Dune's Thoroughfare? Let me see.' He types something into the panel and the monitor lights up with a map and red dots. He picks one, near the Thoroughfare and a name comes up. 'Oh yeah, Carlin Holt. I've been there.' He turns and looks at me. 'Your Mover's a friend of Carlin Holt?'

I'm a little surprised he knew who Carlin was right away. I wasn't prepared for it.

'Wait – *Bo*?' says Pilot, and my pulse quickens as he tries the name out, like he's done it before. 'Your Mover's not *Bo Hill*, is he?'

There's another surge from Bo – fear and anger. I guess that means Pilot's right.

'Whose Mover is Bo Hill?' I jump back with a start at Captain Bash's voice. How long has he been there, listening?

Pilot and I exchange glances, neither of us saying anything.

Captain Bash's warm smile fades, replaced with a stern expression. 'Pilot, answer me. What are you two doing?'

His red eye is on me as he stands up in front of Bash. 'Pat's Mover,' he says. 'It's Bo Hill.'

Captain Bash looks to me, surprised.

Bo told me not to give his name. Now I know why. Bash knows it. I've messed up, I can feel it. And Bo's already furious.

'No one's heard from Bo Hill in eight years,' says Bash.

'No one but Carlin Holt,' agrees Pilot.

They're both looking at me like I'm some kind of relic, some kind of unearthed artefact and it's making me nervous. I look down at my feet.

'Pat,' says Bash. 'Do you know where Bo Hill is now?'

Bo's anger swells in my mind, so bad it hurts. I shake my head.

'He's gonna be at Carlin's tomorrow.'

I look up at Pilot – why would he say that? He said he was going to help me.

Bo's raging, like a wasp inside a glass jar, pinging against my head.

Stop it! I tell him.

But he's too mad. Too upset to communicate. He can't hear me through his own tantrum.

'What's wrong?' Pilot frowns, seeing the pain in my face.

I grab my head in my hands, growling against the onslaught, and force Bo back from me. I push him out of my head, slamming closed my mind to keep him from hurting me any more. And I think about what Bo said – about hostile connections being a danger in the field. I remember how Roth used to hurt Gabby. I would have never thought Bo could do that to me. But he just did. It was a brief glimpse of what Gabby had to deal with and it's enough to scare me. Then again, he told me not to tell them his name. And I betrayed Bo's trust.

I can still feel him, blazing mad behind the door of my mind. I don't know how long I can keep him out, but I hope he calms down soon.

'Why did you say that?' I ask Pilot. 'Why did you tell?'

He smiles apologetically. 'Pat, do you know who Bo Hill *is*?'

No. Bo doesn't tell me anything. I rub my aching temples. I doubt he'll tell me much more after I gave up his name.

131

'He was Constance Ashlinn's first tactician,' says Bash. 'He was a genius engineer, specialising in AI, artificial intelligence. One of the best weapons Shade Unit had in the fight against the Nowbies.'

'Bo?'

Pilot nods.

'Pat,' says Bash. He takes a seat on the chair and faces me, his fingers steepled. 'I would dearly love to meet this man.'

I look away. I already know what Bo will say to that. I can't feel him any more. He's backed off completely. Trying to get a hold of himself, I guess.

'This is a man who could really help us with what we are trying to accomplish here.'

'What exactly is it you think Bo can do for you?'

'BMAC's technologies are extremely advanced, improving every day,' says Bash. 'A mind like Bo Hill's, a mind that knows exactly how these technologies work at their most basic level? He could change everything for us.' They can't be talking about *my* Shadow. My throat feels dry. How could they know more about him than I do?

Bash moves his chair closer to me, pressing his fingertips against his lips while he thinks. 'Pat, what we're trying to do here, trying to take BMAC's Cure facility, it's a big mission. With a lot of moving parts. It's why I'm trying to unify the leaders of Shade Unit. We're a stronger machine if all the parts work together. The machine doesn't work for Shade Unit. It works for *all* Movers and Shadows.'

I like Bash. I like that he's trying to create something for *all* of us. Something to stand against BMAC and the

Nowbies. Something to show them they can't make us do whatever they want. If we'd had something like Shade Unit in my time, maybe things would have worked out differently for me and Gabby.

'And someone like Bo Hill,' Bash says, 'knows how important that work is. He did it himself. Until BMAC stopped him. We can offer him a second chance. Don't you think he'd want that chance?'

I know he doesn't. He wouldn't have freaked out the way he did if he had any interest in helping Shade Unit. But still, I don't understand him. I don't understand how he could hear what Captain Bash and Shade Unit are trying to do and not want to help. How badly did BMAC treat him that he's too scared to stand up to them again? Too scared to even talk about it?

'He won't like it,' I admit. 'He doesn't want anything to do with Shade Unit any more. He's made that pretty clear.'

'Would you let me try to convince him otherwise?'

I check the seal in my mind – the brace that's keeping Bo out. He hasn't been prodding at me to get back in. He's left me alone enough that he's not listening to the conversation any more.

If his reaction to Pilot guessing his name is any indication, then there's no way Bo can be convinced to help Shade Unit. But I need to get back to him, somehow. And Bash and Pilot know how to do that.

'If you take me to him,' I say, 'you can ask Bo whatever you like.'

PAT
2383

A hovercraft drops us off at Dune's Thoroughfare and Bash leads us to the Archivist's door. He knocks, and my hands busy themselves, twisting my fingers, waiting for Bo to open the door. After a few seconds, Bash tries again. Pilot raises an eyebrow at me and I realise I'm fidgeting. I can't help it. Every passing second a new Bo scenario pops into my head, each one worse than the last. Maybe he'll yell, tell Bash exactly what he thinks of Shade Unit. But then another idea hits me – what if Bo doesn't come at all?

I reach out for him with my mind and feel the edges of his own. He doesn't reach back, he's too mad, but still, he's there. He's close. At least I know he's shown up.

There's a screech of metal as the door pulls open and the Archivist peeks around the door, wearing his massive spectacles.

'Oh ho! You're here!' He bounces on his toes like an excited kid. 'Well of course you are. Bo said you'd be coming and here you are!' He's rambling. He's combed his hair. I guess it's been a long time since Carlin's had so many guests at once. 'Come in, come in, come in.'

An amused grin tugs at Pilot's mouth. I'm not the only one who's noticed Carlin's particular brand of crazy. All that time alone with his books, I guess.

He leads us down into the library where Bo sits at the desk. His mood hits me like a blast of ice. And the sour look on his face is enough to tell Bash and Pilot he's not happy to see them. Pilot looks at me nervously and I feel like shrinking behind the stacks. Bo's not even going to try to play nice.

'Well then,' smiles the Archivist, glancing from Bo to Bash, 'here we are. Together at last, eh?'

Bo harrumphs.

I look up at Bash, who's standing beside me. He swallows nervously. This could be worse than I thought.

Finally, Bash clears his throat and stretches out his hand, taking a step towards Bo. He says something I don't understand. He must know Bo's language, same as Carlin. But Bo's not about to bridge the gap because he folds his arms and looks away. I try not to wince, staring at Bash's hand hanging unshaken in the empty space between them.

He says something else, and Bo scoffs.

No one from those days is a hero. Least of all me.

Bash tries to recover, speaking quickly and it's maddening not being able to understand one whole side of the conversation.

Bo raises his hand to stop him. *I'm well aware of the things I did during my Shade Unit days, and I can tell you I'm*

135

not proud of a single one. If you came here to talk me into returning, you've wasted your time.

Bash talks some more and I glance over at Pilot. He's staring, nearly slack-jawed, as he listens and I wonder if he understands these foreign words.

He must, because before I know it, he's opening his mouth and speaking in Bo's language. I recognise the last words – *Constance Ashlinn.*

Constance Ashlinn is dead to me! Bo shouts, so loud and so venomous it stuns everyone into silence. A crinkle forms between Pilot's eyebrows and I can see his admiration for Bo draining. Bash isn't deterred. He opens his arms, his voice ever calm despite the rage coming at him from Bo. *You want my help?* snaps Bo. *Here it is, so pay attention. You cannot stop BMAC because there is no stopping BMAC. The best you can do is stay out of their way.* With that, Bo steps around the desk and plunks himself down in the Archivist's chair, turning his back on the three of us.

I look to Bash, his fists clenched tightly at his sides. Finally, he nods to himself. 'Let's go, Pilot.'

'That's it?' Pilot says. 'You're just going to let him—'

'His mind was made up a long time ago,' says Bash, heading for the door. 'He's not one of us any more.'

Something inside me shrivels up. Bo must look like a coward to Bash, a selfish old wimp who cares about no one but himself. And maybe he is. How else could he tell Bash to just give up?

Bash stops at the door and looks back to me. 'Pat, if you decide to change your mind, we'll be at Ruby's for the night.'

'Ruby's?'

'In the Thoroughfare,' says Pilot.

I'm relieved by the offer – at least they haven't lumped me in with Bo as a lost cause. But I hate that this is probably the last time they'll ever see me. This rude, tense encounter with my Shadow is the last thing they'll remember about me. 'Thank you,' I say. 'For everything.'

Bash nods and leaves, but Pilot lingers at the door.

'When you're ready, Pat,' he says. 'Any time.'

The door upstairs clanks shut and it's just me and Bo. I stare, facing the door. I can't look at him right now. I'm not just embarrassed. I'm ashamed. Because some part of me feels like Bo is my responsibility. He's my Shadow after all. And I let him humiliate the only friends I've managed to make for myself in 2383.

I know you're mad at me, Bo says inside my mind. *But one day you'll see I was right. That man and his boy are going to get themselves killed in their useless fight against BMAC. I've seen it enough times to know.*

When I turn back to face him, he's tinkering with his Eventualies readings. *You want to make a difference for Movers and Shadows? This is going to improve all our lives more than you can imagine. Work with me on this, Pat, I've just made a huge breakthrough.*

What?

Your pungits, Patrick! Didn't you see them?! They were frozen. FROZEN! And here you are, unparalysed, unharmed. Walking and talking as though nothing is wrong! Do you have any idea what this means? He's excited, almost giddy.

No.

137

It means your pungits are still! Pungit movement creates the Eventualies. If we can freeze pungits without harming Movers, it means we can stabilise the Eventualies! I've been working on this for years. At last, I know how to do it!

The Eventualies, I grit my teeth, my eyes still on the door. *All you care about is the Eventualies?*

He looks at me, confused. *Patrick, they can be stabilised. People could go out during the daylight if that happens. We could build a proper city and lives out here for Movers and Shadows. We don't have to fear the consequences of more Movement in the future. What could be more important than that right now?*

'But I don't want to be here!' I shout. I can't believe how oblivious he is, how selfish. 'And you just humiliated me in front of my friends!'

Friends?

Yes! My friends! They were nothing but kind to me and they didn't have to be. And then they meet you and you're nothing but vicious!

Kind? You thought they were helping you, to be kind? He's shouting in his language now, his own frustration rising to meet mine. *They were using you to get to me.*

Why then? What's so great about you that they need to use me to get to you? Huh?

Bo shakes his head, fingers prodding his temples.

Tell me, Bo! Because I don't understand. I don't understand how you could be Shade Unit once upon a time, how you could have believed all the things Bash believes in now, and then become this. This selfish old creep who won't lift a finger to

138

help anyone! What happened to you that makes you hate Shade Unit so much?

Since when is Shade Unit so important to you? he asks me. *Brainwashed you, did they? You were only there a day and listen to you now. Save all the Movers and Shadows if we just work together, yeah?* He leans across the desk, holding his head in his hands. It looks heavy for him, like whatever is in there is weighing him down. Finally, his eyes meet mine and there's pain there. *You want to know where that thinking gets you? Fine.*

I feel him, reaching out into my mind. His thoughts are clear and open, like a big gaping well inviting me to fall into it. Bo's head has never been like this before, never been so unguarded. I peek inside, unsure of what I'll find, and soon the old memories I've caught glimpses of begin to bubble up towards me – running, screaming, First Avin. The wind. He's showing me. His memories are mine to take. And before I can decide if I really want to know, Bo's mind swells around mine until I can't see him in front of me any more. It's like I've fallen – tumbling down into the well of his memories.

I'm Bo. I'm here with Shade Unit, the war has not yet ended. It's dark here. A tiny room with glowing screens, the outside howl of the Eventualies louder than I've ever heard it. The digital symbols in front of me are a glowing mess of numbers and brackets and shapes that mean nothing to me. It's code. I don't know it. But Bo does. The code belongs to him. He wrote it.

A voice over my shoulder says something in words that I don't know. Bo's language. 'She's never late.'

I turn, a young woman with curly hair watches me nervously. I understand her. I've got Bo's ears. 'Something's wrong,' she insists. 'Of all the days, she wouldn't be late today.'

I glance at the time on the monitor. Seven minutes past four a.m. 'She's not even ten minutes late.'

'Have you ever known Connie to be late?'

Constance Ashlinn. Bo's waiting for her. I know it because he knows it. And I also know this woman – Mari – is right. Constance is never late. Something could very well be wrong. But the final code still needs to be complete if they're going to have the vault open to First Avin Bank. Mari can't get distracted.

'If something were wrong, we'd be informed,' I tell her through Bo's mouth. 'If something were wrong, Connie would send a runner.'

Mari says nothing, pacing the tiny room, back and forth.

'Mari,' I say calmly, 'this is just like what happened before Archer Base. You were convinced the entire operation was in jeopardy, do you remember?'

She stops and nods.

'And what happened?'

She tries not to grin. 'We took Archer Base.'

'We did. And we'll take First Avin too. Everything is in place. I sent the runner last night so Connie knows the plan. There's nothing to worry about. Now please, have a seat and help me finish.'

Reluctantly, Mari obeys and sits down at her own monitors. Her fingers fly furiously across the touchscreen and I'm glad to have her working beside me. She's a brilliant programmer, and more dedicated to Shade Unit than anybody – dedicated to Connie. We're here to finish what Blue started. With Constance Ashlinn to guide us, we'll take down BMAC and plunge Avin into chaos.

'What if the runner didn't make it to her?' says Mari.

'He did.'

'What if he didn't?'

'If he didn't, Connie would know. She knew to wait for him. If the runner didn't show, Connie would have sent another one to tell us there was a problem. Now hurry, we don't have a lot of time.'

There's something hidden behind Bo's confident words. An unsteadiness. My eyes flick to the clock on the monitor. Thirteen minutes past four. He's worried too. Now I feel just how suffocating the tiny room is. It's the back of a hovercraft, one Shade Unit has stolen from BMAC. I'm aware of the towering, oppressive skyscrapers just beyond the craft's hull. They're looming over us. Bearing down. We are in the heart of Avin. We are in the enemy's camp.

Two bangs sound against the hull, and a man slides the door open – a BMAC agent. No, wa. He just looks like a BMAC agent. But I know him. That's Stately. He's Shade Unit in disguise. He's my friend.

'We have to go,' he says quickly.

'Go?'

Mari's eyes flash to me – she was right. The 'something wrong' has caught up to us.

'Sirens, can you hear them?' says Stately. 'Burns guesses at least four BMAC vehicles approaching from the north-west. Who knows how many more on their way.'

'They know we're here?'

'We're blown, we have to ditch.'

Panic swells inside me. We can't ditch. We're so close to pulling down First Avin's security defences. When Constance gets here, she'll be able to storm the bank and destroy all the data. We're so close to bringing down the walls BMAC has built around Movers and Shadows. So close to liberating everyone from the Nowbies and the world they've tried to keep us out of. If we ditch now, it's all lost. Everything we've worked for.

'What about Connie?' asks Mari. 'She'll walk right into them if we don't warn her.'

'She'll be coming from the south-west,' says Stately. 'We can try and intercept her.'

'Let's hurry then,' I say, the BMAC sirens growing louder by the second.

'On foot,' says Stately. 'We can't be caught with all this.'

He's right, but I hesitate. The craft is filled with the last six months of work. Six months of hard-won code and stolen equipment. Six months of the most important work we've ever done. And we just have to leave it. Because if they tie this to us, Shelving will be the least of our problems.

Mari's already jumping out of the craft, shoulders hefting bags filled with whatever she could grab.

How did this happen? Everything was planned down to the smallest detail. How could BMAC have found out what we were up to without us catching wind of it first? How did Constance not know? Where is she?

Burns runs up, eyes wide with terror. 'We gotta go!' he barks. '*Now* you guys, come on!'

Snapping into action, I leap out with the rest and I'm

surprised to realise I have no limp. The lights of the approaching BMAC reflect off the glass of the skyscrapers. They're close.

The Eventualies aren't on our side today, pushing and pulling us whichever way it wills. Burns leads us at a sprint through back alleys, trying his best to leave the screaming vehicles behind. No matter how hard we run, how fast, the sirens are never far. They've locked onto us, I realise. Their radar knows where we are.

I glance at the sky to our backs. BMAC's up there. BMAC's searching. The first of their pursuit crafts bursts free of the smoky clouds, black and hard and menacing. It swoops low, and Mari screams.

'Run!' orders Stately.

But there is no running. They've already caught us. Even before they've surrounded us, I know we're theirs. But how? How could Constance miss this? How could she not warn us?

A sudden gust of the Eventualies blows me sideways, and it catches the BMAC craft, hurling it into the nearest building. Glass shatters, raining down from above and we scatter, taking cover as best we can. A beam hurtles towards me and I dive sideways – white hot pain rips through my leg and I scream.

'Bo!' Mari screams.

I glance at my leg – a jagged piece of glass juts from my thigh. It's so large, I want to faint.

Stately's beside me instantly, slinging my arm around his shoulder and hauling me to my feet. The pain is vicious, but we can't linger. The BMAC craft has recovered its balance and is coming. Stately shuffles me along, and we duck down the alley to the right. When I glance back, Mari and Burns are gone. They went the wrong way.

'We have to go back!' I shout to Stately.

'We can't!' he says. 'We have to get to Constance!'

I can't leave them. We're a team.

I take my arm from Stately's neck, hobbling back the way we came. Every step is agony, but I have to get to them. Stately's shouting after me but I can't leave Mari and Burns behind. When I get back to the main street, clutching my burning leg, blood seeping through my fingers, the BMAC craft is on the ground, officers with guns posted around it.

And there are Mari and Burns – each of them held at gunpoint. I want to run to them. But I'm alone and unarmed and there's nothing I can do. The BMAC officers posted by the vehicle pull open the side panel and Mari and Burns are shoved inside. They'll be Shelved, or worse. Tortured first, probably.

Just before BMAC closes the panel and seals my friends inside, I catch a glimpse of someone else cuffed and secured to a seat. Someone I know.

It's Curly – the runner I sent to Constance last night.

BMAC caught him.

That means he never made it to her. She would have waited for his message and it never came. She knew something was wrong all this time. She knew BMAC intercepted our message. She knew Curly told them what we were doing. Where we would be.

And Constance never warned us.

*   *   *

144

Suddenly I'm falling – falling away from Bo and back into myself. The turbulence of it makes me lose my balance.

There's a gasp.

I'm on the floor of the Archivist's library, tears stinging my eyes. Carlin stands by the desk clutching a tray of his spice mull, eyes full of worry. Bo sits behind it, lips tight in a frown.

I wipe my eyes, thinking of BMAC taking my friends away. I don't know them, not really, but through Bo, these strangers have pressed themselves into my heart. They're with me now. 'What happened to them?' I ask. 'Mari and Burns.'

Carlin bites his bottom lip and looks to Bo who never takes his eyes off me.

I brought you back when I did because I don't care to show you that part.

What happened? I can't help but ask.

Shelved, Patrick. Shelved for refusing to provide the information they had on Constance Ashlinn and the rest of us. Held their tongues to the last.

Goosebumps rush over my skin. Shelved. Just like Gabby. I close my eyes, trying not to remember the needle that I always see when I think of the Shelves. Blue and ugly and hungry for Movers and Shadows. The needle that put Rani on the Shelves. It's come for all of them.

'Here now,' says Carlin, as soothingly as he can. He hands me a steaming cup. 'Just a small sip. A good mull will do us all good, yes?'

I ignore Carlin's outstretched arm, eyes on Bo. 'I don't understand. Bash is offering you another chance. A second shot at doing what you and Shade Unit started—'

'Another chance to land innocent people on the Shelves?' Bo shouts, resorting to English now. 'Another chance to be a puppet for Constance Ashlinn?'

'Maybe she didn't know.'

'She knew!' Bo bellows. 'It was her job to know. She sacrificed us so she could get away. She could have helped us and instead she did nothing.'

I don't know how he can be so sure of that. Everything turned to chaos that day. Anything could have happened. I hope he's wrong about Constance, for Bash's sake.

'You said I don't help anyone,' says Bo. 'I trusted people to help me and my friends, and I was abandoned. BMAC, Shade Unit, it's all the same. No one cares about anyone but themselves. So I gave up on all of it. And I've been just fine looking out for myself.'

I don't know what to say. I can still feel the echo of the gash in my leg. The gash that left Bo with a permanent limp. It must remind him of Mari and Burns and Stately every single day. Must remind him of Constance Ashlinn, and how she didn't come to rescue them all. How can I blame him for not trusting Bash when he carries that with him all the time?

'But now we have a chance to help everyone,' Bo says finally. 'You and me. With your pungits, and what they can teach us about the Eventualies.'

When I look up, his dark frown has melted into something softer. He cares about my safety. I can feel it inside his head.

'Stopping the Eventualies won't help me get into the Time Cache, Bo.'

'We'll figure all that out,' he says, taking a cup of tea from Carlin. 'Just trust me, Patrick. I only want what's best for you.'

I see Bo's idea of what's best for me, I get a brief glimpse before his thoughts turn to the spice of his mull. What's best for me is more of the same. More days in his leaky lair. More trips to Carlin. Safe and sound and huddled up in the quiet life we've been building together.

I sip my mull, carefully closing my thoughts off to Bo. He has no intention of helping me get to the Time Cache. He thinks it's as foolish as Shade Unit trying to fight BMAC. After seeing what happened to him the last time he went into the heart of Avin, I can't say that I blame him.

The truth of what I have to do solidifies in my mind. Bo can't help me find my way home. If I want to get to the Time Cache, I'll have to do it without him.

I think of Pilot and the message folded inside his breast pocket. When I'm ready, he told me. I'm not sure that I am. But after what Bo's just shown me, I have no choice, I have to be ready. Bash said they'd be at Ruby's for the night. So that's where I'll go. I have to join Shade Unit.

GABBY
2083

The fluorescent lights of Julie's Eatery flicker. The greasy spoon is one of the few restaurants in my neighbourhood that stays open this late. I've come here late a lot.

This isn't the first time I've had to leave my parents' house in the middle of the night. I discovered Julie's after a bad fight two years ago. It was the only place still open in the little back street I had wandered onto. I've come back after every fight since. $3.49 for a mint chocolate milkshake. I always order one. Work on my ray. When I'm finished, enough time has passed that my parents have gone to sleep and I can go home.

Not tonight.

I scratch anxiously at the skin between my fingers.

This wasn't a typical fight. They threatened to call BMAC. The look in their eyes – I was their enemy. That's how they saw me. Lines will be drawn, Father said. And he drew one, right between me and them.

There's a loud, phlegmy throat rattle and I look over my

shoulder. A sour-faced line cook watches me from the counter. He's here every night. I don't think he's Julie.

'Still good with water?' he asks.

I nod. I keep some money in my backpack for nights like this one. But tonight I didn't have a chance to grab my backpack. So no milkshake for me. I inspect my stinging fingers. I've scratched too hard. Blood, bright and red, beads out from where I've torn the skin.

I can't stay at Julie's for ever. Where am I supposed to go?

Are you asking me?

My muscles tense. My mind too. My Shadow's suddenly back inside my head.

You reached out for me.

He's cold. His rage from the apartment has cooled to something worse. I press my palms to the table, steadying myself. **If I did, I didn't mean to**.

You did.

I wait for the pain, but there's nothing yet.

You reached out because you need my help.

I don't.

You do. Just like you needed me against your parents. That's why you began to Move me.

I shake my head. But a part of me is worried that he's right.

Because without me, who do you have, Gabby?

A tickle forms in my throat. I'm going to cry.

No one.

I try not to look at the empty seat across from me.

Without me, you are all alone.

My eyes burn. I wipe my tears away as quick as I can but still more come. What he says is true.

I think it's time you learned to appreciate that. I think it's time I made you appreciate that.

I take a deep breath. He's going to punish me. He's going to hurt me again.

I think it's time I made you realise how much you need me. Time I made you learn how alone alone can be.

I close my eyes, steel myself against the pain.

But there is none.

Only silence.

Because he's gone again. He's fallen back from me. Alone, he'd said. He wants me to be alone, without his constant, poisonous thoughts. I almost laugh with relief. But he hasn't left me. Not completely. He's lurking, like a shark, gliding silently at the farthest edge of my mind. Watching me.

At least he's quiet for now.

A phlegmy cough splits the silence. Only now do I realise who's standing beside my table – the line cook.

'Are you done looking at the menu?' he asks.

I haven't opened a menu.

'Can I get you something to eat?'

I shake my head.

'Drink?'

I pull my half-drunk cup of tap water closer.

He sighs and looks around the empty restaurant, his patience finally run out. 'All right, kid. I'm not an idiot. I can see you're in some kind of crisis here. And I'm sorry for that, I really am.' He doesn't look it. 'But this isn't Hexall

Hall.' My breath catches in my throat. Why would he mention Hexall Hall? Is it that obvious I'm a Mover? If he notices my surprise he doesn't show it, he just keeps lecturing. 'You can't squat here waiting for life's problems to clear up. This is a place of business. And places of business need money. And if you don't plan to spend any money, then you can't stay here.'

My face feels hot and I know I'm blushing. I'm embarrassed. Can't look him in the eye. Slowly, I get out of my chair and tuck it in, slinking past the cook. His narrow eyes watch me all the way to the door.

Outside, the Eventualies cool my blushing cheeks. The streets are empty. I have no idea what time it is. No idea where to go. But the line cook is watching me from the window.

I follow the direction of the wind. Seems as good as any. I'm trying to decide what to do next. It's very late – or by now, very early. Morning should be here soon. By then I can go to school. That's something at least. I can go to school and figure out where to go from there. I don't have my homework with me though. I briefly think about going back home for it, but I know that's a mistake. Still, I don't have anything. No money. No FIILES that contain all of my Phase Forms. Not even a change of clothes. And I don't have my pungit ray. It's gone. Shattered to pieces, but some of it must be salvageable. I have to go back, if only for that reason. But when?

My Shadow stirs on the edges of my mind. He wants to

weigh in. I wait but he keeps silent, determined to keep punishing me. Let him. I'm enjoying the quiet.

A loud squawk erupts above my head. I jump. I look up and meet eyes with a crow, sitting on a ledge just above me. It's so completely black I almost didn't see it in the shadows.

I realise I recognise this apartment tower. This is where Pat Mermick lives.

Instinctively, I press my back up against the wall, trying to hide in the shadows like the bird. *Don't let him see me, don't let him see me.* As if he could. The tower is easily thirty storeys high. Hundreds of people must live here. The odds that Pat is looking out his window right this moment down at the street below and that he'd catch me here, this late at night, are minute.

But still – my heart pounds.

If he did see me, what would he think? Pat Mermick, with his mother who fights for Movers. He's never been kicked out of his house in the middle of the night, I bet.

Then again, Pat Mermick has his own Movers troubles. I glance back up at the building. It happened here – his father Moved someone. It was all over the news at the time. I've read plenty about it. The storm opened up right above this very spot. Of course, BMAC came. They took his father away. Sometimes I wonder why he did it. He had a family. A nice one. Why would he risk Moving someone when he had everything to lose?

Maybe he didn't have a choice. Maybe his Shadow was more forceful than mine.

The bird watches me. Its head tilts sideways as it takes me in.

I feel a heat rush to my cheeks, embarrassed that I know so much about Pat.

Ice flashes through my head, and I wince – my Shadow. He's circling the name – Pat Mermick.

The bird blinks at me, always staring.

What did you do? its eyes ask, accusingly.

I rub my head, as my Shadow fades back again. *I was born.*

With another squawk the bird leaps off its perch, diving for me. I duck and scream as it swoops low over my head before launching skyward. I watch it float across the street before catching an updraft of the Eventualies and disappearing into the sky.

There are lights across the street. A digital bulletin board glowing in the night like a beacon. I wander over, reading the public notices and advertisements that blink and fight for attention. The smallest are the personal ads:

Missing Cat.

Wanted: New Water Heater

The bigger ones take up the centre of the board and are mostly from BMAC and the city of Avin.

Phase Forms Reminder

Avin Walk for the Now.

The next ad blinks across the board and I frown. A panoramic view of four silos under construction. The Shelves. Big bold red letters flash across the image.

THIS IS NOT ENOUGH.

I know what the ad is for already.

BMAC IS NOT ENOUGH. THE MOVER THREAT IS REAL. PROTECT YOUR PRESENT WITH WE ARE NOW.

Even after they've kicked me out, I can't escape my parents and their We Are Now poison. It feels like it's everywhere and it's choking me.

The image flickers out. The silos break up into a million little squares and burn out before my eyes. The screen goes completely white.

Is it broken?

A new message scrolls across the board.

MOVERS OF AVIN, DON'T LIVE WITH FEAR.

I glance over my shoulder. There's no one on the street but me.

RESIST THE NOWBIE OPPRESSION.

This is wrong. The ads for the public bulletins have to go through the Avin government. They are screened. A message like this would never get through. Someone must have hacked it.

WE WILL NOT HIDE.

WE WILL STAND STRONG TOGETHER.

WE ARE TOMORROW.

WE ARE MANY.

YOU ARE NOT ALONE.

Alone. That's been the word of the night. I bite back the tears. The board is wrong. I'm more alone than I've ever been.

Handprints – black as crows – fill up the screen. A clock tower rises between them. I recognise it. The final message, in red letters, appears.

SHADE UNIT WELCOMES YOU.

And just like that, I know where I need to go.

PAT
2383

The wind from the hovercraft nearly blows me over as it takes off into the sky, leaving me and Pilot on the ground of a crumbled city street. The damage here, just outside Avin's border entry, is worse than anything I've seen in the Movers' sector. The rubble and scorch marks don't look like the scars of a battle – they look like a bomb.

The night sky is lit up here, the city just beyond the border glows.

I found Bash and Pilot. Right where they said they'd be, at Ruby's – a dilapidated shack/restaurant on Dune's Thoroughfare. I told them I wanted to be a runner, and that was that.

I rub my fingers over the insignia emblazoned on my chest: it reads *BMAC*. My nose wrinkles. The sight of it on my clothes brands me a traitor. It feels wrong to use my own body as a billboard for the Bureau of Movement Activity Control, after everything they've put me and my family through, put Gabby through.

'Welcome to the Dark Zone,' says Pilot, Tungsten circling his ankles. 'We are officially out of range for any communication with the Block.'

'What if we run into trouble?'

'Distress beacon,' he says, tapping his red eye. 'It's just a ping really, but at least it lets Shade Unit know if we've hit a snag.'

'And they'll come help us?'

Pilot shrugs. 'Depends on what kind of trouble we're in.'

Great.

'You ready?' he asks me. 'We've got a bit of a hike ahead of us.'

I nod and let him lead me through the expanse of destruction, the city of Avin glowing like a perfect beacon in the distance. We're headed for BMAC Headquarters – the Avin Turbine – to deliver a message to a man Bash has inside. I don't know what's in the message Pilot's carrying and I don't much care. I just want to get to the Time Cache. I feel around my head for Bo – his dreams float in the distance. He's still sleeping. When he wakes up and finds me missing, I'll know.

'So I've been thinking,' Pilot says, eyes ever forwards, 'about what you said to Bash last night. About wanting to come with me into Avin.'

'What about it?'

'You were kind of insistent about it.'

I was. Bash wanted me to go to the Block. Wanted me to train. But I begged him to let me go with Pilot – to get real experience, I'd said, to learn from the best. Bash was sceptical but Pilot said he was happy to take me with him and that was that. I didn't think anyone really noticed that I was being pushy about it.

'So, I've been trying to figure out – what's in Avin you're so desperate to get to?'

'A device,' I admit.

'A device?'

If I'm going to find what I'm looking for, I'll need as much help from Pilot as I can get to navigate the city. 'It's in the Time Cache.'

'The Time Cache?!' He shakes his head. 'You can't get into the Time Cache.'

'Well, what do you care if I try?'

Pilot doesn't say anything, just keeps walking, his brow furrowed. 'The Time Cache is filled with artefacts from the past,' he says. 'What's a Shadow from the distant future care about a bunch of relics from the distant past?'

'I just do, OK?'

'And your pungits, the way they are. You're not a normal kind of Shadow, are you?'

'No,' I agree. 'I'm not.'

'You're some special kind?'

'I guess you could say that.'

'You're from the past, aren't you?'

I stop and sigh, looking down at my feet. 'Pilot, I don't want you to know too much about me. I don't even know what I am and I don't want it to get you in danger too.'

'Well,' he laughs, 'I'm Shade Unit. I already am in danger.'

'*More* danger, then,' I snap.

Pilot holds up his hands in surrender and keeps walking, and I'm relieved he's letting it go.

'So the Time Cache . . .'

Or not.

He raises an eyebrow at me. '. . . You know how you're getting in?'

'I'll figure it out.'

Pilot scoffs. 'Sure you will. The guy who's never seen a borg before will find his way into BMAC's most secure vault.'

Pilot's right. I don't know what I'm up against. But all I can do is find out. And try to solve the problem.

'When we get to the check,' he says, 'make sure you look bored. Even annoyed, if you like. Make it look like you do this every day. Nothing gives away a Mover like a sweaty forehead when the pungit scan starts up.'

'Pungit scan?' I feel the sweat beading at my hairline already.

'Yeah, why do you think they call them checkpoints?'

I hadn't really thought about it.

'There are checkpoints all around the border to Avin,' Pilot explains. 'Sixteen in all. Each one set up with one purpose – keep the Movers out. If you want to get into the city you have to be cleared by the border guards at one of these checkpoints. They scan everyone, making sure no Movers or Shadows are coming into their perfect little Nowbie world.'

I imagine a border guard staring at the mess that's hiding above my head. 'I uh, I think now would be a good time to remind you that I have pungits.'

Pilot laughs. 'Yeah, so do I. But don't worry, that's where Tungsten comes in.'

The little borg gives a chirp as he slithers ahead of me and Pilot.

'He'll hit the border guards' computer with a DOS.'

'What's that?'

'Denial of Service attack. It's a hack. Basically, he disrupts their system briefly by overloading it with requests so that there is a delay in the result. During a scan there's a light above the gate into the city. For a Mover, the light blinks red. Fail. Nowbie blinks green. Pass. Tungsten makes it so there is no blink.'

That's not reassuring. 'Isn't that the same as failing?'

Pilot shrugs, turning down another street. 'Border guards have to scan hundreds of people all day long. It's pretty dull work. They don't really pay attention unless they see red. They are *looking* for red. They aren't looking for nothing. So when they see nothing, they wave me through.'

What if today's the day they notice 'nothing'? 'And you've done this before?'

'Sure.'

'Lots of times?'

'Tonnes.'

'And it always works?'

'I'm not on the Shelves, am I?'

He has a point. But I'm still nervous.

Pilot rounds another corner and I follow, the blue glow of the city is just ahead of us, framed by the walls of dead skyscrapers on either side. It looks like another planet, another universe. So alive and thriving and loud compared to the ruined streets of the Movers' sector.

'That's Checkpoint Four,' he says, pointing at a massive grey door frame sitting at the end of the street, a guard booth beside it. Lines of a dozen or so people mill about, waiting for their turn to be scanned.

'What are they all doing outside the city?'

Pilot shrugs. 'BMAC patrols looking for Movers trying to get into the city, Diplomats and politicians returning from visits to other cities. Cadets coming back from training simulations and things.'

'Training simulations?'

'Sure. They're not gonna let BMAC fire off weapons and loose their borgs in the confines of Avin just for training purposes.' I guess not.

I don't know what I was expecting. Something more, I suppose. A giant building like an airport. But there is no building. Just the large grey frame and a small guard booth no bigger than a closet. 'What's to keep people from just going around the check?'

'What do you mean?'

'There's no fence or anything. Couldn't we just go a few blocks over, away from the border guards, and walk into the city?'

'The border is laser monitored, Pat,' says Pilot. 'If you try to cross without going through a Checkpoint, Mover or not, you're cinders.'

'Oh.'

A barrier lifts and a group of twelve shuffles into the frame. It's then that I notice it is divided into stalls, one for each person. Once they've all stepped into their spots, the barrier falls and there's a hum. A bell rings and the lights that line the top of the frame blink green.

'We all go at once?' I ask.

But Pilot doesn't answer me – he's got his eye on something just above us.

Crows – two of them, perched on a ledge thirty feet up. They lean forwards, beaks pointing down at us, accusingly.

'Breezes.'

'Is that a problem?' I ask.

'Not for long,' he says, winking. When he does, his eye glows red and there's a chirp from Tungsten as the little borg takes off, snaking up the wall towards the birds. 'Looks like BMAC is on extra alert.'

'BMAC?'

'See the bands?' He nods at the birds and it's then I notice the blue bands on their ankles. 'BMAC has what they call their "Murder Squads". A flock of crows they sometimes release to patrol the Checkpoints and detect Movers and Shadows.'

'You mean BMAC knows we're coming?'

Pilot shakes his head, watching Tungsten climb higher. 'I doubt it. We're not the only Movers trying to get into Avin, Pat. Desperate people try to sneak in all the time, trying to get to family in the city or just hoping for a better life than what you get in the Movers' sectors. And then there are other Units sending their own runners, their own moles. Nah, these crows aren't here for us. It's just rotten luck.'

One of the birds, its beady eyes on me, lets out a squawk. I cringe. A bunch of BMAC crows that go by the name Murder Squad doesn't sit well with me.

'Should we, you know, like abort or something?'

Pilot doesn't say anything, just keeps watching Tungsten, eye glowing. The robot snakes his way onto the ledge, slowly sidling up to the crows who are too busy watching us to notice him. There's a sound, like an electric charge, and Pilot's eye surges brighter as Tungsten lets out a whip of red lightning that zaps each crow. The birds shriek and take off into the sky.

Pilot laughs as they fly away and Tungsten slithers back down the wall. 'That'll teach 'em not to bother us.'

I try to smile, but the nerves in my stomach are starting to make me feel sick.

'All right, Tungst,' says Pilot, when the borg is back on the ground with us, 'let's get to work.'

The borg chirps and takes off again, disappearing through the rubble.

'This way, Pat,' says Pilot, heading in another direction, towards Checkpoint Four.

'What about Tungsten?'

'He's got to go his own way, can't have the guards seeing him. Not allowed to bring borgs through the Checkpoint. He'll send the DOS from somewhere near the guard booth and meet us on the other side.'

I follow Pilot and we make our way towards Checkpoint Four and as we get closer I try to do what Pilot said and look bored. But I can feel fear seeping out with my sweat. Especially because the security measures around Checkpoint Four are enough to make me want to puke. There are the guards in and around the booth – eight in all – heavily armoured with the biggest-looking guns I've ever seen held across their chests. They're more like cannons. And there's a nuclear symbol with a warning printed on the barrels. But what upsets me most are the dogs – two of them. Except they aren't dogs. They're borgs, with thick, shiny, chrome-plated muscles and eyes that glow blue. Their jaws – metal with jagged fangs – crackle with an electricity like the current bindings BMAC uses in the time I come from.

'CoyoTanks,' Pilot whispers, and I wish he hadn't. That name upsets me worse than Murder Squad.

We line up with all the others waiting to pass into Avin – BMAC patrols, other cadets like us, some regular-looking civilians. I'm shaking too much to look bored like Pilot wants. I keep my eyes on the dirt, hoping no one notices me and praying that Tungsten is as good at his job as Pilot says.

The screech of a bird makes me jump – our two crows from before sit atop Checkpoint Four.

I glance nervously at Pilot.

He crosses his one normal eye and jerks his neck, making a *bzzzzzzzzzzz* sound. He grins. 'They'll remember.'

I wish I had his confidence but all I can think of is Beauty, my sister's crow. Nothing could shake that bird. Why would these ones be any different?

Stop it, I tell myself. Pilot's crossed into Avin tonnes of times. He knows what he's doing and I have to trust that. Even still, my mind starts reaching for Bo.

No! I close my eyes, shaking my head to pull my thoughts back. I can't risk waking Bo. Not right now. I need to focus and if I wake him up and he feels my fear, he's going to lose it. I can't have that kind of distraction right now. I have to get through this without him.

There's a hum as the group ahead of us are locked into

their stalls beneath Checkpoint Four, the crows perched above watching intently. The lights that line the top – one for each person – are off, and we wait for the results.

I move in closer to Pilot so only he can hear me. 'What happens if one of the lights is red?'

'That means the scan detected pungits,' he whispers. 'There's an alarm and all reds get pulled aside and have to go for an individual exam where they stick you under the rays.'

Getting caught with pungits would be bad. But getting caught with *my* pungits? I might be making a mistake here.

Finally, the lights blink green. Every single one. And the barriers lift, allowing them to pass into Avin.

'Next group,' barks the border guard standing by the Checkpoint, a CoyoTank at his side.

It takes all of my concentration to remember how to walk, but Pilot is as casual as any other cadet as we step up to Checkpoint Four.

'Hey, wow,' he says to the guard, nodding at the CoyoTank. 'Series Five?'

Maybe too casual.

'Seven,' says the guard, bored of the conversation already, staring off into space.

'Seven? Really? They've got us training on Threes at the academy. That's my focus this year.' He taps at his red eye and it's then that I realise the guard's left eye is a strange colour blue. The same blue as the CoyoTank's. He doesn't have all the hardware surrounding the eye like Pilot, but the colour gives away that something's not right. The guard must be connected to the CoyoTank, just like Pilot is to

Tungsten. The guard keeps on staring into nothingness, his blue eye blinking every so often. 'They brought in a Series Six once,' Pilot goes on as we step into our stalls. 'We didn't get to use it or anything, it was just a demonstration, but it was still interesting.'

'Mmmhmm,' says the guard, still staring into nothingness, the blue light blinking and flickering inside his eye. Then his face twists into anger and he lets out a frustrated growl before shaking his head.

There's raucous laughter inside the guard booth and I can see through the window two other border guards goofing off in front of the monitors. 'You owe me a drink!' shouts one of them.

'One more match!' snarls the blue-eyed guard as the barrier comes down and I'm trapped beneath Checkpoint Four.

The lights in the guard's eyes blink again and he leans back against the booth, staring off into nothing.

It's a game, I realise. Just like the ones I play on my droidlet back home. He's playing the guards in the booth. He's not even paying attention to us.

There's a hum as the scan starts and my palms run slick with sweat. One of the crows above lets out a squawk. I want to look up. But I don't dare. I will the bulb above my head to not blink red. I keep my eyes on Avin, as if I do this every day.

There's a click and the hum stops. And then nothing.

A couple of the civilians to my right look up, confused, and to the guard.

'Can we go?' someone asks.

The guard's eyes come into focus, leaving his game behind and he glances up at the lights. They are off. Just like Pilot said they would be.

The guard knocks on the booth.

'What?' shouts one of the men inside.

'Did you get a read?'

He knows. He knows something's wrong.

The guards inside lean closer to their monitors, shrugging and shaking their heads.

'No alarm,' says one.

'No alarm,' agrees the other. 'They're clean.'

The blue-eyed guard frowns. 'Run it again, maybe?'

He knows for sure. And my legs are going to crumple beneath me. If they run it again, who knows if Tungsten can interrupt their system in time? I feel hot. Lightheaded. Before I can stop myself, my mind reaches for Bo.

And he wakes.

He's so startled by my fear he pushes me back with such force that I gasp.

Pilot looks at me.

And so does the blue-eyed guard.

The guards in the booth aren't paying attention. I can hear them laughing and cheering as they go back to whatever game they are playing.

And then he's angry – Bo. He knows I'm gone. Knows I ran away. Ran to Shade Unit. He realises what I've done all in the span of a wink and it's too much for him to process, too much for him to make sense of. All he can do is react. Anger, fear, worry, sadness – it all comes flying at me like a punch to the brain.

I stifle a cry and wince. *Stop it*, I beg Bo. *You'll get me caught.*

You will *get caught!* Bo rages.

I risk a glance at the guard and he's frowning at me. I cough, making a big show of hacking up something caught in my throat. The guard raises an eyebrow.

'I nailed you again, Deeks!' cackles one of the men inside the booth and the blue-eyed guard growls what I assume is a profanity before looking away from me. The barrier in front of us rises up, the city of Avin invites me in.

'One more match!' Deeks barks, and everyone going through Checkpoint Four steps down out of their stalls. I step down too, my feet firmly on the asphalt of the city of Avin.

Pilot's at my side, lips thin with worry. 'You need to get a hold of yourself.'

But I can't. I knew Bo would be upset, but I didn't anticipate this. A torrent of fear and sadness and anger and more fear floods out of him, pounding my brain again and again and again so that I cry out, grabbing my head.

Pilot grabs me by the elbow. 'Pat, they're watching us. Keep it together.'

I breathe slow and deep, trying to send as much calm to Bo as I can, trying to let him know I'm OK. It isn't working, he can feel my fear and it's making him more panicked.

I hear a screech. It's that shrill, angry blast that only a crow can make as the two birds swoop down from their perch and land on the ground by my feet.

Pilot goes still, his body tense as he holds onto me. 'Oh no.'

The crows scream and scream and scream at us, their ugly necks extending as they trumpet their alarm. The blue-eyed guard begins to shout.

Pilot's yanks me hard. 'Run, Pat! We gotta run!'

The guards are running from the booth now, the CoyoTanks springing to life. I've blown it for us. They know what we are.

GABBY
2083

The clock tower. I've seen it before. It's on the edge of Avin, where garbage from the landfill has started to encroach on the city. Lots of Movers live out there on the fringe of society. *I should leave you here*, Father likes to say whenever we pass it, *I should send you to live like all the other vermin. You'll probably end up in Hexall Hall, like the rest of them.*

I stare up at the looming tower – the old Avin post office, boarded up and rotting. I scratch nervously at my finger.

I watch a ragtag trio shuffle into the shadows, shoulders hunched. Movers, I assume. They barely glance at me, too busy picking through a pile of garbage. I've been raised to fear these people. But seeing them now, I don't feel fear. I feel sadness. How many Movers have had to run from homes that didn't want them?

A flock of crows perch above the dark clock face above. The hands don't move. It's broken. Of course it's broken. That's what time does. It breaks everything.

The post office is covered in confused graffiti.

Hopeless words painted beside hopeful ones: *We are all Shelf Meat; Remember: You know there's going to be a tomorrow.* Crow droppings stain it all. Hidden in the swirls of colour and poop smudge, a black handprint marks the right-side wall.

There's a girl there, not much older than me. She leans back against the brick, her sweatshirt hood hiding her face as she picks at her teeth. Her eyes are fixed on an old woman with long, pale blue hair. I've never seen hair like that. The old woman speaks with a couple, man and woman, patting the man's shoulder reassuringly. The man nods, and looks to the woman, who smiles, and the two let the blue-haired woman lead them back towards the girl. She doesn't acknowledge the girl. Just walks by, ushering the couple along until all three disappear into the shadows of the alley. The girl turns to follow. But not before kissing her fingers, and touching the black hand on the wall.

Did they see the message on the public bulletin too? Did they put it out there? Whoever they are, they are following the black hand. All I can do is go after them.

The trio picking through the garbage still ignore me as I pass them. I'm invisible here. Just like at school. There's something comforting in that.

I slip into the shadowed alley. I can hear an echo of footfall on metal. Above me, the blue-haired woman, the couple, and the girl in the hood climb an old fire escape up to the roof.

I follow, gripping carefully to the railing. Don't look down. I don't like heights.

* * *

On the roof of the clock tower, a few dozen people stand around a fire. The back of the clock looms over the group like a rose window. Did they all follow the black hand?

The blue-haired woman walks the couple to the centre of the group, to a steel drum filled with some sort of liquid. They peer into the drum, and the blue-haired woman dips her hand in, pulling out a palm dripping with black paint. The man moves to dip his hand in, but she stops him, telling him to wait. I watch as she walks up to a short staircase beneath the clock. She steps up onto a catwalk that gives access to all the dead cogs and levers casting dancing shadows in the firelight. She comes to the centre of the walkway, turns to face the group. She stands there, calmly looking out at us all. And waits.

Not for long. The heads of the gathered group turn to watch her.

Someone moves in to stand beside me – the girl in the sweatshirt. She pulls the hood back off her face. Striking midnight blue hair cascades over her shoulders. She glances at me out of the corner of her eye. She's pretty. Intimidatingly so. Tall and thin, clear skin and full lips. She's pretty the way Leelee Esposito is pretty. A popular kind of pretty. She looks me up and down and I feel small. Ugly. The way I feel when Leelee Esposito looks at me. But her gaze is different from Leelee's. She's not judging me. She's searching.

For what?

She brings a finger to her lips and turns to watch the old woman. The assembled group has gone silent. The only sound is the crackle of the fire.

'Friends,' says the old woman, loud and clear. 'I want to thank you. Thank you for answering the call.'

I bite my lip. What call have I answered?

'The call,' the old woman says, 'to live out of the shadows. Out of the fringes. To live in society as regular human beings, without having to be afraid of what you are. To be free of Nowbie oppression.' She waits a moment, lets the idea sink in. It's sinking deep into the minds of everyone standing in front of her. Including mine. Even my Shadow takes notice, pulling in for a closer glimpse. Free of the Nowbies. Free of BMAC. It's an idea we've all had, all dreamed of. To hear someone say it out loud sets goose bumps on my arms.

'But how do we do that?' the old woman asks. 'How can we possibly live free in a society that wants nothing to do with us? The aggressive and invasive phase testing forced on us by BMAC not only violates our privacy, our dignity, but now they want to test us more frequently and rigorously. And they want us to smile while they do it.'

Heads nod in agreement, including the girl with the midnight hair. She glances at me. I look away quickly.

'And the vile, hateful movement of the time purists, the so called We Are Now movement, has become more hostile than ever.' Mother and Father. The way they look at me. More hateful every day. Maybe it isn't just them. Maybe it's all of We Are Now. 'Their attacks against innocent Movers and Shadows are on the rise. And BMAC and the Avin government are all too quick to turn a blind eye.'

Shouts of agreement.

'Nowbies. Face. No. Consequences.'

More agreement.

'And they won't,' says the old woman. 'Unless we make them.'

There's an awkward silence, people looking from one to the other. Confused. So am I. How are we supposed to do that?

'Look at yourselves, my friends,' she goes on. 'When was the last time you stood back, and really looked at what you are?'

What I am. Fat. Ugly. Loser. Worthless. A Phase 2 Mover. Maybe Phase 3, now.

I hate looking at myself.

'You may see the weak and tired person that society has beaten down. See the helpless wretch that BMAC and We Are Now want you to see.'

The girl glances my way again. My eyes drop to my feet. I am all these things.

'But that,' says the old woman, 'is not the person I see.'

I look up and the old woman is leaning forwards, her finger pointed at the group gathered before her. She's pointing at all of us. Pointing at me.

'You have a power,' she says.

No, I don't.

'In the history of mankind, we as a species have been stuck. We have been prisoners of time. Second after second, ticking past. And man has had no choice but to tick along with it. Man has lived at time's mercy. Until there was you. No human being has had the ability to defy time the way that you, or you, or you, can defy it. That is power. That is strength.'

The way she talks about Movement as a power makes my stomach twitch. Right where it seized up in my parent's apartment when I tried to Move. I remember the feel of the wind. The way it flowed from me. The look of fear in my father's eyes.

'And BMAC and We Are Now are working hard to make you forget that power,' she says. 'Now look at the faces standing next to you.'

I feel her eyes on me, the girl with the midnight hair. Nervously, I look up to meet her gaze. A grin tugs at the corner of her mouth.

'Faces,' says the old woman, 'that reflect your gift. Brothers. Sisters. Born with the very same power as yours.'

The girl with the midnight hair. Eyes bright as the moon. She is powerful. The way she stands, tall and proud, says she knows it. I want to see myself in her. More than anything, I want to see it.

But I don't.

There is no reflection of me there at all.

'You are not alone. Look around you,' says the old woman. 'You. Are. Not. Alone.'

My Shadow snakes closer, drawn towards the words.

The girl's grin opens into a smile. I smile back. I so want the old woman's words to be true.

'I look at all of you,' she says, 'and I am awed by the collective strength here tonight. If we stand together and use that strength, BMAC and the rest of the Nowbies will tremble in their skins!

'A bully will always beat their chosen victim down,' she goes on – Ollie Larkin's voice echoes through my head,

Goooooooooobaaaaaa. 'Until that victim stands up and says "No more!" We must stand together and draw a line in the sand.'

Father said that very thing: lines will be drawn. What side of it am I standing on?

'Tomorrow, we march outside the city hall,' she says. 'We will march and shout until they hear us. We will *make* them hear us.'

A protest. I've never liked protests. Mother and Father protest about Movers all the time.

'I am asking you,' shouts the old woman, near fever pitch, 'friends, brothers, sisters, to stand up with me and shout from the rooftops, NO MORE!'

Fists fly up into the air. Men and women shouting and cheering.

The old woman holds up her blackened hand. 'This is our mark – a reminder that we have let them keep us in the shadows for too long. It is time we clawed our way out!' She turns and slams her hand down on the back of the clock. 'Join me, and make your mark!'

She barely finishes speaking before the group begins dunking their hands into the drum and they clamber over each other, all of them in a rush to place their palm print beside hers. The clock is covered with black handprints.

This is how it starts, my Shadow says, breaking his silence so suddenly I jump.

How what starts?

The war.

'You gonna get up there?' The girl with midnight hair is staring at me.

I look down at my palm. The war between Movers and Shadows. It's coming.

Sooner or later, my Shadow agrees. *And it will rage for centuries.*

I'm a Mover. Is that where I stand on the side of the line? But if I can get my pungit ray working, if I can cure myself, is my place on the other side?

'Hey,' the girl says. 'Don't you want to make your mark?' Her eyes. Pale blue, like ice. I'm frozen. I don't know what to say.

When I don't answer, she speaks again. 'What's your name?'

My name? 'Gabby.'

'Gabby.' The girl nods. Gives me her hand. I take it. 'Good to meet you, Gabby. My name is Blue.'

PAT
2383

Faster. That's the only thought. Run faster than you've ever run in your life.

Because BMAC is coming.

FASTER! It's Bo blaring in my mind, it's both of us – and I pump my legs as hard as I can, racing after Pilot.

I risk a backwards glance and there they are – the guards from Checkpoint Four – the CoyoTanks with their hideous glowing mouths leading the pack.

'Go, Pat! Go!' Pilot yells, pulling away from me as he sprints for the busy downtown lights of Avin. He moves like lightning, I can't keep up.

You have to! Bo's command blasts my mind like a boot to the face and I cry out, stumbling.

'Pat!' I hear Pilot shout. 'Pat! Keep going!'

Yes. Keep going. I have to keep going but the pain inside my head is throbbing, watering my eyes and blurring my vision.

I'm blinded – a blast of nuclear green explodes to my left and I tumble sideways.

Shock cannons!

When I look back, one of the guards reloads his massive gun, points it straight at me –

Please no—

. . . and before he pulls the trigger, he falls, knocked flat on his back.

'Yeah, Tungst!' cheers Pilot and I see the little borg, uncoiling himself from the guard's ankles and slithering after us.

The guards forget us for the moment, blasting everything they have at Tungsten, but the little borg is fast, dodging every shot.

I don't waste time and scramble to my feet, tearing frantically after Pilot.

Are you trying to get me killed?! I blast at Bo with all my terror and rage and he shrinks back from me, a whimper of an apology on his thoughts.

Pilot bounces on his toes, waiting, Tungsten bobbing around his feet and I can't believe they haven't abandoned me to save themselves. 'Are you all right?' Pilot shouts over the chaos.

I manage a nod, but no, I am not all right.

They'll have alerted the patrols, Bo warns. *More BMAC are coming.*

Pilot brings his hand to his face, flicking something in the circuitry that surrounds his mechanical eye. 'The distress signal,' he tells me. 'Let's hope Bash is listening!'

A Cure Bus – only smaller, sleeker, faster – flies out from between the buildings up ahead. A rush of cold works its way up my shoulders as Pilot and I watch, mouths gaping, the bus's bay doors open to unload a pack of five angry CoyoTanks and their BMAC masters, toting more Shock cannons.

'This way! This way!' Pilot shrieks, darting down the street on the left.

Where does this fool think he is going?

'We're blown, Bash!' Pilot's shouting, his eye glowing red. 'BMAC in pursuit! Send help, Bash! Now!'

There's a hideous mechanical screeching echoing at our backs and when I look, it's the CoyoTanks, heads pointed skywards, howling for reinforcements.

We can see them coming, two more BMAC vehicles heading towards us.

'Breezes,' Pilot pants. 'This is bad.'

My lungs are ready to burst, my legs aching, my mind so bruised and battered by Bo, I can't think straight. And my heart – BMAC in front of us, BMAC behind, CoyoTanks falling from the sky – my heart is hammering so hard, so fast, I'm worried it might shut down altogether. 'What do we do?'

'I uh – I don't – I don't—'

The Promenade, Bo cuts in.

What?

TELL HIM! He sends me stumbling again. *THE PROMENADE. QUICK!*

'The Promenade!' I yelp through the pain.

Pilot looks at me, confused. What did I say? What is Bo doing?

There's a light of understanding on Pilot's face. 'Right!' he shouts as a cannon blast whizzes by our heads. 'This way!' He takes off to the right, down the nearest narrow street, and I follow, begging myself not to look back.

We emerge onto a busy street, thousands and thousands of Avin citizens browsing what looks like an endless outdoor mall. Pilot charges into the crowds, and I try my best to follow, knocking and bumping into everyone in my path.

Behind us, the crowd is screaming as BMAC bursts onto the Promenade.

Hope swells inside me – we're hidden in the masses. BMAC can't find us amongst all these bodies.

But Pilot doesn't slow down. He ducks and weaves as fast as he can.

'Pilot!' I shout after him.

Faster, Patrick, Bo warns. *This is no time to relax.*

I look back and see what they're afraid of – the CoyoTanks. They haven't lost our scent, I guess, because they are ploughing through the crowds, bowling over and trampling anyone in their way, a frenzied determination in their lifeless glowing eyes.

'The covered bridge!' Pilot screams.

When I turn back, I see what he's running for – a white shiny tunnel bridge suspended over the Promenade, translucent walls showing the thick crowds of people shuffling slowly inside.

'No!' I shout. 'We'll be trapped!'

'Just do it!' orders Pilot.

Do it, Bo echoes.

There's no time to argue, the howl of the CoyoTanks closing in, and Pilot and I plunge into the mass of people funnelling in and out of the covered bridge. The walls surround us, tight and claustrophobic, the crowds unable to move out of our way as easily as on the open Promenade. Screams erupt behind us and I look to see a CoyoTank at the tunnel's mouth.

'They're coming!' I scream.

'No they're not!' shouts Pilot.

The CoyoTank tries to come in after us, but the frame of the opening is too small for its massive metal shoulders, and it slams itself against the opening again and again to no success. A second CoyoTank appears, pressing against the frame, pushing the other one. And then a third, all of them ramming themselves pointlessly against an archway that's too narrow.

A laugh of relief escapes me. *Bo, you did it!*

Don't be stupid. It isn't over.

One of the CoyoTanks leaps up, and there's a loud bang, bang, bang, above us as it stalks its away across the bridge, the walls of the tunnel shuddering with each step.

'He's blocking the exit!' cries Pilot as we watch the CoyoTank appear at the other end of the tunnel, sending the frightened crowds running back towards us, pinning Pilot and I together, everyone huddling in the middle of the bridge.

There's more thudding, the entire structure vibrating and creaking as the rest of the CoyoTanks find their way onto the roof, moving towards the centre.

They'll find a way in.

'What do we do?' I say, to myself, to Bo. There's no answer on his end, his mind a jumbled mess of different ideas, none of them helpful. 'Pilot,' I shout, abandoning Bo, 'Pilot, what do we do?'

But Pilot isn't listening to me. He's pushing back the crowd, yelling at them to back off and creating an open space around the two of us and Tungsten. Where's Tungsten? The little borg isn't at his usual spot by Pilot's feet.

There's a high-pitched squeal above us, and the ceiling glows where the CoyoTanks are standing above us. They're coming.

Something grazes my foot and I glance down as a silver ball rolls past along the floor. Tungsten's come apart – separated himself into multiple pieces that have set themselves up in a circle around Pilot.

The CoyoTanks erupt into their unnatural howl. A hole, the size of a fist, opens above us. That glow: it's their lasers. The CoyoTanks are melting away the ceiling.

'Your ears!' shouts Pilot.

'What?'

'Cover your ears!'

I don't understand, but Pilot covers his and begins to count as the hole above us grows wider. 'Three, two, one—'

KABOOM!

An explosion sends me backwards into the crowd as Pilot disappears through the floor. 'Pilot!'

I scramble to regain my footing. Now I see there's an opening in the circle marked by Tungsten. And fifteen feet below me on the Promenade, is Pilot in a pile of rubble. Tungsten is piecing himself back together beside him. He looks up at me. 'Pat! Jump!'

Jump? I can't jump!

Bo's back, urgent. *You have to.*

A growl above me – I look up to see the head of a CoyoTank snarling down, jaws opening. It lunges—

NOW, PATRICK!

I jump, dropping down beside Pilot, landing hard on my knees, my elbow. Everything hurts. But Pilot is hauling me to my feet, screaming at me to run.

We take off as fast as our bruised bodies will allow, Pilot leading us off the Promenade and down a dark side street. A wall rises up in front of us.

'Dead end!'

A CoyoTank howls at our backs. We turn – five furious borg hounds blocking us in.

'Pilot . . . what do we do?'

'I don't know,' he pants.

My back presses against the wall, eyes on the borgs.
Bo?

He's frantic, the desperate solutions pinging through his mind like a swarm of hornets. I catch sight of one of them – scale the wall. Desperately, I glance up the slick stone building, wondering if we could somehow climb it and that's when I see it – another CoyoTank, snarling from the rooftop, a BMAC patrol guard on some kind of motorbike parked on either side of it.

There is no getting out of this. We're surrounded.

Sirens wail in the distance as the CoyoTanks stalk their way down the alley towards us, mouths hissing and crackling with electricity. They snarl as they close in, and there's a terrifying cruelty in the artificial sound of it – BMAC designed them to make that sound.

The first CoyoTank, the one leading the pack, rears up,

jaw widening, and Pilot and I both throw up our arms, waiting for the bite . . .

But there's a howl.

A crash of metal.

I open my eyes as the CoyoTank from the rooftop drops onto the advancing borg, mouth clamped over the beast's neck.

The rest of the CoyoTanks leap into the fight, tearing at the attacking hound. But the CoyoTank from the rooftop bucks and tosses each one, and I see now it's different from the others. It's smaller, slighter, and the glow in its mouth is a hot white, instead of cold blue. The smaller CoyoTank stands over the motionless body of the borg that lunged for us, its head completely removed from the body. I barely have time to process it, barely have time to register what's happening, when it launches after the others, tearing off circuits and metal plating, ripping out wires and pulling off limbs.

And then it's quiet. All that's left is a pile of dead robot parts and the smaller CoyoTank standing victorious over the carnage. It stares at us, its white eyes glowing.

Pilot finally breaks the silence, his face screwed up in confusion. 'I mean . . . what?'

There's a rumble above us and both Pilot and I look up to see the BMAC patrols, two of them, defying gravity as their motorbikes carry them down the wall head first.

When they're on the ground in front of us, all Pilot and I can do is stare. They aren't from the BMAC patrol. Their uniforms are the same as ours, BMAC cadets. The big one giggles to himself, hissing through his teeth, and I recognise him from the shop at Dune's Thoroughfare – it's Rads. The other, a girl with goggles that glow the same colour as the little CoyoTank's. She removes them along with her helmet, blue hair spilling over her shoulder.

The sirens grow louder and the girl scowls at us. 'Well?' she snaps, making room on the seat of her bike. 'Climb on.'

PAT
2383

The bike isn't just a bike – racing up walls and soaring across rooftops as though gravity is just an optional setting, climbing so high and moving so fast I can barely open my eyes.

When the girl with blue hair finally comes to a stop, the sound of BMAC sirens is long distant. I scramble to untangle my legs from the seat and stumble, bending to heave up whatever's left in my stomach.

There's a chuckle behind me, a low, resonant sound.

'Shut it, Rads,' snaps the girl.

I glance up from my sour-smelling puke to see them all staring at me – Pilot sitting behind Rads with a concerned face, Rads smirking, and the girl – well, if looks could destroy pungits, I'd be a Nowbie.

'Are you done?' she asks, petting the head of the CoyoTank that has nuzzled up against her shoulder.

Am I? I guess so, because there's nothing left in me.

I can feel a flicker of embarrassment on Bo's end, but he tries to shield me from it.

Pilot hurries over, placing a friendly hand on my back.

'I'm OK,' I say, shrugging him away.

'We need to get off the street,' says the girl, climbing off her nightmare bike. 'You've made enough of a spectacle of yourselves for one day, don't you think?' She turns her back on us, her CoyoTank and Rads following behind. She walks up to a building that's glowing purple with holograms of dollar signs blinking on and off so obnoxiously I worry it might give me a seizure.

'A wager lair?' says Pilot.

The girl sighs and holds the door open for us. 'They charge by the hour and don't ask a lot of questions. Do you know somewhere better we can go?'

I guess he doesn't because he glances nervously at me.

The girl's right, Bo tells me. *The clientele of a wager lair won't want BMAC showing up to ruin their gambling. This should do for now.*

'It's OK,' I tell Pilot doubtfully, and get up to follow the girl and Rads into the building.

We enter a tiny lobby lined with mirrors. A woman with curly hair piled on top of her head and half her face painted pink sits looking bored at a desk. She jumps when she sees the uniforms, lunging for something under her desk.

The girl with blue hair holds up her hands, 'Relax.' She flips the woman what looks like a data chip and the woman catches it, turning it over in her hands, long sharp nails glowing neon blue. 'We want a room.'

'Dice, cards or forebrawl?'

'Doesn't matter,' says the girl.

The woman looks at a screen in the desk, then taps it. 'Got a forebrawl room open.'

'We'll take it.'

'Only s'posed to be a two-man room. Costs extra for four.'

The girl flips her another chip and a hidden door in one of the mirrors behind the desk slides open. Rads, mouth in a tight grim line, motions for me and Pilot to walk through as the girl approaches the desk. She places two more chips in front of the woman. 'You never saw us, got it?'

The woman nods, counting her chips. We all pile through the door into what looks like an elevator.

'Don't normally allow dogs in here,' says the woman, nodding at the CoyoTank. 'You want yer mutt to stay, there'll be a charge.'

The girl rolls her eyes and tosses another chip as she and the CoyoTank squeeze inside. The borg's too big for the tiny space and I have to squish myself against the back wall, sandwiched between Rads and Pilot, the robot's steel shoulder pressing hard against my chest.

The door opens to a narrow hallway, barely wide enough for the CoyoTank, doors lining the length of it. The girl stops outside the fifth one down. It opens automatically and we all step into a bare room, two plush white chairs facing the wall on the left, which has a screen that's showing a pair of fighters in a particularly savage battle. Forebrawl.

The girl settles down into one of the chairs, and a bunch of holographic lights spring up in front of her face, showing the vitals of the forebrawlers in the match, the time left in the round, the odds on each fighter. You wouldn't know there was anything special about a forebrawl just to look at it. But the match isn't just between the two fighters. There are four of them fighting, the forebrawlers and their Shadows. The years of their Shadows and the number of moves they've anticipated correctly glow in the corners. She scoffs passing through the light and leaning on her knees.

'All right, let's have it then,' she says.

Pilot frowns. 'Have what?'

'The message,' she says impatiently. 'The message you're carrying.'

'Who says we're carrying a message?'

She rolls her eyes and looks over at Rads. He's laughing again. Only this time he's giggling like a little girl, fingers pressed to his mouth daintily – his moods shift faster than I can blink.

'I don't have time for games,' the girl says. 'You've ruined any chance of delivering it yourself, since BMAC will be looking for you the second you set foot outside. If your mission has any last hope of success, it's through me.'

Pilot frowns. 'Who are you?'

'She's Dark Unit,' I say. 'I saw you on Dune's Thoroughfare.'

'Dark Unit?' Pilot looks alarmed.

Rads' giggles turn into full-on laughter and the girl shoots him a warning look.

'Just relax, Red Eye,' she tells Pilot. 'We're not Dark Unit.'

'But,' I point at Rads, 'your arm. The tattoo—'

Rads pulls up his sleeve and reveals the black hand with wings. He licks his finger and wipes away one of the wings with ease. It's not real.

'We were posing as Dark Unit for the sake of our scouting mission,' the girl says.

'Scouting mission?' says Pilot. 'You saying you're Shade Unit?'

She watches him a minute, deciding whether or not it's worth her time to answer. Finally, she tucks a strand of hair behind her ear and leans back in the chair. 'Something like that. We're part of Constance Ashlinn's outpost.'

There's a flash of anger from Bo, but Pilot's jaw drops. 'Constance Ashlinn?'

The girl nods. 'Rads and I were on our way back from Dune's Thoroughfare when your captain reached out to her unit. Apparently we were the only allies close enough to answer your distress call.'

'Lucky us,' mutters Rads, his giggles gone, sulking in the other chair.

'What were a couple of Constance Ashlinn's people doing on Dune's Thoroughfare?' Pilot asks.

Rads sits up, his sour face shifting inexplicably to something more neutral, mechanical. 'Investigating,' he says, matter-of-fact.

'Investigating what? Us?' says Pilot. 'What for?'

The girl sighs. 'Because Constance needs to make sure your captain is running a smooth operation before she agrees to join him in the fight against BMAC. Between those Dark Unit idiots and now this fiasco, I think it's safe to say Constance won't be too impressed with your Captain Bash.'

Pilot's shoulders hunch a bit.

'So now that it's impossible for you to get anywhere

in Avin, thanks to the mess you made on the Promenade, it's my responsibility to run your message. Thank you for that.'

It can't be impossible. I still have to get to the Time Cache. 'You don't need to run it, we can still do this. It's our job, not yours.'

'Well,' she says, loosening the straps on her boots, 'it's my job now, since like I said, you two are now as useful to Shade Unit as a pair of crows.'

She's right, Bo tells me. *You can barely hope to get back to the border, let alone into BMAC Headquarters without being spotted. It's time to stop this Shade Unit nonsense and focus on how you're going to get back home without getting Shelved.*

Home. He means his leaky mouldy hideout. That's not my home.

Bo's mood turns frosty, insulted. *It's the closest thing to a home you have, Patrick.*

That's not good enough for me. I can't just give up.

I look to Pilot, desperate. 'Bash trusted you,' I tell him. 'We can still do what we came here to do. This is our responsibility. Are you really just going to hand it over to someone you don't even know?'

He's still hunched, our screw-up weighing heavily on his shoulders. 'How do I know I can trust you?'

The girl shrugs, pulling off her boots. 'You don't.'

'See?' I say. 'She could be BMAC for all we know!'

'Right,' says the girl. 'Because trashing six very expensive Series Seven CoyoTanks and going through this mind-numbing song and dance with you two is just so much more practical than simply arresting you and throwing you on the Shelves.'

She may have a point, but I can't let her keep us from getting close to the Time Cache. 'Pilot, we don't need her. We'll figure out a way.'

'There is no way.' The girl folds her legs, hands clasped over a knee. 'We're all you've got.'

Pilot shakes his head, defeated. 'They'll have images of our faces from Checkpoint Four. All of BMAC knows who we are.' He finally looks up, his good eye puffy with tears or exhaustion, I can't be sure which. 'I don't even know your name.'

She nods over at her partner, 'That there is Rads.' He grunts, a scowl on his face now. 'This is Tyke,' she says, scratching the CoyoTank under the chin. 'And me?' She leans back in the chair, indifferent to the stress of the whole situation. 'I'm Blue.'

Pilot raises an eyebrow. 'Your parents were big Blue Ashlinn fans, I take it.'

A laugh bursts out of Rads like a trumpet before he covers his mouth, stifling his giggles.

The girl, Blue, just grins. 'Something like that.'

GABBY
2083

'You think we can't do it.'

The girl with midnight hair – Blue – looks at me. She cocks her eyebrow.

'What?'

'Stop the Nowbies. Free Movers from their oppression.'

No, my Shadow tells me. *No, they cannot. I've lived in the future they fight for. Things will only get worse.*

I don't want to believe that. But I know my parents. No protest is ever going to change their mind.

'Is that why you don't want to join them?' Blue nods towards the platform. The collected group are all pressing their blackened palms against the wall.

'No, I—' I don't know what to say. I don't know why I'm not up there. The way Blue and the old woman talk – I don't doubt that they can change things. But me? 'I just don't think I'm the kind of Mover you're looking for.'

'What kind of Mover *are* you?'

I don't know the answer to that.

'Are you the kind of Mover that doesn't mind being automatically treated like a criminal by BMAC?' Blue asks. 'Are you the kind of Mover that likes the way things are?'

'No, of course not.'

'Then you're exactly the kind of Mover we're looking for.' She nods, certain. She holds out her hand for mine. 'Come with me.'

I don't dare move.

She grins. 'You didn't come all the way here just to watch, did you?'

She grabs hold of my wrist and walks me to the drum – I don't stop her, don't know how – and she dunks my hand in. I stare down at my blackened palm, the greasy paint dripping down my arm.

'Might as well wipe it off up here, don't you think?' She moves towards the platform, looking back for me. My feet follow, eyes on my palm. Not alone. That's what the old woman said. This Blue girl wants me to join them. I can't think of a time someone wanted me to join anything.

She reaches the steps and stands aside. 'Go on.'

Resisting the urge to scratch my itching fingers, I step up onto the platform. Black handprints cover the wall like a flock of crows. My father – what would he think of me, signing up to stand against everything he believes in? What would he do if he knew I was here? I glance back at Blue. She smiles at me and motions to the wall.

Idiot, my Shadow sneers. *This girl's brain is fit for crow bait*. There's a chill that seeps in with him. A rippling cold that I know is his laugh.

I don't mean to ask. But the question reaches him all the same. **Why?**

*She has to be a fool to think someon*e like you *could make it in Shade Unit.*

He's still angry with me about not Moving him, I can feel it radiating from him. But still, my cheeks flush. **Why not?**

Look at you. You're not like the rest of them.

I could be.

The cold seeps into my bones. His amusement is growing. *These people fight for Movers. What would they think of a We Are Now child trying to cure herself?*

What would they think? I glance nervously back at the crowd. At Blue watching me. She's trying to do something for all Movers. What I'm doing – trying to find a cure – I've just been doing that for myself.

You're a coward, my Shadow hisses, a barb of pain shooting through my mind.

I'm not a coward, I fire back. But there's no conviction behind it. Because I know he's right. I'm afraid of everything. Of being a Mover and all the trouble that goes with it.

My Shadow digs in deeper. The pain thuds in the centre of my brain. I grab my head.

You know as well as I do, that to these people, you are. And when they find out what you tried to do with your little experiments, he twists my mind harder, *they'll cast you out. And you'll be alone again.*

But maybe if I explain, maybe if I can make them understand—

My Shadow sends another jolt of pain. I groan.

'Gabby?' Blue says, somewhere behind me.

No one will ever understand you, growls my Shadow. *No one but me.*

I grit my teeth through the ache. **That's not true.**

It is. And you know it.

I don't know it. I don't want to.

You don't need these people and their doomed endeavour, he says. *It is not who you are.*

My blackened hand balls into a fist. **You don't know anything about me**, I tell him. **I'll prove it.**

I press my palm against the clock face. My handprint joins the rest.

And rage – blinding, searing, painful – blasts from my Shadow, knocking me to the floor.

'Gabby!'

The assault doesn't let up. I'm hit again and again, inside my mind.

I curl up into a ball. Protecting myself from a force I can't stop.

But at least I proved him wrong.

He doesn't know me at all.

PAT
2383

Pilot stands in the middle of the room, Tungsten next to him, projecting an image on the wall opposite the forebrawl. It's a blueprint for a Cure Bus. This is the message, my ticket to the Time Cache. And Pilot is handing it over to this bored-looking girl, Blue, and her split-personality partner and robo-dog.

'The buses are autopiloted,' he says. 'Before each bus picks up its BMAC crew, it's loaded with the Cure at the Cure facility. Because the facility is the highest level of classified, no BMAC soldier is ever onboard the bus when it moves to and from the facility itself. The crew boards the bus at BMAC Headquarters in the city, before moving out into the Movers' sectors. So nabbing a soldier and questioning him won't tell us where to find the facility.'

Blue folds her arms across her chest, unimpressed. 'This is old news. We've known this for months.'

'Right,' agrees Pilot. 'So we needed to get our hands on the bus itself. Bash and his outfit figured if we could get to the onboard navigation system, we could figure out where the bus was programmed to return to. Two days ago, we succeeded in overtaking a Cure Bus for that purpose.'

She leans forwards, slowly, and I can tell she's giving it her best effort not to look excited. 'And?'

'And,' says Pilot, 'turns out the bus was only programmed to return to Headquarters. After that, it must wait for a command from the facility to return home because there was no information on the onboard computer.'

Blue's face falls, disappointed.

I think of the BMAC vehicle, gutted on the floor of the Block, Shade Unit tearing apart every panel, pulling out every gear. And for what?

Rads explodes with a frustrated roar, making me, Pilot and Tungst jump. The big brute turns on his recliner and tries to rip it from the floor. 'Another dead end!?!?'

'Rads!' snaps Blue. 'Switch out, would ya? *Breezes.*'

Bafflingly, Rads stops shaking the chair, and stands rigid, motionless. I look over at Pilot, who's just as confused, as Rads yawns and lies back easily in his chair.

I turn to Blue, 'What's his problem?'

'Don't worry about him,' she says. It's an order, not a suggestion. I don't like this Blue girl. And neither does Bo, who monitors her suspiciously from the walls of my mind. Not that she cares what Bo or I think, because she's already forgotten me, pacing slowly around Tungsten's projection. 'So that's it, then? The raid was a bust?'

'No,' says Pilot. He reaches towards the projection, zooming in on a part of the image close to the front of the bus. 'We tore the whole vehicle apart and, in the end, we found sand in the bus's filter. Black sand.'

They meet each other's eyes for a moment, and Blue's mouth spreads into a grin as what he's just said sinks in.

There's a warm buzzing at the back of my brain – Bo. I guess Blue's not the only one excited by this news.

What's black sand have to do with anything? I ask him.

Black sand is not something you can come by easily. Only one place in the greater Avin area to find black sand. The old RareCore mine.

'You mean you know where the Cure facility is?' I ask Pilot.

He shrugs. 'It's either at the mine, or somewhere close to it.' He says something to Tungsten, who changes the image on the wall to a map – the city in the bottom right, surrounded by barren empty nothingness. A hundred kilometres to the north just beside the coast, is a red dot marking the RareCore mine. But where are the others? In my time, Avin was surrounded by landfills, landfills that were fed by not only Avin but neighbouring cities. From the look of this map, those cities are long gone.

Rads, still the sleepy version of himself, wanders over to Blue, rubbing his eyes as he looks up at the projection. 'Connie will want to send recon to be sure of it.'

'She won't,' says Blue. 'It's too risky. If BMAC gets a whiff that Shade Unit is close to their facility, they'll shut it down.'

'Exactly,' agrees Pilot. 'Our man on the inside will have to do the recon for us.'

Blue shakes her head. 'How? He doesn't have much security clearance.'

'No,' said Pilot. 'But he's the safety minister for all of

Avin.' He bends down and holds a hand out to Tungsten. The little borg trembles a moment before a hatch in the third sphere opens. Pilot pulls out two vials, handing one to Blue and the other to me to inspect. I stare down at the nuclear blue liquid and shudder. The Cure.

'They are different,' says Blue, looking from my vial to hers. She's right. The liquid in hers is a lighter shade of blue, cloudy where mine is clear.

Pilot nods. 'Pat, you're holding true blue BMAC Cure serum. Blue, you've got Shade Unit's *special brew*.'

'Special brew?'

'It's contaminated,' he says. 'If our man presents a vial of contaminated Cure serum, a safety inspection of the facility would be exactly the kind of thing BMAC pays him for.'

Blue smirks, holding her vial up to the light. 'Contaminated with what?'

'Salt water. Bash's idea. They'll think the ocean's leaking in somehow.'

Rads nods, approvingly. 'It's clever.'

'It's dangerous,' says Blue. 'It's a big risk for our man on the inside.'

'You know about our inside man?' ask Pilot, surprised.

She rolls her eyes. 'Who do you think *got* him inside?'

Pilot says nothing, embarrassed.

'We put Bash in touch with him, and now Bash wants to put him at risk. Constance won't like that.'

'How do you know?' I ask, annoyed. I'm tired of her acting like she has everything figured out, like she can just decide what's best for everyone. 'Can you read Constance Ashlinn's mind?'

Rads chuckles.

Blue looks up at me from behind the vial, a glimmer of something in her eyes. 'Almost.'

'You look like her,' says Pilot and her gaze shifts sideways. 'You look like Constance Ashlinn.'

Blue wipes at her nose, and I can tell she's uncomfortable.

'She's my mother,' she says, nonchalantly.

Pilot's mouth hangs open – mine too. This girl isn't an ordinary member of Shade Unit. Her mother and her grandmother are both FIILES thieves, legends in the war against the Nowbies.

Bo wriggles inside my head, just as surprised as me and Pilot.

He's staring at her like he's just discovered a Martian. 'I didn't know Constance had a kid. She's kinda . . . old, you know?'

'Well, she does,' Blue says quickly.

'So you're named after the real Blue Ashlinn,' Pilot says excitedly. 'She's your grandmother!'

'Yes, well done,' says Blue. 'So, now you know a bit about me. Let's move on, shall we? If our man inside can get what you need, how soon can Bash launch the offensive?'

Pilot stutters, thrown by the quick change of topic, and considers his answer carefully. 'I mean, I don't really know, Bash didn't say.'

'That's something we need to know if our man inside is going to risk his life for this.'

Her voice is fast, loud, direct. Like a drill sergeant and my fists bunch at my sides.

'Well,' says Pilot, 'assuming the facility is where we think it is, and assuming its defences are something we can handle, then I'd guess . . . two days?'

'Two days,' Blue repeats, staring at the map. 'All right. I'll run the message and deliver the vial. You two wait here and when I return, I'll take you back over the border.'

She's on her way to the door, my one shot at the Time Cache going with her.

'Wait!' I nearly shout. 'Pilot, I don't understand how you're gonna let this happen.' But I do understand. I understand perfectly. We got ourselves on BMAC's radar. We're a risk to the mission and everyone involved. But I'm not here for the mission. I'm not here for Shade Unit.

I'm here for Gabby.

Which is why I have to say this next part. 'If you let her take this from you, what is Bash gonna think, huh? That you're a failure, that's what. How will he ever trust you to run for him again?'

Hurt wells up in Pilot's eyes, and I instantly hate myself.

'I know,' he says. 'I screwed up. But I haven't failed. Not yet. Not if Blue gets the intel where it needs to go.'

'Smart boy,' says Blue, cutting me a glare that tells me exactly what she thinks of me. 'Give me a few hours,' she says, flinging open the door, her CoyoTank following. 'Rads'll take care of you until I get back.'

And with a slam, she's gone, leaving the three of us alone in the room together.

'Right then, boys.' Rads, no longer sleepy but brooding about something I can't even guess at, makes his way back to one of the white recliners, and takes a seat. 'What do you say we place some wagers? How deep are your pockets?' He taps on the armrest and the fight stats bloom to life around him.

'We don't have any money,' says Pilot.

Rads harrumphs, turning his back on us to watch the fight.

Pilot sighs and drags his feet over to the other chair, Tungsten circling at his ankles. 'You want to sit?'

No, I don't want to sit. I don't want to relax and watch a forebrawl while my only chance at the Time Cache disappears down the elevator.

My eyes drop to the Cure vial in my hand. Gabby's cure. This little bit of liquid – there can't be more than three drops. This is everything she ever wanted. This little bit of liquid represents so much pain, so much trouble. But it's something else too. It's something that can fix everything. If my sister had this that day that Roth came, if Gabby had it, would any of this have happened?

'You can have it,' I say, shoving the uncontaminated Cure vial into my pocket.

I have no intention of waiting around for Blue.

PAT
2383

I'm going after her. I'm going to follow her to BMAC Headquarters and, once I'm there, I can look for the Time Cache.

Don't be ridiculous, Bo comes in. *You'll be spotted instantly.*

Not with Rads' bike helmet, I think. Rads watches the forebrawl lazily, back to me. His vehicle is still parked downstairs, the helmet balancing on the seat.

Pilot has his eye on me from across the room.

And when did you learn to operate a StrikeBike?

I didn't, but I can figure it out.

I very much doubt that.

Pilot shakes his head, urgently. He already knows what I'm thinking. Because it's bold. It's daring. And just the slightest bit stupid. Exactly the sort of thing Pilot would do.

I reach for the door and Pilot silently leaps across the room to me. 'Are you crazy?' he whispers. 'We're Avin's most wanted. Just let Blue handle the message.'

'I'm not here for Bash's message.'

'Yeah, I noticed,' he says angrily. 'You've completely jeopardised the mission, not to mention compromised me. You know Bash will probably never let me run back into the city, right?'

I don't say anything because I don't know what to say. He's mad, and I understand that. But I don't have time to beg for his forgiveness. I reach for the door handle and realise there isn't one – just a blinking panel on the wall beside it that I have no idea how to operate.

'You're doing well so far,' whispers Pilot.

I glower at him.

Bo! I feel him leap back at the force of my thought. *How do I get out of here?*

He answers me with a pulse that doesn't hurt but still makes me flinch – the mental equivalent of spitting in my face.

How am I supposed to do this on my own?

Pilot obviously sees the desperation in my eyes. He looks away from me. Finally, he frowns. 'Breezes, Pat. You're risking your life going for the Time Cache. What's in there that's worth all this?'

'A way to save someone else's life.'

My answer surprises him, because his frown disappears. 'You're doing all this for someone else?'

'Someone I'm in a position to help,' I say, remembering his words to me back at the Block. 'Isn't that the rule?'

Pilot winces, like he's been pinched with his own logic. He scratches nervously at his neck, and glances back at Rads, happily watching the brawl. 'Well, he's not gonna let you steal his bike. You think of that?'

I nod.

'And your plan for that?'

I don't really have one. 'If you open this door for me, I'll sneak away and he'll never know. He won't even know you helped me.'

Pilot rolls his eyes. 'Oh he'll know.' He points at the blinking pad beside the door. 'That calls down to the front desk. The door doesn't open unless the gambling debt's paid. You'll have to negotiate with Happy Face downstairs to let you out. And I don't have any digibits. Do you?'

'Digibits?'

'Yeah, digibits. How are you going to pay?"

He must mean the data chips I saw Blue use earlier. I feel into my back pocket and pull out Bo's AvinGate. 'Will this work?'

Pilot's eyes light up as Bo lets loose a string of profanities and a million ugly words for 'thief' that I don't know but catch the sentiment of.

Pilot grins, his red eye lighting up. 'I was right about you. You're no ordinary Mover.'

Tungsten sits up, his eyes burning brighter with Pilot's.

'You'll help me?' I ask.

'Hey,' Rads watches us over his shoulder, suddenly realising he hasn't been babysitting well. 'What are you two whispering about?'

Pilot zips up his BMAC jacket and pulls it up over his nose as Tungsten's body separates and the spheres begin to roll towards Rads. 'Rules are rules,' he says. 'Can't break my own now, can I?'

'Hey!' roars Rads, leaping to his feet.

There's a hiss as Tungst releases the chloroform, and I scramble to cover my mouth inside my coat like Pilot.

And then a thud as the giant soldier collapses on the ground.

Pilot gingerly steps over to Rads' unconscious body and picks through his pocket. He lets out a laugh and pulls out two chips. 'Thanks, big guy.'

He takes the AvinGate from me. 'Let's hope it's enough.' And smashes it on the floor.

Bo's anger explodes against my brain and I have to grit my teeth against the pain.

Pilot doesn't notice, sifting through the shattered pieces of the AvinGate. 'Breezes,' he says, and whistles, picking up a little chip. 'A LOEBS chip.'

'Is that good?'

'Pat,' he says, holding the chip up to his red eye. 'A LOEBS chip is . . . it's more than good.'

He waves a hand over the panel and tucks the chip into his pocket.

'What?' the desk woman's face appears on a tiny screen.

'We want out.'

'Four digibits.'

Pilot glances at the chips from Rads. 'Two,' he says.

'But—' I start, pointing to his pocket, but Pilot's already clamped his hand over my mouth.

'You placed the bet,' the woman says. 'The debt's four.'

'We didn't place any bet, our friend did, and as I'm sure you can see, he's not going anywhere. He'll settle up when he wakes, but for now we can give you two, plus whatever our blue-haired friend gives you when she comes back for

207

us. Or we can stay and wait for her and keep these two digibits for ourselves.'

There's a long silence.

Then finally there's a buzz and the door in front of us swings open.

Pilot and I follow Tungst out into the hall, and into the waiting elevator.

'Pat,' says Pilot, patting his pocket. 'Do you know what a LOEBS is? Logic Optimising Electronic Brain System. These things are the brains of borgs. A LOEBS chip like this? This is powerful stuff. We can't just hand this over to some wager lair woman.'

The doors open and we make our way across the lobby, the woman at the desk leaning on her elbow, lazily watching us as we head out the door. Pilot tosses her the agreed two digibits and she catches them. 'Have good day, gentlemen.'

Rads' bike is right where we left it. I hop on and glance at all the controls. It's more of a spaceship than a bike.

'This kinda chip,' Pilot goes on, nudging me out of the way, 'it's almost people-smart. Like a human brain. There's no way BMAC would let this out of the city easily.'

Now I feel sick. I didn't just take something from Bo. I've stolen. *I'll bring it back*, I promise him. But he's not even paying attention to me, trying to stem the flow of memories that are bubbling up from the hidden corners of his mind.

'Bo must have smuggled it out when they T and B'd him.'

I catch glimpses of a memory he doesn't like. A fancy

penthouse apartment. And borg pieces, silver and sleek scattered around the room. 'T and B'd?'

'Tagged and Banned. Identified as a Mover and kicked out of Avin. Usually happens as soon as a Mover is born. But for Bo to have access to tech like this, he must have been an adult when he was identified.'

A borg – a humanoid creature – stands by the window, its chest open, circuitry exposed. And on the floor, curled up in a ball and screaming, is Bo.

The day I connected to him.

I grab my head, unable to get rid of the image. Bo had a life before me. A nice life. An important life. I can see it all. A respected scientist. Innovative. On the verge of a great discovery.

And then I chose him. I lashed out through space and time and dug into his brain and ruined everything he'd built.

'If he was an adult,' says Pilot slowly, trying to sort out his thoughts as he fumbles with the controls of the bike, 'then that means he can't be a Mover. Movers are born that way. That means Bo's a Shadow. You . . . you can't be Bo's Shadow if *he's* a Shadow.'

My eyes begin to sting, thinking of Bo's leaky lair. A dank cave compared to the luxurious apartment he had before I connected to him. That means I ruined Bo's life.

Bo stretches towards me, trying his best to suppress the memory of my birth. His anger has shifted, giving way to concern for me. *You had no more control over this than I did. The arm doesn't choose the hand, Patrick. They are built together. It's the same with us.*

209

'You're from the past,' Pilot goes on. 'And Bo's a Shadow. You're his Mover, aren't you?'

I nod.

I've put Bo through so much, I'd understand if he just washed his hands of me altogether. But I know why he can't. It's the same reason I never could. We *are* a part of each other. As vital as an organ.

The bike rumbles to life and Tungsten rolls up onto the seat, ready to go.

'Breezes,' says Pilot. 'What happened to you?'

Come home, Bo begs me. *You don't have to do this.*

You know I do.

'It's a long story,' I tell Pilot. 'But I can fix it if I get what I need from the Time Cache.'

'Who is it?' he says. 'Who are you doing all this for?'

'A friend.' My dream, the one I keep having, creeps up on me, and Gabby's eyes are staring up at me through the glass before the final needle, they're asking me to hurry. My hand reaches into my pocket on its own, closing around the Cure. 'BMAC Shelved her,' I tell him. 'Because of me. I have to go back and stop it.'

'Go back?' says Pilot, surprised.

This is foolish, Patrick. You know it as well as I do.

'Yes,' I say, trying to ignore Bo.

'In time?!'

I nod, and lift my leg over the seat, settling in behind Tungsten and leaving room for Pilot.

He blinks at me, and his feet shift, like he can't decide whether to step forwards or back. 'You know what happens if BMAC catches you and gets a load of your pungits? If they figure out you're a Mover who travelled by their Shadow? We're not just talking about the Shelves, you know.'

'I know.'

Pilot lets that sink in for a minute and then shrugs, climbing onto the bike. He pulls his kerchief up over his nose, covering his face. 'As long as you know.'

PAT
2383

The lights of Avin whiz past in a blur of colour from behind the blue-tinted visor of Rads' helmet as Pilot speeds us through the streets. It's so different to the Avin I left – bigger, brighter, denser. It's all so tightly-packed, I couldn't see it properly from outside in the Movers' sector. There're more skyscrapers than in my time, wedged wall to wall so that they're practically just one big clump of steel and concrete, more lights so that the night almost looks the same as day, and more people, so many more people, filling the streets to bursting so that Pilot has to drive the StrikeBike along the sides of the buildings so that we're parallel with the ground and my muscles feel like they're tearing, straining to keep me from falling off.

'How much further?' I shout over the thunder of the bike.

'You tell me,' he says, tapping his eye.

At first, I don't know what he means, and then I notice a light blinking in the corner of my visor. Taking my cue from Pilot, I tap the spot and a grid lights up in front of my eyes, a map of Avin. A red dot on the left, moving fast – us – and a stationary blue dot on the right just a few blocks away.

'There's just a blue dot,' I tell him. 'Is that it?'

'That's Blue's StrikeBike,' Pilot explains. 'Is it moving?'

'No.'

'Then she's at BMAC already. That's where we're headed.'

As the red dot closes in on the blue, I notice crowds of people begin to disperse and the buildings around us start to become more spaced apart. The colourful commercial lights give way to a sterile white lighting.

Pilot rounds a corner and the Avin Turbine rises before us, lit in bright white and rising so high I can't see the top even with my neck craned all the way back. I was just at the top of that tower. Just two weeks ago. I left my time at the top of that tower to come here. Part of me wonders if I got up there again, could I find my way back?

No, interrupts Bo. *You couldn't. Because you can't get into the Time Cache, Patrick. It's impossible.*

I ignore him. I'll find a way. I have to.

It's a fool's errand, Patrick. Quit making yourself the fool.

Pilot follows the road that circles the base of the tower. It's so immense, it's at least two blocks wide. BMAC uniforms mill about the base, between the tower and the buildings that surround it. Cadets run in synchronised packs, officers mingle and salute one another. I glance at my visor. We're nearly on top of the blue dot. Ahead of us, I see a sea of StrikeBikes, parked neatly to the side of a grand stairway that leads up to the main entrance into the Avin Turbine.

The rumble of the bike quiets to a purr as we slow. Pilot parks the StrikeBike and Tungsten slithers up from my lap onto Pilot's shoulder.

'THIS is BMAC Headquarters?'

'This,' nods Pilot. 'And everything for the next eight blocks.'

Breezes. In my time, BMAC had one building outside the city, plus the silos. I notice them now, the silos, peeking through the gaps in the buildings – their brightly lit white domes marking the perimeter of BMAC's new territory. I shiver, remembering the chill of the air inside them, the Shelves and Shelves of marbled pale feet. They had six silos in my time. Now, there must be thirty of them. BMAC is practically its own city.

Pilot's off the bike, pulling his scarf off his face.

'Are you crazy?'

'Covered face sticks out more here,' he says, marching down the street. 'Get moving. Look like you've got important business.'

I haul myself off the bike and stumble after him, my legs wobbly after the crazy ride. 'Where do we go?'

'Nowhere yet. Just look like you're in a hurry and no one will pay any attention.'

'But the Time Cache . . .'

'Yeah, it's in the Turbine. High security in the Turbine. We shouldn't just waltz in. The training school is back that way. When class lets out, this place will be swarming with cadets going back to their residences, dropping off papers, reporting to superior officers. We can blend into the crowds and slip into the Turbine with the rest of them.'

I walk stride for stride with Pilot, trying to copy the way his arms are suddenly swinging, the way his legs march militantly. He looks the part. I'm not sure I do, with my awkward imitation walk and oversized helmet still on my head. Tungsten wriggles his way into Pilot's shirt, hidden from sight, as Bo continues to lecture me from the centre of my brain.

Even if you managed to get into the Time Cache – which you won't—

You don't know that.

Oh yes, I do, Patrick. I know exactly what you're up against in there and I know you are no match for it. But even if you were, even if you did manage to get inside and find this Punch of yours, you still don't have a person with the pungits you need to get back there.

He's right about that. And I have no idea where to find them. But I can only deal with one problem at a time. One foot in front of the other. At least with the Punch in my hand, going home is possible. Without it, I'm stuck for good.

'Here we go,' says Pilot. Hordes of BMAC cadets spill out of the training centre onto the street. They march just like Pilot, determined and focused, all of them busy with important matters. Pilot turns abruptly to follow a group of especially grim-looking cadets, and I nearly fall over trying to turn fast enough to join him. There's about a dozen of them, making their way back towards the front of the tower. I hold my breath. Flanking the sides of this particular group are CoyoTanks. Then I notice their eyes

215

– they all have yellow glowing eyes to match their borgs. They must be some kind of CoyoTank squad.

'Series Five,' says Pilot, admiring the menacing borgs.

There's a hum inside my head, quiet and distant, coming from Bo. It's so absentminded on his part, so involuntary and subtle, I would have mistaken it for white noise, but because I'm super on edge, I'm more sensitive to it than usual.

Infrared scanners, stun bites, REM processor, level 2 cognisance, Titanium exoskeleton. It's a laundry list of the make-up of the CoyoTanks.

How can you tell all that?

Bo doesn't answer me, just keeps cycling through the CoyoTank's features like he can't help himself.

As the group rounds the front of the tower, several of them break off, climbing the steps to the front entrance. Pilot and I follow them, passing through the front doors and into what was a grubby ticket kiosk the last time I was here. Now, it's a grand marble entrance way, with towering ceilings and columns and a massive BMAC symbol carved into the wall opposite us.

The cadets leading the group salute the pair of guards leaning casually against the front desk. The guards nod and return to their conversation, disinterested as we make our way down the grand hallway to the left. I guess our uniforms are good enough for the guards because they don't even notice us. No one notices us. We blend in with all the other cadets. The click of the CoyoTanks' paws echo as we march past metal doors, each of them easily two storeys high, lining the hallway. They all have their functions clearly marked, bevelled into the metal: Office of Movement Identification and Registration Ministry, Office of Movement Investigations, Office of Special Investigation, Office of the Movement Compliance Minister, Office of the Shadow Registry, Office of the Shelving Warden.

Pilot grabs hold of my shoulder to pull me back from the group. The cadets march away without us and we stop just outside one of the doors – this one marked Office of the Minister of Movement Health and Wellness.

'Health and Wellness?' I whisper.

'Yeah. Don't want us dead before they Shelve us. After all, capital punishment is illegal.' Pilot shakes his head. 'Like there's a difference.'

Hardly. To be Shelved, you might as well be dead. I think of Gabby, her feet cold and veiny, lying among the thousands of others on the Shelves.

Pilot pushes open the door and walks into the ornate office, right over to a wall that's lit up with notices and articles on all things Mover-health-related. The others in the office, several officers waiting in chairs, a few others working behind a desk, glance over at me. I swallow and stand awkwardly beside Pilot.

'Take off the helmet,' he mutters to me.

'But—'

'But nothing, you look like a freak. Just take it off and face the board.'

I do what he says and as soon as the helmet is off, the eyes of the room go back to what they're doing.

'What are we doing here?' I ask him.

'Making sure,' he says. 'Do you see her?'

'Who? Blue?'

He nods.

As casually as I can, I risk a glance over my shoulder and do a quick scan of the waiting room.

'No.'

Pilot frowns. 'Me neither.' Ever the Shade Unit soldier, he's still worried about his mission. 'I'm sure she's here, we saw her bike. This is the office of the Health Minister. This is where our guy is. She's supposed to be here.'

Just then the door to the office flies open and everyone drops what they're doing, removing hats and holding them to their chests, heads bowed. A round, sour-looking man, dressed in a BMAC uniform with all kinds of medals and badges, stands in the doorway.

Pilot elbows me. 'That's the High Minister of BMAC,' he says, like that should mean something to me. It doesn't. I've never heard of the High Minister, but I hold my helmet over my heart and bow my head as quickly as I can.

The High Minister storms across the room, past the main desk and over to one of the doors at the very back, throwing it open. Inside stands another decorated officer and a cadet. Behind the cadet is a slender CoyoTank with glowing white eyes. Tyke. The cadet's eyes find mine across the room – she's tucked her hair inside her hat, but it's her, Blue.

And she's not happy to see us.

'What's all this, then?' roars the High Minister. 'Contamination?! Impossible!' He slams the door so hard behind him that the walls rattle.

'She did it,' Pilot breathes beside me. 'She delivered the message.'

'We should go,' I say. Blue knows we're here. She could come after us at any second.

'OK,' Pilot agrees, nudging me towards the door.

We make our way down the hall, round one corner and then another. Pilot leads us up a back stairwell and finally we emerge onto a new floor. Our footsteps echo on the concrete floor through a massive, dark cavern.

There are children.

Groups of school children running around from one glass display case to another.

'It's a museum,' I say, realising.

'BMAC Museum of Movement Control,' says Pilot. 'A celebration of their years keeping the likes of us in line.'

The ceiling is easily four storeys high. An enormous ball – a hologram – hangs from the centre. It's composed of a million delicate glowing quills, or spikes, jutting out in all directions. Several groups of students stand beneath it, listening to teachers that look like BMAC officers explain. I hear one say, 'There are no numbers on this clock, but there are hands, more than any one person can count.'

'That's a clock?' I ask Pilot.

'Eternity clock,' he says. 'It tracks all of time – time that's passed, time that will be, and all the alternate timelines.'

On each hand, a golden ball slides up and down silently and from that new hands grow, branching outwards. I watch as one of the balls glows brighter than the rest, a new hand sprouting from its centre.

'Alternate timelines?'

'Sure. See the golden orbs?' he says, pointing. 'They sense changes in the radiation from the world's pungits. When there's a split in a timeline thanks to Movers, the clock records and tracks it by growing a new hand.'

I watch as more hands sprout out of the thousands of glowing orbs and wonder about all the Movers – Movers like me and Gabby – and all the consequences that follows one of those little glowing balls.

'Pat? You coming?' Pilot stands in front of another hallway opposite the clock, Tungsten poking his head out his collar. 'It's this way.'

But I can't move. The statue beside Pilot has frozen me in my tracks. A statue of a woman – a woman I know.

'That's Agent Hartman.'

'Huh?' Pilot looks over at the stone woman. 'Yeah, Beadie Hartman.'

That face, that smug, merciless face – the same face that haunts my dreams – makes my fists clench. 'Why is there a statue of Beadie Hartman in here?'

'You're kidding, right? She discovered pungits.'

The Archivist said something similar. 'Except no, she didn't.'

Gabby did.

'Well, history says she did. And BMAC loves her for it. She's the reason BMAC can identify all of us. The reason they figured out how to cure us.'

'What?'

'Sure,' says Pilot, staring up at the officer's ugly face. 'Without Beadie Hartman, there's no knowledge of pungits. Without that knowledge, there's no Cure.'

It would devastate Gabby to know that her greatest discovery becomes the biggest threat to Movers' survival. Devastate her to know that Hartman took all the credit and turned pungits against us. I want to tear the statue down.

Why did everyone think it was Beadie Hartman who discovered pungits?

A rush of sick radiates out from my gut, through my legs and arms and out through my toes and fingertips. I grab hold of my knees.

'You all right?' Pilot asks.

'I showed Hartman the pungits.'

'What?'

'Back when she arrested me, I traded pungits for my safety and my mother's.'

And now everyone thinks Hartman discovered them. It's my fault BMAC has pungits.

My fault they have the Cure. I betrayed Gabby.

Bo drifts into my mind like smoke. *You did what you had to do, Patrick. It was survival.*

But Gabby didn't survive. Not really. She's on the Shelves.

'Breezes,' Pilot breathes. 'I mean . . . I don't . . .' He trails off, not sure what to say.

What is there to say?

He puts a hand on my back. 'It's OK.'

'What?' How can he say that? How can he even look at me?

He shrugs. 'I just mean . . . How could you have known?'

Tears sting my eyes, grateful for his kindness. I don't deserve it. I did this to the future. He should hate my guts.

'Now, come on,' Pilot says. 'We need to hurry.'

We make our way through the museum, heads down to keep from being recognised. Finally, Pilot leads us to another grand room, with children pressing their faces up to a glass window.

'Through there,' says Pilot, nodding at the window.

On the other side of the glass, I see it. A massive circular vault door, bigger than the Eternity Clock, made of polished, glimmering steel, blinking with a thousand different lights measuring who-knows-what. A pair of CoyoTanks stand guard on either side of the door. Their operators stand beside them – BMAC officers. But they don't look like your average officer. Their eyes glow blue and their faces are covered in all kinds of circuits and metal.

They aren't *ordinary BMAC officers*, Bo chimes in. *They are borgs.*

'Those are borgs?' I choke.

Pilot nods. 'If you think CoyoTanks are bad, those GuardBorgs are a whole other level. At least CoyoTanks are stupid. That's why they need people to pilot them. But those GuardBorgs?' He taps his pocket with the LOEBS chip. 'They're problem-solving smart. They don't need anyone driving them.'

That's not the half of it, Bo tells me. *The vault operates using a neural network and a complex system of genetic algorithms. It's a system that works the same way as a human brain. But better. Faster. Smarter.*

What does that mean?

The vault knows it has to keep you out. By any means necessary.

How do you know that?

I know because before you, it was my job to design systems and intelligences just like that.

I gape at the intimidating steel door. The image of Bo curled up on the floor of his penthouse apartment, borg parts scattered around him, plays in my mind. Before me. Before I was born and made him my Shadow. It becomes clearer.

You worked for BMAC, I realise.

He's silent on his end, and it's enough to confirm my suspicions.

I did, he admits. *I helped to create the intelligence that operates this door.*

Bash's interest in helping me so he could get to Bo becomes so clear, it's almost blinding.

You cannot get into the Time Cache, Patrick, he says. *It's not just my opinion. It's a near impossibility.*

A black pit of hopelessness opens up inside of me.

'So what do you want to do?' Pilot asks.

I don't know what to do. I knew it would be hard, but what Bo's just told me—

So that's why you didn't want me coming here, I tell him. *You knew how the vault works.*

Again, Bo's silent, the truth of it hanging heavy in the empty space between us. A lump swells at the back of my throat. I suddenly feel tired, every limb too heavy to stay standing. I want to collapse, to curl up in a ball on the floor and give up.

I'm the reason Gabby's on the Shelves. The reason her discovery is being used against Movers. I'm responsible for so much bad and no matter how hard I try to fix it, it's not enough. I've come all this way, and it's still not enough. Not even close to enough to fix what's happened.

Every night, in my dream, Gabby's eyes beg me to stop it.

How am I supposed to save her?

'Pat,' says Pilot, looking nervously through the glass. 'Pat, I think we should go.'

He's nervous because of the GuardBorgs.

They're watching us.

PAT
2383

The GuardBorgs, once statue still, are stepping towards the viewing glass, their glowing blue eyes locked onto me and Pilot.

'What are they doing?'

But Pilot doesn't say anything, backing away slowly, not daring to look away.

The eyes of the GuardBorgs flare, and they lift their guns, their CoyoTanks whirring to life.

'We're blown!' Pilot shouts, and he takes off running. 'Pat! Go! Move!'

The GuardBorgs sprint towards us, my heart leaping into my throat and I race after Pilot. They recognise us. They know who we are.

Checkpoint Four would have security footage of you, says Bo. *The GuardBorgs must have been alerted to your faces just like the rest of BMAC.*

There's a hideous crash and screams from the museum patrons, and when I look back, I see the GuardBorgs haven't bothered with the door – they rise from the shattered window glass, that blue gaze never leaving us.

They'll alert the rest of BMAC that they've found you.

This is bad. We're in the heart of BMAC Headquarters. If the whole force knows we're here, how are we supposed to get out?

I pump my legs as fast as they'll go, barrelling past the statue of Hartman. Pilot is faster, pulling away from me as he races beneath the eternity clock.

We just have to get back to the StrikeBike. If we get to the bike we have a chance. If we get to the StrikeBike we can—

The CoyoTanks land in front of Pilot, blocking the door out of here. Pilot skids to a stop and I nearly run into him.

Behind us, the GuardBorgs stomp towards us. They aren't running. They know they don't need to.

'Pilot . . .' I say, shrinking as the furious bots tower over us.

He moves in close to me, gaping helplessly at their emotionless faces.

'What's gonna happen, Pilot?'

He doesn't say anything. And I can tell by the fear in his eyes he has no idea.

There's a click and whir from inside their heads, their dead, glowing eyes spinning. Suddenly my pungits are there above my head, and Pilot's too. There's no hiding now. They know what we are.

The GuardBorgs hold out their left arms in perfect sync, opening their palms. They each hold what look like marbles – electric blue marbles. They glow the same as the eyes, and lift up into the air, hovering over the borgs' open hands.

Pilot begins to shake.

'What is that?'

'Neural binders,' he rasps.

The borgs flex their fingers and, like lightning, the little balls shoot straight at my head, and there's a pain – an icy cold bite blistering the sides of my head at the temples. I cry out, and the cold spreads through my body, sending me to my knees. Pilot moans beside me and we're both on the floor, clawing at our heads.

Patrick, I feel Bo thinking. My name pours out of him, again and again. I can feel him clinging to me, desperately trying to hang on.

The cold freezes my brain so that I can't think, numb to my own mind so that I can't feel my arms, my legs – and my Shadow.

Bo? I want to reach for him, but I can't. I can't do anything.

Then I'm moving. My body gets to its feet, without any command from me. I'm not standing up, I didn't try to stand up. But my body does it all the same. Pilot stands too, his face pained, the little blue marbles glowing on either side of his head.

Panic rises in my throat as I tell my arms to move – beg them to even twitch – but nothing happens. A constant coolness pulses at my temples where I know the neural binders have attached themselves. And Bo, he pings around the inside of my skull, searching for me, begging me to answer.

I can't answer him.

My brain has been commandeered.

The GuardBorgs stare at us blankly. The one on the left taps a finger to Pilot's chest and a shock jolts through him. There's a clatter as Tungsten falls lifelessly to the floor. The GuardBorg picks him up and then my body turns, and so does Pilot's, and we begin to march, the CoyoTanks leading us out of the museum, the GuardBorgs at our backs. We're led through winding hallways and up an elevator with no buttons so that I have no idea where we are. Not until the doors open again. The brightly lit opulence of the main level is long gone – up here it's dark, with only dim lights lining the hallway, and the lights of Avin spilling through the floor-to-ceiling windows on our left. It spreads out beneath us like a carpet and I know where I am now. I've seen Avin from this height before. We're on the observation deck of the Avin tower. Except here, in 2383, it's not a tourist attraction. It's something else altogether. Something dark and cold and secret.

Something like the Shelves.

I feel nauseous. But I couldn't throw up even if I wanted to. Are they going to Shelve us?

A double door at the end of the hallway slides open, and white light pours along the floor towards us. A round silhouette stands in the light.

'Ah!' the silhouette says. 'Here we are. Excellent timing. Let's settle this now, shall we?'

As Pilot and I move towards the voice, my eyes adjust to the light and I recognise the face of the High Minister. I expect him to be furious, but he's smiling, apparently pleased.

'Hurry up, hurry up,' he says, waving an impatient hand at us. Our feet carry us over the threshold and into a sterile-looking operating room, a row of a dozen metal slabs lining the centre of the room.

My vision blurs a moment and I'm dizzy with fear. They are going to Shelve us. They are going to Shelve us and I can't lift a finger to fight them. I can't do anything.

Oh, Bo, help me.

But Bo can't hear me. My mind won't let him.

Another man – tall, well-dressed, stern-faced – waits for us. And beside him, eyes blazing, is Blue.

'Now then, Minister Mathis,' says the High Minister. 'I do share your concern about contamination at our facility, but our officers have reported no incidents in the field with the current shipment of the Cure.'

Minister Mathis – Shade Unit's inside man – doesn't even look at us. We're as insignificant to him as we are to any other BMAC superior. We have to be. Because his mission, I'm sure, comes first. 'Well, High Minister, my analysis of this vial clearly indicates that the Cure contains traces of salt water. The chloride alone is enough to completely alter the chemistry of the intravenous solution.'

Blue stands like a soldier, stiff as a board with her CoyoTank at her side, her chin held high. But her nostrils flare as she stares at me.

'I fear a leak at the facility could—'

The High Minister holds up a hand to stop Minister Mathis. 'What, if any, effect does salt water have on the effectiveness of the Cure?'

Minister Mathis makes a choking sound, throwing open

his arms and I realise he's stalling, trying to come up with a lie. 'I simply don't know. I need to run an in-depth investigation and I can't do that without the security clearance required to access the Cure facility.'

'Consider this the first part of your investigation, Minister Mathis,' says the High Minister, motioning us forwards. My feet begin to move and the GuardBorgs escort Pilot and I over to the metal slabs at the centre of the room where we both climb up without a fight. One of the GuardBorgs drops Tungsten with a clang onto a tray of tools, the little borg's eyes dark. He's offline. My body lies down on the cold hard table on its own, and I'm freezing but still the sweat beads on my forehead. 'Thank you, Guards, that will be all.' The GuardBorgs obey and leave the room, but the cold in my head doesn't go with them. I'm still a prisoner inside my own body. 'Now then, Minister Mathis,' the High Minister says, 'if you can demonstrate for me the consequences of this possible contamination at the mines, then I'll consider upgrading your clearance.'

Blue's eyes dart to Minister Mathis who looks confused. 'Demonstrate?' he says. 'On these boys?'

'Border infiltrators,' shrugs the High Minister. 'Typically a Shelving offense, but why waste the opportunity for you? Come now, I'm a very busy man. Prepare the syringes.'

I try to swallow the hard ball of panic swelling in my throat, but my brain won't let me.

I was wrong. They aren't going to Shelve us.

They're going to cure us.

PAT
2383

I try to fight the binders, squirming against the cold that's frozen my mind. It's no use. My body won't listen to me.

I look hopelessly to Pilot, he's still as stone, his wild eyes telling me he's trying to fight free with everything in him.

The High Minister steps up to Pilot's table, and beckons Mathis forwards. 'Minister Mathis?'

Minister Mathis doesn't even glance at us as he walks calmly to a cabinet on the side wall and removes a number of tools before joining the High Minister. He stands over Pilot. We're nothing more than lab rats to him. We have to be. His cover depends on it.

Blue refuses to meet my eyes, keeping her stare on the far wall. The mission is what's important. To her, we're just collateral damage.

Minister Mathis selects a pungit ray from his tools and points it into Pilot's face. His pungits reveal themselves – hordes of tiny black flecks flowing into his head.

'A textbook Phase 1 Mover,' says the High Minister,

cheerfully, like a fisherman pleased with his catch. 'On your mark, Minister Mathis.'

Minister Mathis nods and puts the ray down, replacing it with a little black disc. Just like the kind I'd seen on the Cure Bus. The High Minister leans closer to Pilot, inspecting his red eye while Mathis takes the Cure vial and – so quickly and fluidly I almost miss it – slips it up his sleeve. In his other hand he has another vial, a slightly deeper blue than the ones Pilot had shown me. I glance over at the cabinet, still open, and see there are Cure vials inside. He's replaced the contaminated vial. He clicks it into the disc, and the centre glows white.

Pilot watches from his prison of a body, powerless to do anything as Mathis presses the disc to the inside of his elbow. With another click, the light dims, and Pilot's body begins to shake.

I want to scream, but no sound comes out. All I can do is feel every bit of terror and pain and grief as it rips through my body, unable to escape.

'Very good,' says the High Minister. 'A successful treatment, wouldn't you say, Mathis?'

He nods. 'Appears to be.'

Pilot's twitching begins to subside, his eyes closed as he sleeps. Minister Mathis points the ray at him again and the pungits that had once been there are gone.

It's done.

Pilot is cured.

The fat man laughs. 'An alarmist, you are, Minister Mathis. But I suppose it's your job to be.' He waves a hand at me. 'Once more for posterity, eh?'

Minister Mathis appears above me, a crease between his brows. His hand brushes my shoulder and I feel the faintest squeeze. An apology for what he has to do, I guess.

So this is it. It all ends here.

What will I be without Bo? And a shoulder squeeze is all the sorry I get.

Minister Mathis points the ray at my face—

No, wait—

They'll see—

There's a gasp from the High Minister as Mathis's frown switches to amazement.

'What in the ever-loving breeze . . .' breathes the High Minister.

My pungits.

The High Minister's eyes are wide as he stares at me. 'Mathis, have you ever . . .?' His voice trails off, his mind too busy trying to make sense of the chaos above my head.

Minister Mathis ignores him. 'You're gonna want to take a look at this.'

At first, I don't know what he means – how could the High Minister be looking any harder? – and then Blue steps closer to me and I realise Mathis wasn't talking to the High Minister.

She's standing over me, her eyes bright as if she's seeing me for the first time. The beginnings of a grin tug at the corner of her mouth. 'Well, that's a surprise.'

'What do you want to do?' Mathis asks her, and I suddenly understand she's in charge now.

And so does the High Minister.

'What is all this?' the old man growls. 'Mathis, who is this cadet?'

233

Blue and Minister Mathis ignore him, and Blue's fingers work at the neural bindings on the sides of my head. 'We better get him to the Aberrants.'

'The what?' barks the High Minister as Mathis helps her. 'What are you doing? Don't touch those! Guards!'

Blue's eyes dart from my pungits over to the High Minster, a flash of anger and annoyance there. 'Tyke,' she says, and that's all she has to say. The CoyoTank moves like lightning, blocking the way to the door for the High Minister.

Suddenly the icy chill in my brain is gone, a rush of heat as the neural bindings come loose and my body tries to repair the damage.

On instinct, my mind reaches out for Bo, and he's there, relieved to have me back.

'Guards!' bellows the High Minister, but Blue is already behind him, her hands grabbing hold of the sides of his head. The High Minister cries out and tries to thrash against it, but he's too late. He crumples to the ground, trembling, until he's finally lying still and silent, the neural bindings glowing at the sides of his head.

Mathis helps me sit up, my head aching so bad I can hardly manage it myself. 'Can you walk?'

Can I? I don't know. My mind is in so much pain, I don't know if I can remember how.

'It doesn't matter,' says Blue, stepping over the High Minister. 'He has to. We need to get out of here, now. How long do you think before someone notices the High Minister hasn't come back from his meeting with you?'

'Not long.'

'We can't leave him here.'

'The gurneys,' Mathis says, pointing to several suspended metal beds parked against the wall. 'We can put him on one of these with a sheet over him. Same for the boys. They'll look like any lab subjects or Shelf prisoners that way. No one will think twice about it.' He pulls at one and it floats away from the wall, gliding easily under his direction, and pushes it over to me and Blue. 'Get him up.' They lift me onto the gurney and lay me down, and then do the same to Pilot.

'Tungsten,' I rasp, reaching for the little borg.

'Lie still,' she snaps at me. 'You're Shelved, all right?'

'Please, Tungsten.'

She notices what I'm reaching for and with a scoff she snatches him up from the table and tucks him under my arm so that he's hidden from sight. 'There. Now shut up.'

I'm happy to do what she says. My head hurts too much, the effort to speak only makes it worse.

Mathis glides up beside us with Pilot still sleeping. He pulls the neural binders from Pilot's head, but he doesn't stir. Cured. Pilot is cured. The enormity of it washes over me and I close my eyes, wishing the truth of it away. And with my eyes closed, I'm suddenly tired. So tired. And everything starts to fade.

'My cover's blown for this,' Mathis says. 'What's Connie gonna say?'

'To save another Aberrant?' Blue's voice is distant as I drift off to sleep. 'She'll say it was worth it.'

PAT
2383

When I wake up, it's dark and there's a dank smell, and the faint blue glow of monitors and computer screens is the only light to see by. Am I back at Bo's?

No. You're not back.

Voices I don't know speak quietly somewhere in the room. 'I don't like the idea of launching an offensive if we're not exactly sure where the facility is.'

'We are sure. The High Minister said it was at the mines. Go back in there, wake him up and ask him yourself if you don't believe me.'

'Yeah, right. Like I want the High Minister seeing my face.'

'What are we going to do about him?'

Someone sighs. 'One problem at a time.'

The pain in my head has eased off, but my muscles are sore. With a lot of effort I manage to turn my head. That's when I see him.

'Pilot!'

He sits, slumped against the wall, chin in his chest. Tungsten lies on his lap, looking up at him but Pilot doesn't see him. Doesn't care.

'Pilot?'

'I wish I could have at least said goodbye to her, made her understand what was happening.' He covers his face, pulling his knees up to his chest so that Tungsten has to jump off. The little borg looks at me, his glowing red eyes conveying as close to concern as a robot can.

Pilot is cured. Because of me.

'You're up,' someone says.

I roll over and there's Blue, standing beside Tyke in the middle of what looks like a dark cement basement. Behind them, several pairs of curious eyes watch me.

'Where are we?'

'Where BMAC can't get to people like us.'

The other eyes belong to a raggedy-looking group of misfits. One face is familiar – Rads, arms crossed and scowling at me from his seat on the couch. I guess he hasn't forgiven me for taking the StrikeBike. Sitting by his feet is a girl, about the same age as my little sister Maggie, who waves. Across from them, more interested in the monitors that are lined up along the walls than me, is a muscular guy with long hair, a child's doll in his lap. Beside him is another young man, maybe just a few years older than me, with industrial earmuffs on his head. Sitting just behind them, I recognise another face – Minister Mathis. He smiles weakly.

'Like us?' I ask.

'The Movers and Shadows,' says a voice, a dark figure

appearing in a doorway at the far end of the room, 'who are more.' There's a rumble from Bo, a tremor that I don't understand. When the figure steps into the light of the monitors, I see an old woman, hair as blue as Blue's, and I realise what his problem is – Constance Ashlinn. 'We are the Aberrants.'

I'm not sure if I should be relieved or worried. Constance Ashlinn *is* Shade Unit, she's one of us. But the rage emanating from Bo, the memory of her betrayal, makes me wonder how safe I really am.

And Constance can tell. 'You know who I am,' she says with a grin.

'Yes.'

'Then you know I'm someone you can trust.'

Bo's anger is explosive and I wince from the force of it.

'You don't think so?' she says, taking my flinch for doubt.

And I guess I do have doubt. Bo showed me what happened that day outside First Avin. I lived it through him. Felt the fear. The disappointment. 'I've been warned not to.'

Her grin disappears, surprised by my answer. 'By who?'

I hesitate, not sure how much I should say. But Bo has no hesitation.

Tell her, he orders me.

And so I do. 'Bo Hill.'

She doesn't say anything, but she doesn't look surprised either. 'Bo Hill. Never did forgive me for that nasty business outside First Avin, did he?'

'He told me you betrayed him,' I say. 'Told me you could have warned them and you didn't.'

'I tried to,' she snaps. 'But there wasn't time.' She sighs, rubbing a hand through her long blue hair. 'A decision had to be made. BMAC was coming for us and I had to get the Aberrants out. If BMAC ever got their hands on them – I couldn't let that happen. Getting them out, that was the most important thing. '

More important than saving your friends?

It's a valid question, so I ask it for Bo.

'Yes.' She doesn't even pause to think about it. 'As hard as you've tried to keep what you are from BMAC, I've worked a thousand times harder to protect people just like yourself from them.'

My eyes shift between the expectant gazes around the room, trying to figure out what she means, what all these people are, but I don't understand.

'Relax, Patrick,' Blue says. 'We know.'

'You do?'

'I saw your pungits,' she says. 'They're not normal. Just like all of ours.'

Like theirs? But how can that be?

Constance grins, and it's the same grin as Blue's. 'You thought you were the only one, didn't you? Sorry to disappoint you, young man, but you are not alone when it comes to your Movement gifts. Everyone in this room is blessed with a – shall we say, *unique* arrangement of pungits. Each one of us can't be defined by BMAC's simplistic phase statuses. We are beyond the phases. And the pungits grant all of us different talents, each one unique and special.'

Special talents?

I sit up, shaking my head. 'No, you don't understand—'

'Oh, I understand, young man,' says Constance, 'I've spent a dozen lifetimes finding Aberrant Movers and Shadows like yourself, finding them, collecting them, so that I can protect them.'

'But I'm not what you're saying,' I tell her. 'I'm not a normal Mover.'

Constance laughs. 'Haven't you been listening, young man? No one in this room is normal!'

Blue sits on the edge of my cot and points at Mathis who leans against the wall, watching me. 'Mathis is one of our best talents. He's what we like to call a Spitter. He can spit his pungits off himself and onto someone else temporarily. That's why he's able to work in BMAC. They can test him all they want, he just throws his pungits, and they think he's a Nowbie.'

I stare, slack-jawed, and Mathis nods casually, like it's no big deal.

Blue points over to the little girl who waves again. 'That's Hope. We call her a Super Mover. She can Move any Mover or Shadow from the future. Doesn't have to be connected to her.'

'The big guy over there?' says Blue, nodding at the one holding the doll. 'We call him Zombie. He can't Move, but he can take over his Shadow's mind, using him like a puppet.'

Zombie holds up a finger, 'Never without permission.' He notices me glance at the doll. 'This? I use her to pinpoint which limbs I want my Shadow to move,' he explains, a little embarrassed. 'Helps me concentrate.'

Used like a puppet? That sounds sinister.

'That's right, Zombie,' Blue beams, proud. 'And beside

him is Psychic. He's what we call a Watcher Shadow. Like Zombie, he can't Move, but he can get into Movers' heads – any Mover, in any time – and listen to their thoughts.'

I shrink back a little, the idea of that unsettling me.

'Ah, don't worry,' says Psychic, tapping his earmuffs. 'I hear Movers' voices all at once and it's too loud to zero in without concentrating really hard. The headgear helps me block it out.'

I nod, but it doesn't make me feel better.

'It's pretty painful for the guy,' Blue assures me. 'Ever had to listen to thousands of people yelling at you at once?'

'That sounds awful.'

'It is,' she agrees.

Psychic nods. 'It's not great.'

'You remember Rads?' Blue asks.

I nod.

Rads isn't smiling any more. He's scowling, like he's ready to rip my head off. 'He's what we call a Puppet Mover. He's got Movers like Zombie across a bunch of different times that jump into his head and take over. Eight of them, by my last count, right?'

'Nine,' he says.

'Sorry, nine. That's why he's a little uh . . . moody. To be honest, I'm not sure I've actually even met the real Rads.'

Rads sniffs and his eyes are full of tears. 'You think I'm moody?'

This is all stuff I don't understand – can't understand. Movers who control their Shadows like puppets? Who can read other Movers' minds? Shadows who don't need Movers? Even Bo is having a hard time processing all this, his anger giving way to confusion. Our relationship, Mover to Shadow, must seem so simplistic to people like these.

Suddenly, phase testing and statuses seem stupid – all these mechanisms of control carefully designed by BMAC and yet here are these people, the Aberrants, existing outside all those careful controls.

'Are you OK?' Constance asks, seeing the confusion on my face.

'It just sounds . . .' I struggle for the right word. 'Hard.'

'It's a blessing and a curse,' Blue says, 'to be an Aberrant. Worse for some of us than others.'

'At least there's the Cure,' says Psychic, and I blink at him.

'The Cure?'

'Yes, the Cure,' says Blue. 'For some of us, the Cure offers the only relief there is. Aberrants like Rads and Psychic. These guys haven't taken it yet, because they don't agree with the way BMAC has control over it—'

'Yeah, but if this noise gets any louder,' says Psychic, tapping his headphones, 'I'm catching the first Cure Bus I see.'

'But,' Blue goes on, 'we've helped plenty of Aberrants receive the Cure over the years.'

I guess my face gives away just how confused I am, because she smiles.

'But' – I say, not understanding – 'but Bash. You're helping *Bash*. And Shade Unit. They want to destroy the Cure.'

Blue shakes her head. 'Bash and Shade Unit still see the Cure as a BMAC control, a way to oppress them.' She sighs, eyes focused on nothing as she thinks. 'I can't blame him really, I used to think like that too.'

'But not now?'

'No,' she says. 'For some people, being a Mover isn't so easy. A Mover told me that once, a long time ago. And I never forgot it. Bash and Shade Unit, they don't understand that the Cure has its place. That it's needed.'

I do understand that. I saw how much Gabby wanted it. How much it would have helped her.

'Aberrants learn quickly that the enemy is BMAC. Not the Cure,' says Blue.

I think of Gabby, and all the volunteers lining up for the Cure Bus. If Bash destroys the Cure, what happens to all of them? How many Movers out there need it? How many of them are like Rads and Psychic? How many are Aberrants?

'So why are you working with Bash,' I ask, 'if you don't want to destroy the Cure?'

'Because BMAC can't have control of it,' says Constance. 'Bash isn't wrong, they do use it to try to control us. And that cannot stand. If Bash and his forces can lead us to the Cure, then so be it.'

'So you're using him.'

'To protect my Aberrants,' she says, 'Yes. Can't you see, Patrick, why protecting my Aberrants from BMAC takes priority over everything? Why it took priority over Bo Hill?'

I do, says Bo.

Bo's anger and confusion has given way to something else – something I can't quite figure out. Regret maybe. Regret mixed with . . . forgiveness.

What BMAC could learn from Movers with abilities like these, says Bo, *what they could use them for, against their own will, against the rest of us. It doesn't bear thinking about. I understand now.*

I don't know that I could be as understanding as Bo, but I can feel that it's not easy for him. His leg is still twisted. His friend Mari is still gone. Because of Constance Ashlinn. 'What about you?' I ask Blue. 'What makes you . . . different?'

'I'm a Loop Mover,' says Constance.

'A what?'

'I can Move myself up from my past,' Blue explains.

'We call her the vampire,' says Zombie. 'Cos she can basically live for ever.'

I feel my forehead crinkle. 'I don't understand.'

'Constance is not my mother, Pat,' says Blue. 'She's me. Just older. Or, I guess more accurately, I'm her. Just younger. Like a loop, when I get old, I pull up my younger self. Been doing it for centuries.'

'With Shade Unit's efforts ramping up and myself getting on in years,' says Constance, 'I felt it was time to Move my younger self up, to take over my work if something happens to me, like if I get Shelved again.'

Shelved again. Blue Ashlinn. She's not Blue's grand-mother.

Blue nods. 'And when I get older, I'll reach back and pull up a younger version of myself. On and on and on.'

The little girl, Hope, grins at me. 'See? A vampire.'

A Loop Mover. I remember the pictures the Archivist showed me and Bo, the same blue-haired girl in different times. The idea makes me dizzy. 'So . . . how old are you?'

Constance shrugs. 'Three, maybe four hundred years? It's been such a long time, I lost track along the way.'

'And you?' Mathis looks at me expectantly. 'What's your talent?'

'Me?'

'Sure,' says Blue. 'We told you ours.'

I shake my head. 'No, I'm not— I mean I don't have a— talent.'

Blue rolls her eyes. 'Patrick, this is a safe place for people like us. We saw your pungits and it's OK. You don't have to hide it any more. You can trust us.'

Because they think you're like them, says Bo. *Because they think you're the same. You're not like them.*

No, maybe not. I'm not beyond the phases like they are. But we're not regular Movers any more either. Not since the Punch changed the pungits and you Moved me here.

Blue saved me – twice. She told me her secret. I owe her mine.

So I tell them. I tell them about Gabby, about my little sister and Commander Roth. About the Punch and how it brought me here. And how it has to take me back to the start. To fix everything.

I hope my secret doesn't disappoint them. Because Bo's right, I'm not the same as them.

But I also hope, even after everything Blue's done for me, that by confessing what I am, why I'm here, she'll help me again.

PAT
2383

When I'm finished, the room is silent. The Aberrants stare at me, not blinking, not saying anything. Awkwardly, I glance over at Pilot – he hasn't moved, head still in his chest, Tungsten sitting nervously in his lap. My story hasn't even made him look up. My heart aches for him. Will he ever be the same again?

'Roth.' Constance's voice is almost a whisper, and she shakes her head sadly. 'That maniac.'

'You knew him?'

'I did.'

'Then you know about the Punch?'

She nods. 'I thought it vanished with him. This was . . . *breezes* . . . thirty-five, forty years ago now. My older self had just Moved me up because she was afraid of Roth and his experiments.'

Leonard told me about Roth's experiments in the future. About how they hurt Movers beyond all repair. Just so he could figure out a way to get back to Gabby. It makes me wince just thinking about it.

'Pungit experimentation,' Constance says with a hollow laugh. 'He was supposed to be trying to *help* Shade Unit against the Nowbies. He seemed so dedicated to the cause that my older self, stupidly, introduced him to the Aberrants she had united at the time. She thought, what with our pungits working differently than most, we could help him and his experiments.'

I can't even imagine what a man like Roth would do with the Aberrants. 'What happened?'

'There was one young man, an Aberrant who had an ability that was basically the opposite of yours, Mathis. Instead of throwing pungits, he could steal them. And that talent became the inspiration behind Roth's Punch technology. Roth held the young man prisoner until he could figure out how to harness his abilities. I helped the Aberrant escape, of course, but the damage was done. Roth was obsessed with figuring out how to steal pungits, and he started experimenting on Shade Unit members. Never imagined he actually managed to make the blasted thing work.'

'He did,' I say. I wonder how much she knew about what he did to those Movers and Shadows he experimented on.

'So this Punch,' says Blue, 'you need it so you can get back to the past and save your friend who started all of this pungit insanity?'

'Yes.'

'And *if* you get your hands on it—'

'That's a big if,' points out Mathis.

'If,' agrees Blue, 'then you need someone else's pungits to get back to the time you came from?'

'I don't like it,' says Zombie. 'Just who are you gonna get to give up their pungits for you?'

In truth, I have no idea. I'm not even sure how I'd find them. But if I don't have the Punch, it doesn't matter much anyway.

'The bigger question,' says Rads, 'is who would let you?'

'No one,' answers Constance, firmly, and she frowns at me. 'No one in their right mind, anyway. It's not right. It's unnatural. I'm sorry, Patrick, but taking another Mover's pungits, that's something BMAC does. Not us.'

'But, you don't understand. I'm not—'

'Not what?' Constance interrupts me. 'Not asking to steal the connection of one of your own? You might as well ask to steal the breath from someone's lungs. How can you expect us to justify that?'

I guess I can't.

Blue glances at me, an apology in her eyes, and it makes me lose my grip on what little hope I was holding onto.

Bo is silent on his end, but I can feel him agreeing. I can't just steal someone else's pungits. And even if I could, how would I ever find someone with a Mover in the right time and place?

My chest feels tight, my uniform is strangling me.

I try to breathe. The room is too small. I have to get out. I jump up off the table and my vision blurs, head pounding – the neural binders bruised my mind.

Blue holds out a hand to steady me. 'Easy, Patrick.'

But it's not easy. None of this is. There's no answer to saving my family or Gabby that's easy.

I rip my arm away and stumble for the door, throwing

it open to a dark and narrow cement hallway. Gabby's eyes, staring up from the operating table, begging me to fix it, bore into my brain and a sting begins to form at the back of my throat.

I lean against the wall for support and something in my pocket jabs uncomfortably into the back of my thigh. I pull out the Cure vial Pilot gave me back at the wager lair. I forgot I was carrying it. What I wouldn't give to have had this before everything started. To just stick it in my arm and be done with being a Mover.

Bo drifts into my head, a cooling presence, trying to soothe me, but it's no use. I've ruined everything. Ruined Gabby, ruined pungits, ruined Pilot. How could I possibly fix everything? Everything I've tried to fix just turns into a bigger mess.

Bo's still quiet, doing his best to calm my mind.

Go on, say it, I tell him. *'I told you so.' You want to say it, so say it.*

He doesn't.

'Stop it!' I growl, pushing him back from me. *Stop acting like you care. You never wanted me to succeed. Stop pretending to feel sorry for me!*

I'm not pretending, Patrick.

I wish that he were.

There's a chirp, and I'm surprised to see Tungsten in front of me. He cocks his little silver head, confused by my outburst.

Someone clears their throat and I look up to see Blue, standing in the hallway, with Pilot, his arm draped over her shoulder. He takes his arm back and does his best to move on his own, hobbling along the wall and lowering himself to sit beside me.

My palm closes around the Cure. I don't want him to have to look at it. Don't want him to know that I thought this little bit of liquid could protect my sister Maggie, could protect Gabby from their Shadow. But there's no way to get back to them. I suppose I have to accept that now. And I feel guilty for even thinking about using it on myself.

He keeps his eyes on the floor, his red one dull and dark, a very different boy than the excited, energetic one I'd met back at the Block.

'Pilot.' My eyes well up and I wipe the tears away, ashamed that I'm the one crying after what I've done to him. 'I'm so sorry, Pilot.'

He holds out a hand for Tungsten, who slithers into his lap and nuzzles against his chest. Pilot's face is blank. As if I haven't said anything. And I can't blame him for not wanting any apology from me.

I let my head fall back against the wall and I stare at the ceiling, willing myself to stop crying. 'I should have never dragged you into this. Bo was right. I should have just accepted that this place, this time, is my life now. I can't fix anything. It's impossible.'

Pilot sighs, petting Tungsten. 'You're wrong.'

'What?'

'About not being able to fix anything,' he says, quietly. 'You're wrong.'

'No, I'm not. Weren't you listening? Constance said—'

'I know what Constance said.' He shrugs weakly. 'So what?'

'So what? Pilot, of all people, you should know I can't just *take* someone's pungits. And even if I could, how would I know how to find them? It's impossible. I'm just . . . Nothing I've done is going to change anything. Everything that brought me here, it just . . . stops.'

He looks at me then, the first time since he lost his pungits, and the light in his red eye flickers. 'Only if you let it.' He sighs, and looks back down at Tungsten. 'You know I wasn't always like this? On my own? I had a family.'

I guess he can see the shock on my face because he nods like he expected to see it. I don't know why I'm so surprised. Of course he had a family. He came from some-where, didn't he? I can't believe I never wondered about it before now.

'In Avin,' he said.

My breath stops. Nowbies.

'I was pretty young when the war ended. I don't remember a whole lot from those days. But I do remember my mother and her brown hair and the way her clothes always smelled like soap. She always tried to get me to drink her cactus and potato smoothies. They tasted like feet. I remember my dad. He could juggle oranges. When the war ended, a man came to our home. My grandfather, I think, but I don't know. I remember how upset they all were. My parents and the old man. And I knew it was cos I was a Mover. They'd kept it secret somehow, my parents. I don't know how they did it. Maybe things were really disorganised at the end of the war, but they managed to hide it all the same. Anyway, the old man, when he came to our home, he told my parents I would have to go away. I was scared, but not as scared as my parents. They cried and begged him not to make me go. You know what he said?'

I shake my head.

'"Impossible." I'll never forget the way he said it. "Impossible." And my parents . . . they just cried. They didn't argue. They just cried and held me until BMAC came. I remember the grey of their uniforms. Their grip on my arms hurt. And my parents . . . they didn't fight. They didn't try to come with me. It was like I wasn't even me any more. I was just . . . a Mover.'

More hot tears burn my eyes.

'I remember,' he goes on, 'after BMAC dropped me off in the middle of Dune's Thoroughfare, I was all alone, except for . . .' He grabs his head, and sniffs, trying to suppress his own tears. 'My Shadow was there with me. And I remember, I was thinking that it was impossible, for me, young as I was, to survive out there, alone in the Movers' sector. My Shadow, she sent me this feeling. This warm, glowing, bright feeling. She didn't want me to give up. Because she didn't think it *was* impossible. Not for us.' He looks so sad when he says it, it makes my heart hurt worse for him. 'Now, I've lost my pungits. Lost my . . .' He stops himself, he can't even say the word 'Shadow', it's too painful. 'Movers would say that makes me a Nowbie. Nowbies would say I'm still a Mover.'

'But I don't care what anybody says, I know what I am. I'm a Mover. And I'm not gonna stop fighting because of this. So you can't stop fighting, either,' he says. 'Because it's only impossible if you think it is.'

I want to believe Pilot's right and that I can save everyone back in my time. But so far, all I've done is screw everything up.

'You said nothing you do changes anything, but you already know that's not true,' Pilot goes on. 'You told me you're the reason Beadie Hartman discovered pungits.'

I wince at the reminder and glance over at Blue. Her eyes go wide but she doesn't interrupt.

'You doing that,' says Pilot, 'changed the world.'

'Great,' I mutter, tears stinging my eyes again. 'For the worse.'

'Maybe. But if you already changed it once, you know you can change it again. Maybe this time for the better.'

'How?'

'Fix it,' he says. 'Save your friend. Don't give Hartman the pungits.'

I blink at him, suddenly aware of just how much is at stake. If I can save Gabby, if I can stop Maggie from Moving Roth, then I never go to BMAC, I never show Hartman the pungits – I look down at the blue liquid almost glowing in my hand – and BMAC never gets their hands on the Cure.

Blue crouches down, her eyes fixed on mine. 'Can you do that?'

'I don't—' My mind races, my heart hammering. Saving Gabby doesn't just keep her from the Shelves. Saving Gabby means saving all of us. And it's fallen to me. 'I mean—' Can I? After everything?

Blue's gaze is intense, I can almost see the gears of her mind turning.

I nod, my voice cracking. 'Yeah. I mean, yes. Yes, I can. But without the Punch—'

She stands, heading back to the door. 'We'll get you the Punch.'

'You can't. The vault door is too smart.' Bo told me that.

'We'll find a way,' she says, like it's barely a footnote. 'I've been rewiring AI my whole life. How do you think I got Tyke to stop taking orders from BMAC?'

I glance at the CoyoTank sitting vigilantly by a door down the hall I hadn't noticed before. I never did wonder why he was so obedient to her and now that I know, Blue is even more intimidating than she already was.

I shake my head, remembering the bigger problem. 'I'd still need someone's pungits—'

'I'll get you the pungits.'

'How? You know where I can find pungits that reach back to 5th of March, 2083?'

She stops, her hand on the door, and takes a deep breath through her nose. 'I've been Moving myself up through time since 2017, Pat. I'm connected to every year since.'

I blink, trying to comprehend just how her special Movement works, how that helps me. 'What are you saying?'

She turns back, her eyes flashing. 'I'm saying for the pungits you need, you can have mine.'

PAT
2383

'Blue, wait!' I scramble to my feet, pocketing the Cure and catch the door before it closes.

'Have your what?' Constance stands in front of Blue, arms folded.

'Jacket,' she says, a little too quickly, and pulls it off her shoulders, tossing it back to me with a warning look. 'All he's got is that stupid cadet uniform. He's going to need something else to wear. Him and Pilot.'

'We'll find them something to wear,' says Constance. Her eyes shift to me then. 'Are we all right now?'

'He just needed some air,' says Blue.

I stand there, gaping, not sure why Blue is lying.

The old woman nods. 'I'm so sorry about your friend, Patrick, I truly am. I so wish you could help her. But I think you'll find that here with us, with Shade Unit, you'll be able to help a lot more people.'

'He knows that,' says Blue with a smile, and turns back to me.

I just stare back. What is she doing?

There's a chirp at my ankles and Tungsten coils around them. Pilot's still in the hallway. I hear him grunt and when I glance back he's there, struggling to get up.

'Hang on,' I tell him, and hurry over to help him stand.

'I'm OK,' he says, waving me off, wincing as he rises on shaky legs. He's in worse shape than I am. The residual pain from the neural binders must still be in his head, like it is for me, but the physical effects of the Cure have taken a lot out of him.

He catches me watching and frowns. 'What? I said I'm fine.'

'I just—' I don't know what to say. He's not fine. He'll never be fine. 'I just wanted to say thank you. Thanks for what you said. About how I could still fix things.'

He shrugs. 'It's the truth.'

I wish I could fix what's happened to him. I wish I never made him come to BMAC at all.

'It's so quiet.' He leans against the wall and rubs his head, furiously. 'Inside my head, now that my Shadow—' he stops, tugging at the roots of his hair. 'God, how do the Nowbies stand it?'

I don't answer him. He doesn't expect me to. Bo's been inside my head all my life. I can only imagine what it's like for Pilot without his Shadow – an empty, gaping silence.

On impulse I reach out for Bo – he's been very quiet – and when I find him he's closed himself off from me, like a person with their back to you in the dark.

I'm here, Patrick, he assures me, before turning back in on himself.

Something's wrong. Something has upset him.

I have to go back, Bo, I tell him, wishing he would just understand. *If these Aberrants can help me do it, I have to go.*

If, he repeats, and I hate that he doesn't believe we can do it.

Fine, Bo. Be that way. I've got this far without your help, I can go the rest of the way too.

Without my help?

You're not the only person in my life! My mind is on fire I'm so angry, the pain from the neural binders increasing. *I have a family, and friends! People I love! I can't just stay here because you want me here!*

Bo backs away from me, I can feel the hurt coming from his end. I didn't mean to be so angry with him. The truth of it is, losing my connection to Bo scares me more than anything I've done so far.

'Are you all right?' Pilot's staring at me, one eyebrow raised, and I realise I'm scowling.

'Sorry,' I tell him. 'Head hurts.'

He nods and continues to make his way towards the door on his own. I follow close behind, just in case he needs a hand. Before we make it, the door flies open and Zombie, Mathis and Psychic storm out, marching by us with purpose.

'What's going on?' Pilot asks.

'They're going to rally Bash and the Block.' Blue stands in the doorway, an excited glint in her eye.

The three men stop by the door Tyke is guarding, and pull it open.

'What is all this?' splutters a voice I recognise. 'Do you know who I am?'

The High Minister. They drag him out by the arms, Connie following, as the old man kicks and shouts.

'What are they doing with him?' I ask.

'He's the key into BMAC.'

'Into BMAC?'

'It's happening. It's what we've all been waiting for since the war ended. Shade Unit is finally moving in on the Cure facility.'

'Now?!'

'We're ready for it,' says Blue. 'We've been planning for this for years. We just needed the final piece of the puzzle – the location of the Cure facility. We can't afford to wait any longer.'

'What about our plan?'

'I'm already in contact with my earlier self. March 5th, 2083.'

My breath catches in my throat. I nod.

'She's ready for my say-so, we just have to use the Punch to transfer my pungits.' Blue glances over her shoulder before slipping into the hall with us and closing the door gently behind her. 'We're going to get into that Time Cache' – She watches Zombie, Mathis and Psychic disappear around a corner, and then looks me in the eyes – 'and we're going to get you home.'

GABBY
2083

'Are you all right?'

Blue leans over me. She has her hand pressed gently to my forehead. My head aches. Beyond the platform, the other Movers watch me with concerned faces. I turn my head and see the wall. The handprints. The black smear where my hand fell away. My Shadow – he managed to take me down again. He's so strong. So much stronger than I am.

How long until I can't control him at all?

'Gabby?' says Blue. 'Can you hear me?'

I force myself to sit up. It makes my brain hurt more. 'Yeah, I just, I'm sorry.'

'Don't be sorry.'

But I am. I don't know what I was thinking. Coming here. Joining this Movement. How am I supposed to fight the Nowbies when I can't even win the battles in my own mind? My Shadow's right. I am a coward. I'm not like these people. I'm the daughter of We Are Now members. If my father knew where I was right now . . . calling BMAC on me would be too kind a punishment.

'This was a mistake,' I say, getting to my feet. 'I should go.'

'Go? You just got here. Your handprint—'

'I can't.' My voice is louder than I mean it to be. Blue watches me, surprised. 'It's not – I mean, I'm not—'

'You're not what?' she asks. 'One of us?'

'I just shouldn't be here. I have to go.' I hurry off the stage, pushing my way through the crowd. I'm so embarrassed. So ashamed.

So foolish.

Leave me alone.

I'm sorry for what I had to do back there, but I'm glad you're finally understanding your situation.

My situation?

You are what you are. Nothing will change that.

And what am I?

Mine.

Tears sting my eyes. I come to the fire escape. Rush down the stairs.

'Gabby!' Blue calls above me. 'Wait!'

I don't. But Blue is faster than I am. She catches up easily. 'Hang on a second, will you?'

Her eyes search me, trying to get me to look at her. I don't want to look at her. Don't want to talk about it. 'Please, I just want to go.'

'But what happened? One second you were making your mark and the next . . . What made you change your mind?'

I breathe in the cold night air. How do I explain? How

do I tell her she's got the wrong girl? 'I'm just not meant for this kind of thing.'

'What are you meant for?'

The question catches me off guard. I don't have an answer to that. Don't know that I ever will.

She looks up at the sky. 'Do you believe in destiny?'

I don't understand. All the same, I don't know that I do. But I'm not sure if that's what Blue wants to hear. 'Do you?' is all I can think to say.

She bites her bottom lip. Rubs her arms. 'My Shadow isn't like yours,' she says.

That's for sure.

'My Shadow and I, it's . . . it's a complicated relationship.'

Maybe we have more in common than I realised.

'Anyway,' she says, 'sometimes I wonder, if the reason I was born so different from everyone else – I wonder if it's my destiny to do something great. Do something bigger than most people.'

I've never thought about it like that. Never thought that being stuck with my Shadow, the kind of Shadow that he is, could be for a reason.

'Like what?'

Blue shrugs. 'I don't know. I just know I was born a Mover to do something important. Tomorrow, I think I'm going to get to do that something.'

'At the protest, you mean?'

'I don't know. Like I said, my Shadow doesn't work like yours.'

'You don't know anything about my Shadow.' I don't know why I said that. I didn't mean to snap at her.

But Blue doesn't seem offended. 'No,' she says simply. 'I guess I don't.'

I wish I could feel the way she does. That I was born this way to do something important. I think of my pungit ray, lying on the floor of my bedroom. If I can make the ray work – if I can see the thing that makes a Mover Move, then maybe, just maybe, I could cure it.

A cramp seizes my mind. *There is nothing to cure!*

There is. And I will.

Except my pungit ray is at the apartment.

Blue stares at me. I'm wincing.

'You're not like other Movers, are you?' she says.

I shake my head. 'No. I don't think I am.'

She grins. 'Good. I like that.'

At least one of us does.

'That's exactly why I think you should come to the protest tomorrow,' she says. 'How long before the Nowbies find out about Movers like you and me? You think they'll be happy about it?'

Movers like her and me? Just what kind of Mover *is* Blue?

'How long before they try to Shelve us all, or worse, cure us!'

'Cure us?'

'Yeah,' says Blue, bitterly. 'Wouldn't BMAC love that. Getting rid of us all with a pill or something.'

I scratch my finger. 'Would a cure be so bad?'

Blue looks at me. It's like I've transformed into some hideous beast. 'What?'

'Not all Movers are so happy with their Shadows.'

She opens her mouth to argue. Stops herself. She looks

harder at me, like she's trying to figure me out. 'What's wrong with yours?'

I almost laugh. What *is* wrong with my Shadow? Too many things to count. 'I just don't think you should be so sure other Movers won't want a cure for their condition. It's not so easy for all of us.'

She lets that sink in for a moment, looking back up towards the sky. 'You know, you're the first person who's ever said that to me,' she says finally. Then she smiles at me. 'I'm impressed, Gabby. You're a lot more surprising than you look.'

My gaze falls to my feet. I hadn't meant to impress her. I just spoke the truth.

'That's exactly why we need you,' she says. 'You understand things we haven't even thought of.'

'No,' I insist, 'you don't need me. Other Movers could tell you—'

'You're not like other Movers,' she says again. 'I can tell. You're like us.'

'Us?'

'You can help so many Movers and Shadows, Gabby. Maybe some Movers want a cure, but that doesn't mean BMAC won't keep Shelving us! Doesn't mean We Are Now freaks won't keep blowing our businesses and our homes to bits with Nitromerc and trash bombs!'

That word. I saw it back home. On the jars in the boxes. Nitromerc.

'What did you just say?'

'I'm saying the Nowbies would do anything to get rid of Movers like you and—'

'No! About the Nitromerc.'

'It's a synthetic compound. Used in jet propulsion. But— What about it?' She watches me, frowning.

It's time to use force, Father said.

I have to stop him.

You can't.

'I have to go,' I tell Blue.

'Wait. Where are you going?'

'I just have to go!'

'But, Gabby, stop!' I glance back up, and she's leaning over the railing. 'Will you consider it? Joining us?'

I nod. But only so she'll let me go. When she smiles, I hurry down to the street below. I can't join Blue. Not tonight.

Tonight, my destiny is leading somewhere else.

PAT
2383

The Aberrants' transports are parked in a hangar above ground. Pilot, Tungsten, Blue, Tyke and I crouch low by a workbench strewn with spare parts and tools, watching silently as Constance shouts orders at Mathis, Psychic and Zombie, who are struggling to drag the High Minister aboard a hovercraft marked with BMAC's seal.

'BMAC?' I whisper.

Blue nods. 'They'll use the security codes provided by the High Minister to get into BMAC Headquarters.'

'Provided,' I repeat, watching the impressive fight the old man is putting up.

'He'll cooperate. If he doesn't want Mathis to spit his pungits onto him and make him a Mover.'

'He can do that?'

'Well,' shrugs Blue, 'only temporarily. But the High Minister doesn't need to know that. Once they're in, Psychic can try to take down the defence systems that guard the Cure facility. When they do, Shade Unit will be waiting to attack.'

'How does Psychic know how to do all that?'

Blue shrugs. 'He doesn't. But someone,' she taps her temple, 'someone in the future with more advanced tech knowledge will help him.'

Just then, the High Minister breaks free of Mathis's grip, and manages to swing at Psychic's face. Psychic ducks, but it's enough to knock his earmuffs loose. He readjusts them, making sure they are securely fastened, and I wonder what kinds of voices whisper in his head.

Bo waits on the fringes of my mind. He hasn't paid much attention to me since I got mad at him. And even now he seems distracted, more interested in whatever is happening in the world around him than the world around me. It's just as well. I'd rather he ignore me than put doubts and fears into my head.

'Once they get him secured onboard, Constance will finish double checking the outside reinforcements of the HC. Then they'll load up and double check the onboard computers,' explains Blue. 'Daytime Eventualies make for dangerous flying, and Constance is going to obsess over the HC's safety features. While they are distracted with the computer, we can sneak into the cargo hold.'

I glance back at Pilot, who shrugs, Tungsten's red glowing eyes blinking nervously.

'Why all the secrecy?' I ask her. 'Why don't you want Constance to know what we're doing? What *you're* doing?' As grateful as I am for Blue's help, her decision to give me her pungits without talking to Constance makes me uncomfortable. 'I mean, you guys are connected. Doesn't she already know what you're thinking anyway?'

'Don't be dense,' says Blue. 'We have *some* privacy from each other. We don't just wander aimlessly through each other's heads without an invitation. We have more discipline than that, obviously.'

I try not to blush. That's how it works for me and Bo. I guess Constance and Blue operate on a higher level than we do. She's an Aberrant, after all.

'I just meant,' I say, 'shouldn't you discuss it with her first? This affects her too, doesn't it?'

Blue turns away from me. 'She won't want me to do it.'

I had a feeling that was the issue. And now I'm even more uncomfortable. 'Why not?'

Blue doesn't move, but I can hear her take a deep breath through her nose.

'Blue?'

'Because it means I die.'

At first I don't think I understand her right. Die? 'What do you mean you—'

But she's gone before I can even ask, sneaking across the hangar floor towards the HC, waving at the rest of us to follow. Mathis, Zombie and Psychic are gone, already onboard, and Constance has her back to us, tightening a bolt on the side of the craft.

Blue huddles close to a nearby StrikeBike and holds her hand out for us to stop. We do, crouching down behind her, the quiet grinding of the gears in Tyke's head like a purr beside my ear.

My mind is racing. Die, she said. Both of them. But how can that be? I remember what Psychic called her – a vampire. Blue can't die. She's been alive for centuries.

Constance finishes tinkering and heads onto the ramp into the HC. Blue motions for us to follow her again. When we're behind the HC, Blue sets to work loosening a panel at the back, opening a cramped space, barely wide enough for Tyke to wedge himself through.

She nods for us to get in and Pilot doesn't argue, he and Tungsten climbing into the dark, pressed up against Tyke.

'Wait,' I say. 'What did you mean back there? What are you—'

Her hand clamps down on my mouth, and I can hear Psychic's voice as he disembarks, doing one last check on the outside of the HC.

Blue shoves my head hard, down into the cramped space and I wriggle in beside Pilot, Blue shoving in beside me, closing the panel with a click. In the dark, I can just make out her face, thanks to the little bit of light from Tungsten and Tyke's glowing eyes.

'Blue,' I hiss. 'Answer me. What did you mean back there?'

'I meant what I said,' she snaps. 'Now *shh*.'

'But—'

Her elbow rams my gut as Psychic's voice gets closer, the hull of the HC clanking from whatever he's adjusting. I can feel the Cure vial in my pocket, digging into my hip bone. The three of us lie side by side, silently in the dark, until the clamouring stops and Psychic's voice fades away from us.

'But you're a Loop Mover,' I say, as if she needs reminding. 'You can live for ever, you said so yourself.'

She stares up at the roof that's just inches from her nose. 'Until I break the loop.'

'I don't understand.'

Blue turns away from me, her knees pulled up into her chest as the HC rumbles to life.

'Pat,' says Pilot, 'if she gives you her pungits, then that's it. She can't Move her younger self up when she gets old. She can't continue the chain.'

It takes me a second to process but finally I get it. By giving me her pungits, she's giving up her immortality.

'If I tell Constance,' says Blue, 'she'll try to stop me. Constance has spent her whole life protecting Aberrants, Pat. She's part of a legacy of Blues and Constances that have protected Aberrants for hundreds of years. And she'll want me to keep that legacy alive. If I help you, I can't do that any more. The whole thing will stop with me. And she won't like that.'

The magnitude of what Blue is planning to do for me sinks in, and my armpits soak through with a nervous sweat. 'Why would you do that for me?'

'I'm not doing it for you,' she snaps. 'I'm doing it for everyone else. You said you can change history so Beadie Hartman never discovers pungits. If you can do that, you can stop BMAC from getting their hands on the Cure. We can keep it from BMAC and the Aberrants can protect it.'

My throat feels dry. The weight of what she's telling me is starting to feel too heavy. 'I think you need to talk to Constance. I mean, if you told her, wouldn't she feel the same way you do? You're the same person!'

Blue shakes her head. 'Constance is old, Pat. Her whole

life has been protecting the Aberrants. She's too old to change that now. She *won't* change it now. I have to make this decision for us.'

'But, how do you know it's the right one?'

'When I first realised what I was, what I could do,' she says, 'I always wondered *why me*? Why was I born so different from everybody else? There had to be a reason. I made that reason fighting for Movers and Shadows, fighting to save them from the Nowbies that want to hurt us. That's why I made Shade Unit. And then I discovered other Movers that were different, unique like me, and I thought maybe that was the reason. Maybe I was born to protect them.' Her voice is shaky. The HC vibrates as it lifts off, rattling my bones. 'I've been fighting for Movers for almost three hundred years,' she says. 'I keep myself alive, decade after decade, because I think it's the only way I can protect all of us.' She turns over then, her eyes meeting mine. 'Until you. If you can go back, if you can keep the Cure from BMAC, then we won't just be protecting Aberrants. We'll be protecting all Movers.'

My throat is so dry I'm afraid my voice has evaporated altogether. She's talking like I'm some kind of saviour. I can't be. I'm not going back to save *all* Movers, I'm going back to *save my sister and Gabby*. I can't let Blue do this for me if she's doing it because she thinks it's fate.

'Blue, I—'

There's a groan from the HC's hull and the whole craft lurches sideways, tossing the three of us like luggage. My head rams the side. There's a grunt from Blue as her back collides with the wall and Pilot yelps when my elbow hits his stomach.

The wind outside the vehicle screams, ramming the HC and threatening to take the whole thing down.

'The Eventualies!' Blue yells over the noise. 'I told you they were no joke!'

My stomach flips as the HC drops altitude so suddenly, I'm weightless for a split second, and then my head slams into the roof, Pilot's foot coming down hard on my shin.

'How much farther?' I shout.

'Ten minutes!'

In that little space, ten minutes is an eternity, and by the time I feel the HC dropping again, my whole body is bruised. The HC shakes and rattles and surges as we try to land in the pounding winds, and I close my eyes, begging myself not to throw up all over Blue and Pilot.

Finally, the HC's engines stop rumbling. We must have landed, but it's hard to tell since the vehicle is still shaking from the strength of the Eventualies. Outside, we can hear the voices of Mathis, Constance and Psychic. They've left the HC.

'Where's the High Minister?' I ask.

'He's with them,' she says. 'Bound and covered up.'

Bound. The neural binders.

'Now what?' asks Pilot.

'We wait.' Blue props herself up on her elbows, her lip bloodied. 'It's the middle of the day, Headquarters will be deserted. Plan is to use the High Minister's codes to get them into the Defence Minister's office. Once they do that, we'll head to the Time Cache.'

'How will we know if they've done that?' I ask.

'If there's no alarm after a few minutes,' she says, 'we'll know.'

Great.

'Once they are inside, we have to move fast. BMAC will be so busy with Shade Unit attacking the mines, they won't be watching their own Headquarters. But it won't take long for the system to send out an alert. Hopefully the strength of the Eventualies slows them down enough to give us time.'

'What about all the borg security?' asks Pilot.

'If Psychic can take down BMAC's defence systems, that should disrupt the GuardBorgs and CoyoTanks,' she says. 'They shouldn't be a problem.'

You can't be sure of that. I nearly leap out of my skin, Bo jumping into my thoughts so suddenly he might as well have screamed.

What are you doing back? I don't need your help.

Patrick, you cannot be certain those borg securities will be disrupted by what these Shade Unit people are trying to do.

I want to yell at him again, want to tell him to mind his own business and stop putting doubt into my head. But Bo's an expert in borgs and I can't bring myself to ignore him.

'Are you sure?' I ask Blue, nervously.

'Pretty sure.'

That doesn't give me a lot confidence.

This is a mistake, Patrick.

I'm beginning to worry Bo's right. I'm mad that he's done it again, made me doubt myself. Made me doubt Shade Unit. Made me doubt Blue. *Do not get off that HC*, he tells me. *Just stay where you are.*

Why?

'They're inside,' grins Blue. 'Let's go.'

'Blue, wait.'

Before I can stop her, she kicks open the cargo-hold panel, and the Eventualies rush in, instantly blistering my skin with dust and debris. I cough and sputter, trying to shield myself from the onslaught. I climb out after her, the rush of the wind deafening in my ears.

'Blue!' I shout. 'Maybe we should—'

Blue stands a few feet ahead of me, statue still, her blue hair whipping in the wind.

And just ahead of her, surrounding the HC, standing between us and the BMAC building, are twelve furious CoyoTanks.

PAT
2383

The winds scream, drowning out the wail of BMAC's sirens. My skin and my eyes burn, battered by sand and pebbles and dirt and garbage. Blue was right. Daytime Eventualies are no joke. If I didn't know it was the Movers' wind, I'd be sure I was standing inside a cyclone. It's all I can do to keep my feet on the ground.

But the CoyoTanks – they are boulders. Solid. Immovable. Glowing eyes narrowed on me, Blue and Pilot.

'I thought you said they'd be disabled!' shouts Pilot beside me.

'They should be!' she says. 'Unless Psychic can't get into the system . . .'

One of the CoyoTanks, the one standing in front, snaps its jaws in warning.

Blue stares ahead, straight at the lead CoyoTank. And it stares back, the rest of them watching us stock-still and ready to pounce.

My heart hammers behind my ribs. *Bo . . .*

I can feel him there, in the meat of my brain, my fear mixing with his own. *Wait.*

Wait? Wait for what?

Then Tyke squeezes out of the HC. The lead dog jerks upright in surprise. Slowly Tyke stalks his way past me and Pilot to stand protectively beside Blue. The other borgs shift positions, obviously excited now, eager to punish their traitorous brother. And Tyke is up for the challenge. I think back to the first time I saw him, in the alleyway, the way he took on six CoyoTanks by himself.

But this is double that many.

The lead dog slinks towards Tyke, head low and snarling. Tyke moves to meet it as the rest of the dogs begin to circle.

Just wait . . .

I am waiting. Waiting for the first move. For the crash of metal. For the brawl to begin.

And it does. The lead CoyoTank lunges at Tyke's neck and Tyke is ready, dipping his head low and tossing the monster over his head.

And then the world explodes.

The waiting CoyoTanks jump into the fray, heavy armour thunking against itself, artificial snarls and the scream of tearing metal competing with the howl of the wind. The sand and dust flying into my eyes makes it hard to see, but between stinging blinks I watch as Tyke hurls one dog after the other, glinting metal teeth ripping into the wires of one borg and then the next. But the dogs keep piling on.

'Tyke!' Blue screams, and for a second I worry she's going to jump in to the tangle of snapping jaws.

Pilot's hand grabs my shoulder, his fingers digging in. 'We have to go!' he screams. The borgs are distracted. Now's our chance.

'Blue!' I shout. 'Blue! Let's go!'

But she can't turn away from the fight, or take her tearful eyes off Tyke as he struggles against the rest. He's losing. There are just too many. We don't have much time.

Pilot and I take hold of her arms, tugging at her to run. 'Blue, we have to go *now*!'

One of the CoyoTanks, one of the few waiting on the fringes of the battle, turns its head in our direction. It lets out a mechanical yip, and the other three waiting CoyoTanks turn their gaze on us.

'Blue!' I scream, and that sets them off. The waiting CoyoTanks leap into a sprint, and Blue's tear-stained eyes finally see them and me, pulling at her arm.

I don't have to say it again. Blue takes off running, Pilot and I trailing behind her. She darts left, away from the fight and to the doors of the BMAC Headquarters beyond. I don't know where she's going. I don't know if she knows. But we follow her just the same. The winds hammer our bodies as our feet pound the ground, the CoyoTanks closing the gap with every step.

'Look out!' Blue screams, just as something carried by the wind, something big, the piece of a rooftop maybe, comes swooping over me, nearly taking off my head.

There's a yelp, and when I look back, the giant piece of debris has smashed into one of the CoyoTanks, sending it sprawling so two of the others trip and fumble over him.

Pilot pumps a fist into the air, 'Yeah!' but it's too soon

to celebrate. Through the dust and sand I can see the rest of the CoyoTanks in pursuit.

Tyke lost the battle.

Hang on, Bo says inside my head, and a wave of nerves from his end ripples across my mind.

Ahead of me, Tungsten's glowing red eyes pop out of Pilot's collar, and the little borg slithers down his body and to the ground, coming apart into separate sections. I leap over one of the little silver balls as it rolls past, headed for the borgs.

The little borg's body parts spread out across the advancing line of CoyoTanks.

Pop!

Light bursts at the foot of one tank, sending it somer-saulting.

Pop! ·

Pop!

Two more on the right go down.

But the little borg's charges aren't enough. The fallen CoyoTanks get right back up, slowed but not stopped.

Ahead of me, Blue pulls away, too fast for me and Pilot, until I can barely see her through the haze of debris.

Another piece of debris flies at us, and Pilot swerves, trying to duck, but trips and goes down, his leg coming out and catching me, taking me down with him.

My chin hits the ground hard, my palms torn and bloody. Beside me, Pilot lays over the thing that tripped him up – Blue. She clutches at her forehead, bloodied from where debris hit her.

There's a low rumble, and when I look up, the CoyoTanks

have surrounded us, a terrifying snort hissing through their artificial nostrils.

Patrick— Bo can feel it, feel my terror. It's hurting. But I can't control it.

Just hold on, Patrick.

One of the CoyoTanks steps up to me, its titanium jaw open as it throws back its head and lets loose that unnatural howl. The rest of the borgs join in, creating a nightmare chorus. I scramble back, pressing against Pilot and Blue.

The CoyoTank lowers its head, jaws open.

I can't breathe. Can't think.

The jaws opens wider.

A buzzing of gears.

Wider.

A hiss of hydraulics.

Wider still. Too wide. Until it almost looks like the bottom jaw is barely hanging on.

A plume of steam explodes out the right back leg. More hissing from the rest of the pack, more steam.

The other CoyoTanks' mouths drop open, limp and useless as the light in all of their eyes blinks out.

The three of us sit there, pressed into each other, staring up at the motionless CoyoTanks. They've stopped. How have they stopped?

Blue is the first to move. 'They're offline,' she says, bewildered.

My chest rises and falls in panicked bursts and I press my hand over my heart, trying to stop it from pounding.

'Shade Unit?' asks Pilot.

Blue pokes at one of the open jaws as Tungsten, back

together again, slithers through the circle of dead borgs and up to Pilot.

Blue shakes her head. 'I don't think so.'

Bo bursts into my thoughts, his fear almost blistering. *Are you all right?*

And now that I'm not running for my life, now that I'm still and calmer, I feel his end more clearly. Fear yes, but more than that. Hope. Determination. A focus on a difficult task. I can see, briefly, what he's looking so hard at. Screens. Screens in a small dark space.

This was you, I realise. *You stopped them.*

A wave of relief floods out of him, and it's enough of an admission for me.

I see the screens and something else – the Avin Turbine. It's huge through the window of some kind of vehicle. Bo's looking at the Avin Turbine. At BMAC Headquarters.

You're here?!

There's a rumble over the sound of the wind, and above us, a Cure Bus, the same one I boarded and that Shade Unit raided, descends from the sky.

We are.

PAT
2383

The Cure Bus ramp door lowers with a hiss, and Rads steps out, a massive shock cannon slung across his chests.

'A little breezy out here!' he shouts, waving us over.

We dust ourselves off. Tungsten climbs onto Pilot's shoulder, and we hurry to join him boarding the bus.

Inside the dark space is Bash and the woman, Opal, who processed me at the Block, dressed all in black with the mark of Shade Unit stitched onto their shoulders, black handprints painted onto their faces. Carlin stands in a corner, wringing his hands nervously. And there beside him is Bo – he's bent over a pair of screens.

'What are you doing here?!' I blurt out.

You've nearly got yourself killed too many times for my liking. And you have no idea what you're getting yourself into with the Time Cache.

'Bo and Carlin showed up at my door not long after I found out we were moving on BMAC,' says Bash. 'Bo made me a deal, he'd help Shade Unit, if I helped him find you.

Good thing too, since it looks like Constance and her team can't get into BMAC's system.' He grins over at Pilot, looking for agreement, but Pilot drops his eyes to his feet, shuffling a little more behind me.

Bash's grin is replaced with a frown – he doesn't recognise this Pilot. Quiet. Serious. Sad. So different from the Pilot he sent into Avin. Bash doesn't know.

I watch Pilot, but he refuses to look up at me and I realise he's embarrassed. I wonder how long he'll avoid telling Bash that he's cured. My pocket suddenly feels heavy, and I'm aware of the Cure vial I'm carrying. The far wall glows faintly, lighting up the blue of countless vials just like mine.

'Miss Ashlinn.' Carlin's voice is barely a whisper. He claps his hands together like he can barely contain himself.

Blue looks at me, unsure.

Carlin moves towards her, holding out his hands. 'I cannot tell you what an honour it is to meet you at last.'

'Uh, Blue, this is Carlin,' I say by way of introduction. 'He's sort of a fan of yours.'

'You're my life's work,' he says, taking her hand to kiss it.

She pulls away. 'Charming.'

I try not to laugh as Carlin does his best to regain his composure, but he's too starstruck to do anything but gawk at Blue, who's decided not to notice.

'What's that?' She points at the object Bo's holding in his hand. I recognise it immediately – I'd seen him tinker with the same type of thing every night before bed.

'Pulse Block,' I answer.

'What's it do?' she asks.

That I can't say. *Security*, is all Bo ever said.

'It disables borgs,' explains Opal. 'Borgs and almost anything else not running on blood and oxygen.'

Blue nods. 'So that's how you took out the CoyoTanks?'

Bash laughs. 'No, the electromagnetic pulse on these suckers is only good for about six feet on one or two borgs.'

'Then how did you stop the CoyoTanks?'

All eyes turn to my Shadow, who's busying himself with the cube.

'Bo Hill,' says Pilot.

Blue's eyes go wide and it's the first time I've ever seen her look intimidated. 'You're Bo Hill?'

But Bo hasn't been paying any attention to the conversation. His focus is on the Pulse Block, his mind a mess of numbers and symbols that I can only imagine is code. Code – and the Time Cache.

Bo, I tell him. *You said it was nearly impossible to get into the Time Cache.*

Nearly. There is one way and I'm not confident, but it's the best chance we have of getting you inside.

You can do that?

I'm going to try.

I'm speechless, bewildered at this sudden change in Bo. What made him change his mind?

He can hear what I'm thinking, and he lifts his arm to point at my head. *You're so determined, I know that now. Even without my help, you'd just keep trying. I guess the only way I can protect you is to try and help you.*

Bo gets up and rummages on the shelf beside the unit

282

holding the numerous Cure vials, and picks up something small and black. *If I could change things, Patrick, for Mari, believe me, I would. You have a chance to do that.* His eyes meet mine, a fierce determination behind them. *I realise now that I owe it to Mari, and I owe it to you, to help you do that.* He takes my hand in his and presses the object into my palm — a small disc. The cartridge that administers the Cure. *I think you'll be needing this when we get you home.*

My eyes sting. I'm so grateful, so relieved, so happy to have Bo here, on my side, that I feel like I could storm BMAC and break open the Time Cache right this second.

'But,' I say out loud, 'you said you don't think we can get into the Time Cache.'

We can't, no. The vault would recognise us as intruders and launch its defence systems. The only thing that the vault permits in and out is the GuardBorgs. Bo taps the sides of the Pulse Block and it pulses with a glowing white light. *So, we'll just have to catch ourselves one.*

'*Catch* a GuardBorg?'

Blue's head whips round to look at me. 'He's kidding, right? No Mover can get close to a GuardBorg.'

Opal nods in agreement. 'Those things can sense pungits a mile away.'

They can, agrees Bo, holding the Pulse Block out to Pilot, *which is why there's only one person who can help us.*

GABBY
2083

I've never thought of Avin as beautiful before. But here, on the streets as night gives way to morning, everything is washed in a quiet hazy blue. The streets are empty. Even the crows seem to be asleep.

The flags above the city hall ripple as the Eventualies move through them. The wind feels strong today.

I stare up at the old building. It's one of the few buildings in Avin older than fifty years. It has a dome of mirrored glass, made to resemble a drop of dew, reflecting the stormy sky above it. It's beautiful. Hard to believe that anyone could bring their anger here.

But they do. There, between the two tungsten turbines that first measured the Eventualies, Movers and Nowbies come to protest each other. My parents have marched here many times. It's where Blue and her Shade Unit will march today.

I walk across the courtyard to the base of the first turbine.

Today. Tomorrow. Next week. It doesn't matter.
What doesn't?
What you're trying to do. The war will begin.

A soda can lies crumpled at the windmill's base. Several more strewn round the other. Still more cans lie abandoned in the tulip planters.

It's already begun.

I pick up one of the cans. It's completely crushed. Stomped on and flattened. I run my finger along the smooth bottom and my fingernail catches a seam where none should be. I dig in my nail. A panel lifts up. Inside, a light blinks green.

Trash bomb.

Sadness washes over me. This was what the Nitromerc in my parents' kitchen was for. They made these to hurt Blue and the others.

Nothing you do here will make a difference.

But it will. To Blue. To my father.

I press the slot beneath the tiny green light with my little finger, and just like any standard droidlet, the chip pops out.

I snap it between my fingers and the green light inside the can grows dim. I pick up the next one.

What will he say when his plan doesn't work out in the morning? I can see my father's face in my mind – see it twist the way it always does when he looks at me. But tomorrow it will be different. Tomorrow it will turn a deep shade of red. It will burn so red with fury that he might explode. And he won't know that it was me who put that look on his face this time.

I can make the difference.

Yes, you can make a difference, my Shadow says. *Unite us. Bring us together. And we will change the fate of Movers for ever.*

No. If I can do this here, for Blue, and the rest of them, maybe I can do it in the future too. I can do it alone. If I can just get home to recover my pungit ray.

You'll never make it work, my Shadow says darkly.

Yes, I promise myself. I will.

I pull out my silver droidlet. Check the time. 4:45 a.m. Father will be going to work soon. He'll wait for the news broadcast of victory, for them to report on a trash bombing, which will never happen. Mother will sit in front of our TV, waiting just like him. She won't leave for her shift until the middle of the afternoon. I won't be able to get in until she's gone.

What do I do until then?

Beyond the dome of the town hall, the skyscrapers of Avin reach towards a cloudy sky. In the middle, and a bit to the left, I see Romsey. I guess I'll just go to school.

PAT
2383

It's strange being inside BMAC when it's quiet like this. It's daytime, so everything is shut down and silent. But we need to overcome the Headquarters' high-tech borg security.

I stand nervously with Blue, behind Bo, trying to make sense of the numbers and symbols he's tapping into a glowing monitor. Rads and Opal watch the door, Shock cannons at the ready. So far, Bo's knowledge of BMAC's security systems has got us through the building without any problems. But I can feel his anxiety rising. We're deep in BMAC Headquarters now. Everything he's done to get us this far, those same tricks won't work against the borgs.

I hold my breath, watching as his fingers fly across keys, hoping he can finish whatever it is he's trying to do. Bo's led us to the BMAC Museum Office of Registration and Preservation, a big dark room full of switchboards and screens. This, according to Bo, is where objects are registered and prepared before being deposited in the Time Cache. Beyond Bo's monitor is a glass screen, and on the other side is a cleanroom – long white sterile counter, Tungsten lying lifeless in a tray.

'Uh-oh,' mutters Rads as I suddenly become aware of the echo of shoes stomping down the hallway. Rads and Opal step aside as Constance storms into the room, Psychic and Zombie behind her. Beyond them I can see Mathis pushing a bed. The High Minister is sitting on top with tape over his mouth, looking furious.

Bo stands up slowly, and I can feel a surge of nerves radiating out of him.

'What the breezes do you think you're doing, Captain?' she growls at Bash. 'Shade Unit is marching on RareCore right now and we need to get control of BMAC's defences.'

'I made a deal,' he tells her.

'A deal with who?'

Bo clears his throat. Constance looks up, and her face goes pale at the sight of him.

'Hello, Connie.' I almost laugh from surprise. English sounds strange coming out of his mouth.

'Bo.'

'Having trouble hacking into the system, are you?'

She glances back at the scowling High Minister. 'Just a bit of a defiant streak, is all.' She turns to Bo. 'You're back, then?'

'No,' he says simply, and sits back down to face the monitor.

'Bo, I—' she stops, not sure what to say, and I can feel the war of feelings swirling around Bo's brain – so many years of anger, of hate over what happened to his friends because Constance chose to protect the Aberrants instead of him. But also, a new understanding of why she did what she did.

288

'The High Minister's cooperation won't be necessary. The Tanks are all disabled,' Bo says. 'The shields will take some time.'

'You know how to take them down?'

'When I'm finished here,' he tells her.

She looks to Bash, who shrugs. 'I made a deal. Bo needs to retrieve an item from the Time Cache first.'

Constance frowns, too accustomed to giving orders to know what to do with herself.

Bo grins, unable to help taking a bit of pleasure in her discomfort.

Blue and I exchange a glance. If Constance doesn't like this, she really won't like what Blue is planning to do with their pungits. But Blue looks away from me, focusing hard on what Bo is doing on his screen. She's determined to go ahead anyway. And however uncomfortable it makes me, I'm grateful that she is.

Bo enters another string of numbers into the computer and behind the glass a mechanical arm lifts Tungsten from the tray, placing him neatly on the counter as the tray descends back inside. There's a hiss and a click as a panel in the wall next to Bash opens up and the tray returns to us.

'Now what?' asks Blue.

'Items for the Time Cache have to be processed and sterilised before their storage request can be sent out to the GuardBorgs,' Bash explains.

I watch as our item, Tungsten, is sprayed with something yellow by the robotic arm, then dried and polished and placed carefully in a glass box.

My eyes flick to one of the many screens that surround

us – there's one I've been checking incessantly since we arrived. It shows Pilot, in the museum, beneath the Eternity Clock, all alone in the dark. Pilot didn't hesitate when Bo laid out exactly what his role in this had to be. He agreed without so much as a pause. And I know it's because of Bash, because he wants to prove to his captain that he's still Shade Unit even though he's cured. But Bash would never abandon Pilot because of that. When Bash realised what had happened to his best runner, he didn't say anything. He just grabbed Pilot by the back the neck, and hugged him close, hanging on tight, a fierce anger in his firmly set jaw. It was then that I realised Pilot and Bash weren't just friends, they were like family.

I watch as Pilot stares up at the Eternity Clock, its arms growing and changing with each passing second. And with each passing second I wonder how many of those new arms are my fault, how many different ways the clock has seen what we're about to try to do play out.

Bo's typing stops, and everyone watches him, the silence in the room deafening.

It's coming.

No sooner does he announce it, then a door in the clean room slides open, and a GuardBorg approaches the counter. Its icy dead eyes are trained on the glass, its skeletal face grinning frighteningly at me.

'Can he see us?'

The GuardBorg's task is the safe transfer of the item to storage in the Time Cache, Bo assures me. *It's too focused on the task to notice anything going on outside of that.*

But its dead stare doesn't break as it approaches Tungsten, lifting the glass box. Still, Bo must be right, because it doesn't seem bothered by our presence. Doesn't seem to notice. I suddenly feel an uncomfortable similarity between me and the GuardBorg. How many dangers are lurking outside my focus right now? I glance again to the monitor showing Pilot.

'How's our boy?' Bash asks.

'In position,' says Blue.

The GuardBorg turns and leaves, carrying Tungsten out the door it came from.

Bo nods at Bash who points to Opal. Opal pulls the collar of her jacket close to her mouth. 'OK, Pilot.'

On the monitor, the red of his eye glows a little brighter and I know Opal's message has got through.

Pilot makes his way to the Time Cache, lifts his hands to his mouth and shouts into the dark. 'Hellooooooooo!' I hope Bo's right about this.

A long shadow spills across the museum floor, falling over Pilot. He freezes, and within seconds, the other Time Cache GuardBorg steps into sight.

'This is foolish,' says Constance. 'Bo, this is a bad idea.'

The GuardBorg marches up to Pilot. My teeth clatter in my mouth at the memory of the GuardBorgs before they grabbed us the first time.

Bo's head turns to look at me and I realise I'm squeezing his shoulder. I let go and grab hold of his chair instead as we all watch the GuardBorg, one arm out for Pilot. He stands firm and I feel the urge to shout, to tell him to run. But he doesn't budge, letting the GuardBorg seize him by the throat and lift him into the air.

The borg's eyes glow as it scans for Pilot's pungits and Constance lets out a curse. 'Breezes.'

Blue takes a deep breath beside me and I glance over, meeting her nervous gaze. Maybe Constance is right.

Pilot's feet touch the ground as the borg's scan is complete, but its hand doesn't leave his throat.

'It won't let go,' says Constance.

It knows his face, Bo tells me. *It recognises him from your stunt at Checkpoint Four. But without the pungits, poor dope can't make sense of the situation.*

This was what Bo was counting on. But the question is, how will the GuardBorg decide to react?

The two of them stay there, as if time is standing still, while the robot's mind tries to work out a solution.

And it does.

With its free hand, it opens up its palm.

'Running out of time here!' warns Blue.

The GuardBorg is holding neural binders.

'Bo,' I say nervously.

Then the second Time Cache GuardBorg, carrying the glass case with Tungsten inside, appears. It marches across the foyer without so much as glancing in the direction of Pilot and its partner.

Wait for it.

'Captain!' says Constance. 'That's your man in there.'

The neural binders lift into the air, and the memory of the crippling pain, the complete helplessness, floods my mind.

'Opal,' says Bash, 'tell him to activate the block.'

Not yet! Bo shouts in his language.

But Pilot doesn't have time. If the neural binders take control, he won't be able to activate the Pulse Block.

Bo catches my thoughts. *If the second borg doesn't get within range this whole thing will be for nothing*, he snaps.

Pilot's hand reaches slowly into his pocket. And the GuardBorg doesn't miss it. Its grip tightens and Pilot squirms.

The second GuardBorg marches closer, focused on its task with a brisk determination. Five steps from Pilot. Four steps. Three.

The binders move from the borg's palm, settling at the sides of Pilot's head.

Now! shouts Bo.

'Now, Pilot!' Opal orders.

He pulls the glowing block from his pocket. There's a ripple in the air around them. The Guard drops Pilot and he crumples to the floor as both borgs freeze, their knees buckle, and finally collapse, eyes dull and dead in the dark.

PAT
2383

The room is silent, save for the sound of my own pulse in my ears. The Pulse Block worked. But we're still only on step one.

'All right now,' Bo says in English, swivelling in his chair to face all of us, 'tell the boy he needs to access the occipital panel at the back of the skull.'

I watch Pilot on the monitor as Opal relays the instructions, and he pulls open the back of the GuardBorg's skull.

'Now, do you see the small blue rectangular panel? It should be glowing.'

'He does,' says Opal.

'Tap it twice, and that should release the LOEBS chip.'

I watch carefully as Pilot works on the screen, my eyes searching the fallen GuardBorgs for the slightest twitch or tremor. I realise Bo knows what he's doing with these borgs better than anyone, but still, after everything that's happened, I can't shake the nerves.

'Once he's removed the LOEBS chip, he can transfer

the chip from the little borg, but he'll need to make sure the unit is steady on its feet.'

Pilot digs into his breast pocket for Tungsten's LOEBS, feeding it into the dead GuardBorg's brain and closes up the back of the skull. The GuardBorg's eyes come to life and my bottom lip stings because I'm chewing on it too hard.

The GuardBorg sits up suddenly and Pilot jumps back. It shakes its head, trying to stay balanced.

'Did it work?' asks Blue.

The GuardBorg stops wobbling, steadying itself with one hand, and slowly turns to look at Pilot. The eyes glow white, alive and alert.

'Bo?' I ask.

And then the robot tilts its head, just like I've seen Tungsten do a hundred times before, and I can see Pilot smile on the monitor.

'He's online,' confirms Opal.

'All right then,' says Bash, 'everyone cross your fingers.'

I watch as Pilot hands the new and improved Tungsten the glass box containing the little borg's old body, and Tungsten stands on shaky legs.

'When he's stable,' instructs Bo, 'he can approach the Time Cache.'

'What happens then?' I ask.

'Hopefully, the vault recognises our decoy as part of a routine item storage, and opens up. Once the decoy is inside, it can retrieve the Punch.'

I watch as Tungsten walks off screen, in the direction of the Time Cache, and my toes tingle with excitement. For the first time, home is within reach. It won't be long now.

On another monitor we can see the giant vault door that protects the Time Cache. Tungsten walks into view. He enters the guardroom. I notice that the glass has already been replaced from when the GuardBorgs chased after me and Pilot.

Tungsten stands there, holding the glass box, as the centre dial on the door begins to glow. The inner ring begins to spin, and then the outer. A white light at the centre falls on Tungsten.

I hold my breath.

All at once the light disappears, the glowing dial goes dark, and Tungsten is left standing.

'Is that it?' asks Constance.

Just then, there's a series of clicks, echoing loudly through the halls, and the door begins to slide open.

I laugh. 'It worked!'

I can hardly believe it as Tungsten steps over the threshold and disappears into the darkness. When I see him again, I'll have my way home.

Blue's hand grabs hold of my arm. 'Do you see that?'

'What?'

She points back at the monitor with Pilot. He's standing at the edge of the screen with his back to us, looking off through the doorway that leads into the room with the Time Cache.

'There.' Her finger taps the screen where the second GuardBorg lies in the middle of the room.

Its eyes are glowing.

'It's awake.'

'How is it awake?' I shout at Bo.

'I don't' – Bo stammers – 'the Pulse Block disables smaller borgs for at least twenty minutes. These GuardBorgs, they're stronger than I—'

Without thinking, I sprint for the door, pushing through Rads and Zombie, Blue shouting behind me. 'Opal, tell him to get out of there!'

I barrel down the empty hallway, the sound of feet chasing after me.

'Patrick, wait!' cries Blue, not far behind.

Just ahead, the Eternity Clock comes into view, and I can see the GuardBorg, see it rise, the neural binders lifting out of its open palm.

'Pilot! Look out!'

But the GuardBorg is too fast – the neural binders shoot across the room and hook to Pilot before he even has a chance to turn round. He collapses, the GuardBorg on top of him in an instant, slinging him over its shoulder and carrying him through the open doorway into the Time Cache.

'Patrick!' Blue's beside me now, both of us running as fast as we can, the shouts of Bash and Rads and Zombie and the others echoing behind us. I glance back and see them all, Shock cannons cocked and loaded, racing to catch up.

Bo's in my head, telling me to stop.

But I can't stop. Pilot already paid the highest price for helping me. I can't let anything else happen to him.

I tear through the doorway to see the Time Cache, its massive vault gaping open into a black chamber. The GuardBorg stops in front of the vault, looking back at me and Blue before it disappears inside.

'Come on!' I shout to the others.

Patrick, Bo booms, *do not go into the vault. It wants this!*

I'm already disobeying, plunging into the darkness, Blue right behind me. The others are coming. They'll be here any second.

'Pilot!' I shout into the murk. He can't answer because of the binders, but I can hear the pounding of the GuardBorg's footsteps, and I keep running.

Until the screeching of metal echoes behind me.

I look back, and so does Blue, just in time to see Rads, Bash, Opal, and Zombie disappear behind the vault door as it thunders shut, sealing me and Blue inside.

PAT
2383

The air inside the Time Cache is cold, stinging my skin, and goosebumps bud on my arms. *It wants this*, Bo told me. The cold sinks into my bones.

I blink back the dark, forcing my eyes to adjust. We're standing between shelves. Shelves and shelves and shelves holding different artefacts I can't begin to make sense of. There's a dim light from somewhere above. I glance up and see what looks like the Eternity Clock. But it's different – it pulses with a blue light, and illuminates the ceiling so that I can tell the vault is one big circular chamber.

Bo sees it inside my mind, and he recognises it instantly. *The central cortex*, he says. *The brain.*

I remember what he told me once, about the Vault. About its intelligence. And Bo catches the memory.

Yes, he says, answering a question I didn't ask. *It knows you're in there.*

My muscles tense beneath my freezing skin. This is bad.

'Look there,' whispers Blue, pointing to a sign above the aisle. Numbers that read 2300-2400. 'Years,' she says. These artefacts must be from 2300 to now. Through the shelves I see more aisles, just like this one, leading towards the centre of the chamber. And somewhere, in another aisle, is another year – the year I came from.

Blue grabs my arm, pointing beyond the aisle where the light from the Vault's brain beams down onto an open space. The GuardBorg stands in the centre, Pilot in its arms.

'Come on,' she says, creeping towards them.

Before I can take a step to follow, I hear a sound I recognise. It stops me in my tracks. The buzzing of an electric charge. I glance back the way we came, and there on the wall is a panel, blinking with lights.

'Blue,' I whisper. 'Wait.'

A bolt of blue lightning explodes down the aisle, lashing out towards us. I throw Blue on the ground, landing on top of her.

'Stay down!' I scream, crawling frantically away as another blast strikes.

'What's happening!' cries Blue.

Another blast. And then another. Through the shelves more lightning flashes. 'The walls! It's coming from the walls! Get to the centre!'

We crawl our way towards the end of the aisle, strike after strike cracking just above our heads.

Blue rolls sideways, into the closest shelf, pulling at the lid of a giant crate.

Up ahead, I see the GuardBorg. The whips of lightning shoot past it, above it, around it, colliding with a rod that reaches up to the cortex. But the lightning doesn't come close to touching it.

The Vault isn't after the GuardBorg, says Bo.

The GuardBorg lays Pilot down onto what looks like an operating table, and it's then that I notice the other tables, lined up in the centre of the room.

'Hey!' I shout. 'Let him go!'

The GuardBorg looks back at us, watching us struggling to crawl beneath the incessant lightning strikes, before turning on a monitor attached to the table.

The other tables, I see now, aren't empty. Something lies on each, covered by a sheet, and out the end of each one, between flashes, I see what I've seen in the silos back in my time.

Feet.

Pale marbled feet.

Shelved bodies.

BMAC is keeping some of the Shelved in the Time Cache. People. Real People. Placed here like objects. Who else is lying in here? Why is the Time Cache also a tomb?

Trophies, Bo says. *BMAC's most prized prisoners.*

'Pat, stay down!' Blue jumps up, holding what looks like an early model of a Shock cannon, and fires back towards the panel on the wall that makes the lightning. It explodes with a hiss, but the other panels keep firing, the whole vault lighting up like a firework display. At least our aisle is clear.

I scramble to my feet as Blue turns it on the GuardBorg, 'Shut down!'

The green plasma explodes from the gun but the

GuardBorg turns around just in time to see it and ducks out of the way. The blast collides with the central cortex, but doesn't leave a mark.

The GuardBorg rises from where it fell, and Blue reloads, firing again, an inch too far to the right.

She reloads and takes aim, and the GuardBorg stalks towards us.

'Shoot it!' I scream. 'What are you waiting for, shoot it!'

'It's out of ammunition!' She tosses the gun, diving back for the crate. The GuardBorg breaks into a sprint.

'Hurry, Blue!'

She pulls another cannon, a later-looking model, and tries to load it but we're out of time. The GuardBorg stands a couple feet from us, lifeless eyes glowing white as it lifts its arm towards us. Something pokes out its wrist.

'What is that?'

Blue trembles, shrinking back from the robot. 'Neutraliser.'

I close my eyes, waiting for the blast.

I hear it before I feel it. A loud, heavy CLANG of metal on metal.

No pain.

I haven't been hit.

I open my eyes and the GuardBorg is on its back, pinned by another one.

Tungsten.

Tungsten holds the GuardBorg's arm as it fires uselessly into the air. The robots roll over each other, slamming into the shelves and sending crates and artefacts crashing to the floor.

Go, Patrick, Bo urges me. *Now!*

'Blue, come on!' I take off at a sprint, racing for Pilot. The centre of the vault is a shooting gallery, lightning exploding from every direction. I keep low, careful to keep in line with the panel Blue took out. Pilot lies there, eyes wide open, staring up at the ceiling, the lightning crashing above him.

'Hang on, Pilot!' I grab hold of the binders, tearing them off the side of his head and he screams, rolling off the table and clutching at his head. I know how bad his pain is, I've felt it, but there's no time to rest. We have to keep moving.

'Pat,' shouts Blue, helping me support Pilot. 'We have to get back to the door!'

The only lightning-free exit is blocked by the GuardBorg and Tungsten, pushing each other into the shelves and firing blast after blast. The GuardBorg throws itself into Tungsten, pinning him to the floor. Tungsten thrashes, but it's no use, and the GuardBorg rips Tungsten's left arm off. Tungsten flails, his shoulder sparking and crackling, and throws the GuardBorg sideways.

Bo's mind races, and I see the GuardBorgs in his mind, see them how he sees them – their make-up, like a schematic. The occipital panel.

'Tungst!' I shout. 'The panel! At the back of the head, the panel!'

Tungsten leaps, his knee coming down on the GuardBorg's neck, pinning it as he drives his good right hand into the back of the GuardBorg's skull, wrenching the panel and everything behind it out. Instantly, the GuardBorg falls limp, the lights of its eyes blinking out.

My heart pounds against my ribs. Who'd have thought the little borg had it in him.

'Good work, Tungst,' pants Pilot, barely loud enough to hear over the lightning. 'It's a good look for you.'

Tungsten looks back at us, tilting his head, and I can't help but grin.

'Come on,' shouts Blue, lifting Pilot by the arm. 'Let's get out of here.' Tungsten hurries back to us, letting Pilot lean into him and supporting him with his one arm.

'You guys go,' I say. 'I'll be right behind you.'

Blue shakes her head. 'We're not leaving you.'

'I still need to find the Punch.'

Pilot lets his head fall against Tungsten's shoulder and closes his eyes, wincing and swallowing through the pain. When he opens them again, he shrugs, pretending like nothing's wrong. 'Lead the way, then.'

We're surrounded by shelves, all of them identical to each other. And above each is a sign. One sign, in particular, makes my pounding heart skip a beat. *2050 – 2150.*

'Over here.'

We hug close to the shelf, avoiding the lightning that whips down the aisle. My fingers graze over every item – bizarre-looking gadgets and tools that I don't want to imagine the purposes for. It's hard to believe that while I was living my normal life, normal school days, normal friends, normal phase testing, BMAC was busy collecting all this.

My hand falls on a wooden crate, and between the flashes of light, I see the writing scrawled along its side. *Hartman 001.*

My mouth goes dry.

'What?' asks Blue, watching me. 'Is that it?'

I try to pry off the lid, but it won't budge. Tungsten gives Pilot to Blue and reaches over me, cracking it open like a peanut shell.

Files and gadgets and bags marked *Evidence* spill out onto the floor, along with a jumble of wires and tubes and circuits. My breath catches in my throat – Gabby's pungit ray experiment. I bend down and pick up one of the tubes, my hands trembling. She used to cart this thing to class every day. Her one hope of curing herself. Of saving herself from all the trouble her pungits caused her.

This was hers. Proof, all the way in 2383, that Gabriella Vargas existed.

'Patrick?' asks Blue. 'Is that it?'

I shake my head, a lump forming in my throat. I turn over the spilled contents of the crate, sifting through pieces of evidence.

And there, tangled up in the circuits of Gabby's creation, is a clear plastic evidence bag.

Inside, glinting in the lightning, is a round, metallic disc, just bigger than my palm. The same little disc I watched blast holes into BMAC Headquarters. The same little disc that took hold of my pungits and sent me here.

The Punch.

And with it, the crown Roth used to try to steal my connection.

'Uh, guys?'

I glance up to see Pilot and Tungsten, looking up towards the cortex. 'I think it's time to go!'

The cortex glows brighter, and out of its centre, crawling across the ceiling and spilling down the walls, are hundreds and hundreds of what look like metal insects.

SpiderBorgs.

Coming right for us.

'Run!' I scream, grabbing the Punch and taking off for the door.

The SpiderBorgs are fast, impossibly fast, and we run as hard as we can, Tungsten hoisting Pilot over his shoulder and shooting his neutraliser at the advancing hoard. It's no use – every borg he blasts is replaced by ten more. They crawl over everything, consuming whole shelves in their mass, swelling towards us like a titanium wave.

The cortex! Bo bellows inside my brain. *Patrick, you have to take out the cortex!*

'Tungst!' I scream, pointing at the glowing brain above us. 'Shoot it now, Tungst!'

The borg takes aim and fires, the blast hitting dead centre of the cortex.

The giant ball's glow surges brighter, and the SpiderBorgs don't stop spilling out.

You need something stronger! Bo tells me.

LIKE WHAT!?

The Punch!

I pull the device from my pocket, strapping it to my palm as I run.

'It's over here!' screams Blue, coming to the end of the aisle. I follow her as she rounds the corner, and nearly slam into her when she stops.

More SpiderBorgs. A heaving writhing mass between us and the vault door.

Tungsten fires into the hoard, blasting several borgs. The rest of them begin to advance on us.

The Punch, Patrick!

My fingers claw at the sides of the disc. I don't know how to turn it on. I don't even know if I can. It's been hidden away for so long – who knows if it still works?

PATRICK!

Instinctively, my hand closes over the disc and presses it hard against my palm. I feel a heat, and when I open my hand, a light flickers in the disc's centre.

It does work.

The first line of SpiderBorgs scramble over my feet and I lift my hand towards the cortex as the heat in my palm begins to burn.

The light explodes from the disc, slamming into the cortex with an explosion of blue and white light, so bright it's blinding and I have to shield my eyes.

Metal pings the ground like rainfall as the spiders fall dead, and when I can finally open my eyes, the lightning has stopped firing. The SpiderBorgs lie in piles, falling from the ceiling where the cortex hangs, mangled and fried.

A loud series of clicks, the grinding of metal, echoes through the chamber, and light spills in where the vault door slides open.

'Breezes,' says Pilot. 'What year did you say you come from?'

PAT
2383

They're all there, waiting on the other side of the vault – Bo, Constance, Bash, Rads, Zombie and Psychic – staring slack-jawed at the cortex smoking above us.

Only Bo moves. 'You haven't got much time, Patrick.'

'That's right,' says Constance, hovering behind him. 'There's no time. Not after *this*!' She waves frantically at the smouldering Time Cache. 'This was supposed to be a covert operation, Bo. Covert! BMAC is already on its way! You need to take down the RareCore defences. Now!'

'Soon!' snaps Bo, taking my hand firmly in his.

'Not soon!' screams Constance as an alarm blares overhead. BMAC is here already. 'Now, Bo!'

'No,' says Blue calmly. 'There are Movers inside. We need to get them out of there.'

'What? In the Time Cache?'

Blue nods.

Constance looks to Bash full of concern. 'We can't leave them.'

Bash has switched to combat mode, wearing a deadly frown as he gives orders calmly to the others. 'Zombie. I want you to go back to Mathis and Opal. Take the High Minister to his office and tie him up, BMAC will find him soon enough. Get yourselves back to the transport and bring it round by the side entrance. Psychic, you and I will recover the Movers and bring them down to Zombie.'

Psychic nods, and Zombie takes off, already obeying orders.

There's a rumble somewhere outside the Turbine. Whatever forces BMAC has deployed, from the sounds of it, they're not wasting any resources.

Bo's grip is tight, both his hands squeezing mine. *We have to do this now, Patrick.*

I look into his stormy grey eyes. I understand now. Understand why he fought me so hard on trying to leave. I'm not just leaving Bo here in the future. I'm leaving Bo for ever.

Fear and sadness seize my heart.

His eyes are wet. And he smiles.

I don't know what to say, and a lump swells in my throat, so painful that I couldn't say anything even if I wanted to. I grab Bo, and he hugs me back, our grip on each other so tight it hurts.

Thank you, Bo. For everything.

Thank you, he says. *For helping me change the world. Because of you, we can take the day back from the Eventualies.*

You're sure you know how to stop the winds?

He nods. *It may take a bit of tinkering, but it's nothing I can't handle.*

I have to smile. I'm glad to know that even if I'm not here, part of what me and Bo did together *will* be here, making life better for Movers and Shadows.

Bo turns away from me, trying to pretend he's not wiping his eyes. There's no point in pretending. I see inside his head. See and feel everything that's happening inside him. And it's like he's losing a son.

But he's not.

We're more than family.

'Pat,' says Blue. 'My Shadow is ready for you. We need to do this.'

I look down at the Punch in my palm as the boom of shock cannons explodes around me.

BMAC is here.

Bash and Psychic hurry into the Time Cache as Constance readies her weapon, taking aim at the BMAC agents opening fire from the hallway.

'Patrick!' screams Blue. 'Patrick! We have to hurry!'

'Inside,' orders Bo, pulling me back towards the Time Cache. Blue is quick to obey, Tungsten slinging Pilot over his shoulder and following us inside, out of range of the guns.

Blue stands in front of me and I hand her the crown.

'What do I do?'

I think back to Commander Roth, to that moment he had me by the throat on the observation deck of the Avin Turbine. The moment before Bo saved me.

'You have to wear it,' I say.

She places it on her head, and I hold my palm, the Punch inside it, against the crown.

'Will it hurt?' she asks.

The pain was the worst I'd ever felt. As if my very flesh was cooking to a crisp. I don't want her to be scared. But I don't want to lie.

'Yes.'

She swallows. 'Let's get it over with, then.'

I press the Punch against my palm and feel its heat against my skin.

'Pat!' Pilot leans against Tungsten, Bo standing with them. I try to memorise their faces as the thunder of BMAC's cannons shake the walls.

'Say hi to your friend for us,' he says with a grin.

I nod, blinking away the sting in my eyes.

Blue presses her lips together. 'I'm ready. We're ready.' She grabs my wrist, turning it over to look at the Punch.

'If you need our help,' she says, 'the Aberrants will be there for you.'

The promise surprises me. I realise there are more of them, more Movers and Shadows like Zombie and Rads and Psychic, back in my time.

Patrick, interrupts Bo, ducking as a plasma blast sails through the vault door, sending one of the shelves splintering in all directions. *It's time! Do it now!*

Blue and I duck as shrapnel flies over our heads.

'I can't!' I shout. I can't just leave them here. Can't leave without knowing they'll be all right.

Blue grabs hold of my arm, digging in her fingertips. 'This is bigger than all of us!' she shouts. 'This is for all of us.'

For all of us. For the chance to fix everything that's

gone wrong. I reach a hand into my pocket, making sure the Cure vial and cartridge are still there.

My chance.

My responsibility.

I take a deep breath and press the Punch to the crown.

Light explodes from the Punch and the familiar pain rips through my body, into my brain, searing hot and numbing all at once. It's a whirlpool inside my head, a vicious torrent, pulling me and ripping me, and my one anchor is Bo, tethered to me as the Punch tries to rip us apart. The force is strong, too strong for my wounded pungits, and I feel my grip on Bo coming away.

Something else is taking his place.

A lot of somethings. Hundreds of voices spilling into my head from Blue. Some close, some far. I realise with blinding clarity just how different she is, just how much stronger her Movement abilities are. The voices are Blue. All the different versions of her through time. All of them connected and crying out in pain.

And one, reaching up for me through the pain, reaching from far away.

It pulls on me. On my mind. Hard.

The world feels like it's bending. Ready to break.

And then it does.

In one clean, bright and brilliant snap.

PAT
2083

The pain has disappeared. The sounds of battle are gone with it.

I open my eyes and I'm lying on my back.

The Time Cache ceiling is gone, replaced by a cloudy sky.

'You OK?'

Blue.

She leans over me, snapping her fingers.

I prop myself up on my elbow. We're on a rooftop. The Eventualies weave in and around me, gently, like a hug from an old friend. The Avin Turbine, the one I've grown up with all my life, rotates its propellers above the city's skyline. My Avin.

I leap to my feet, and my head starts to spin, making me stumble. There are voices. So many voices inside my head. All the different versions of Blue speaking through time. How does she live like this?

'Easy there,' says Blue, catching me by the arm. 'Do you have it? Let me see the Cure.'

'Where are we?' I ask, my voice groggy.

'The old Avin post office,' she says. 'On the outskirts of Avin.'

'What time is it?'

She checks her droidlet. 'Nine-thirty. I'm late for a march at city hall. I can take you with me but I don't know if—'

'Nine thirty.' I try to remember – Ollie and I were on the roof yard watching Gabby when the sky opened up last time. That was first recess. That means my sister, Maggie, Moves Roth sometime around ten. I have to get to her before she does.

'I don't have much time.'

GABBY
2083

He's watching me.

Pat Mermick.

He's sitting on the bleachers with Ollie Larkin. Staring. I scratch nervously at my fingers. Why is he watching me?

Why do you think?

I begin to sing.

My Shadow's voice is tense in my mind. *Why, Gabby?*

I quiet my thoughts. Close off my mind. Just a few more hours and I can go home. A few more hours until I can get the pungit ray.

My Shadow's chilly laughter swells inside my head. *You think you can hide it from me? You think I can't see where your silly daydreams take you? See the way you imagine this boy walking you home? Holding your hand?*

A wave of embarrassment crashes over me. So hard and so hot, it steals my breath.

Kissing you?

Pat's frowning at me. And for a terrifying second I'm afraid he's seen my thoughts too. I feel red heat in my cheeks. I look away.

Ollie Larkin's voice echoes across the roof yard. 'Isn't that right, Gooba?'

You, my Shadow says with disgust. *You know he could never care about you.*

A lump forms in my throat.

Nobody cares about you.

'Goooooooooooooooooooooooooba.'

Nobody but me.

I shake my head. 'You're just trying to upset me.'

I'm trying to make you understand. Listen to them, listen to how they laugh at you.

Blue didn't laugh at me.

The girl wanted to use you, to manipulate you to fight her war for her. Along with all those other fools.

That's not true. It can't be true. I can change things. I know I can. I don't have to be as alone as I've been.

With me beside you, you wouldn't be alone. You only need to Move me!

'Leave her alone, Ollie.'

Pat.

MOVE ME! My Shadow tightens his grip. I grab my head.

'Watch it, Shelf Meat!' Ollie Larkin shouts at Pat.

'What are you going to do about it, Real-Time?'

MOVE ME!

A sound, like the world is ripping open, splits through the pain in my mind, through my Shadow's voice, through Pat and Ollie fighting.

I look up towards the sky.
The clouds begin to spiral above us.
This is Movement activity.

PAT
2083

I run as fast as my feet will go, dodging the people of Avin as I race through the streets, from Hexall Hall back down town, Blue on my heels. I see the sky above the Romsey Institute. The clouds have begun churning, just like they did the last time.

It's starting.

There are the front doors to my school – it's been a lifetime since I've walked through them. Maggie's inside. Gabby's on the roof. I can stop this.

I crash through the doors and stand frozen in the foyer. The building rumbles as the storm above grows stronger.

'What now?' Blue pants beside me. 'What are you looking for?'

'My sister.' Maggie.

'Well?' says Blue. 'Where is she?'

She ran into my school. That's what she did. She told me. She hid in a locker.

I stare down the first hallway, the endless rows of lockers.

My school is 64 floors high. 27,000 students. That's 27,000 lockers.

She could be anywhere.

'I'm telling you, she came this way.' I know that voice. It's one I never thought I'd be happy to hear. Mrs Dibbs. She storms up the hallway to my left with another teacher, banging on the lockers. 'She ran right in here and just kept on running.'

The other teacher sighs, impatiently. 'Are you sure it's not a student?'

'She couldn't be more than six,' snaps Mrs Dibbs. 'Is the Romsey Institute a kindergarten now?'

Maggie.

'MAGGIE!' I scream out, and Mrs Dibbs turns round.

'Mr Mermick, shouldn't you be at recess?'

I push Mrs Dibbs out of the way, pulling at lockers. 'Maggie! Maggie, I'm here!'

Blue does the same, throwing open doors on the ones with no locks.

'Pat?'

There, at the end of the hall, climbing out of a locker, I see her. Her clothes ripple in the breeze. Her hair is still in the braid Mom did for her this morning, but the wind threatens to tear it loose.

My sister.

'Pat!' she sobs, running towards me. I scoop her up into my arms and she sobs and sobs as the building rattles. 'BMAC took Mom, Pat! They took her! I didn't know where else to go.'

'It's OK, Mags. I'm here now.'

'We need to hurry,' says Blue. 'Do you have the Cure?'

'What the breezes!' gasps Mrs Dibbs behind me, as a piece of the ceiling crashes to the floor.

'Maggie,' I say, wiping away her tears. 'Maggie, you've gotta calm down, OK? You've gotta stop it. You've gotta stop Moving.'

'I don't know how!' she wails. 'My Shadow said he'd help me. He said—'

'I know what he said, Mags. He's a liar.' I hug her tight. 'Maggie, do you trust me?'

She nods, wiping at her eyes.

'Speed this up,' Blue says. 'BMAC will be on the way.'

I reach into my pocket and pull out the vial Pilot gave me back at the wager lair. 'I can make the Move stop, Maggie.'

She looks down at the blue liquid in my hand. 'He doesn't want you to.'

'Do you want me to?'

She nods.

I click the vial into the disc Bo gave me. Then I take hold of her arm, and press the cartridge to her skin.

This is for Maggie.

For Mom.

For Pilot, and Blue, and Bo.

And for Gabby.

GABBY
2083

My head is pressed to the concrete, waiting for the tremors to stop.

The roof yard is silent. Everyone waiting for the next strike.

The lightning. It shook the whole building.

I glance up at the sky. The clouds – the tight spiral they'd formed has started to uncoil. The sound of the thunder begins to fade.

What was that?

'You OK?'

Pat Mermick. He stands over me. Holds out his hand. 'It's OK,' he says. 'I think it's over.'

PAT
2083

Maggie sleeps in my arms outside the Romsey Institute. We're in an alley across from the school. We can see the students spilling out the front doors in a panic. Blue stands over us, staring up at the sky as the storm clouds break apart.

'Come on, Mags,' I say, smoothing her hair. The Cure is working through her body. How long before she wakes up?

'BMAC vehicles,' says Blue, as their sirens grow louder around us.

It doesn't matter now. The Move didn't happen. BMAC has been called to a false alarm.

I glance up, my neck craning skywards to the top of Romsey. Somewhere, up there on the roof, is Gabby.

But not just Gabby.

'You're up there, on the roof, aren't you?' says Blue.

I nod. Somewhere up there, is me. The me before all this started.

'I don't think you want to be around here for BMAC to figure that out.'

No. I suppose I don't.

'Pat?' Maggie shifts in my arms and I look down as her eyes blink open. 'What happened?'

'It's OK now, Mags. You're safe.'

She sits up, grabbing her head. 'But Mom—'

'Mom will be OK, Mags,' I tell her, the sirens growing louder. Now that Maggie's pungits are gone, she isn't a Mover. BMAC will release Mom.

'But you won't,' says Blue, 'if you stick around here.'

BMAC. They aren't here for me. But still, Blue's right. I don't want to risk them noticing two Pat Mermicks.

'What is she talking about, Pat?'

I smile at my sister, but my heart is hurting. There's so much to tell her. To tell Mom. And I don't know how much of it she can possibly understand. I'm not even sure how to begin.

GABBY
2083

I follow Pat outside the Romsey Institute, where the entire
school has emptied out onto the streets of Avin. There's a
pounding in my head as my Shadow growls inside my mind.

You cannot ignore me for ever.

I can try. At least until I figure out how to get rid of him
for ever.

That chill ripples through me, the feel of his laugh. *Who
would you have if you got rid of me? Nobody.*

I have to stop walking. The pain is exhausting.

'Gabby?' Pat's hand falls on my shoulder. 'You all right?'

His brow is creased, his eyes searching me. Is he mad
at me?

His hand squeezes gently. 'Gabby?'

No. He's worried about me.

My throat is dry. I can't find my voice. So all I can do is nod.

A siren calls his eyes away. A BMAC vehicle pulls up.
'I think it's safe to say classes are cancelled.' He looks back
at me. 'You want me to walk you home?'

Home. My parents will be there. I can't go home yet.

I shake my head.

He frowns again. The worry is still there. I'm worried too. I don't know where to go.

You have nowhere to go, my Shadow hisses. *You have nobody.*

'You want to come to my place?' Pat asks.

The offer takes me by surprise. Before I can think to answer, someone calls his name.

Pat and I turn and there's a little girl running towards us.

'Maggie?' he shouts, near panic. 'Maggie, what are you doing here?!'

I look back the way she came. Somewhere across the street. The alley, maybe . . . there's someone standing there, watching us.

'It's OK, Pat,' his sister is saying. 'We don't have to be afraid any more.'

'What?'

Not some*one*. There are two of them watching us, obscured by the wall of the building. I step closer, trying to get a better look.

'It's OK,' she says again. 'We don't have to be afraid. We can go get Mom and tell her so.'

'Get Mom? Maggie what are you talking about? Where's Mom?'

'With BMAC.'

My breath stops.

'BMAC!' Pat grabs hold of her shoulders, 'Why?!'

'Pat, don't worry. I'm not a Mover any more so BMAC

can't be mad,' she says, looking back to the figures in the alley. 'You told me so yourself.'

'Maggie,' Pat's voice wavers, 'you're scaring me. Who is that?'

Maggie waves at the alley people. I have a better view now. It's a boy and a girl. The girl waves, and it's then that I see the colour of her hair.

'Blue?'

I step closer, getting a better look at the boy.

And my heart stops when I see he's wearing an expression I know. A face that can't belong to him.

Pat?

PAT
2083

Gabby. She stands there, in front of Romsey, staring. I step back behind the wall. She doesn't need to see me. None of them need to see me. She's safe now. And so is Maggie. Because I stopped the Move.

I made it so Roth never came here.

Made it so we never have to go on the run from BMAC. Together. Never have to give Beadie Hartman the secret to Gabby's pungit ray. Or the Punch.

Made it so Bo will never have to Move me.

And Gabby will never be Shelved.

None of it will ever happen.

Thanks to Bo. And Pilot. And Blue.

Gabby will never know. About any of it.

She's safe.

'I know her,' Blue says. 'I know your Gabby. You say she's the one who makes the Cure?'

I nod. In the year 2097, Gabriella Vargas will discover the Cure for Movement.

She grins, shaking her head. 'I knew there was something about her.'

I pull the used vial and cartridge from my pocket. Gabby's cure, commandeered by BMAC. I wonder if I'll ever get a chance to tell her what I've seen in the future. And if I do, will I want to?

'The Aberrants, you and I, will protect Gabby. We'll keep her and the Cure safe.'

I nod.

'It's not over, you know,' says Blue. 'For any of us. So long as BMAC is in power, Movers will still be Shelved. Our work isn't finished.'

No, it isn't. Until the Shelves are shut down, until BMAC is destroyed, it won't ever be finished.

I watch from the shadows as the boy standing with my sister grabs her hand. That's me. Before all of it. It's a weird feeling, watching myself walk away with Maggie. He'll take care of her. I know he will. I've given him everything he needs to keep her safe.

'So there are two of you now,' Blue says, watching the other me. 'In one time.'

I'm no ordinary Mover any more.

Blue grins. 'I guess that makes you an Aberrant.'

I guess it does. 'You said, we have work to do,' I say. 'The Aberrants.'

She nods. 'We do.'

I am an Aberrant.

And that means BMAC needs to be scared of me.

ACKNOWLEDGEMENTS

A very special thank you to my superhero editors who turned their brains to scrambled eggs with me, trying to wrangle the time-travel monster! Charlie, Eloise and Chloe – thank you for all the awesome you do.

And to my family, Ian and Mae, for living with Pat and BMAC for so long.